THE SO15 FILES

NOVELLAS 1-3

BY JACK **PROBYN**

 Published by: Cliff Edge Press, Essex.

ISBN: TBC

First Edition

Visit Jack Probyn's website at www.jackprobynbooks.com.

MEET JAKE TANNER

Born: 28.03.1985

Height: 6′1″

Weight: 190lbs/86kg/13.5 stone

Physical Description: Brown hair, close shaven beard, brown eyes, slim athletic build, scar on his cheek

Education: Upper Second Class Honours in Psychology from the University College London (UCL)

Interests: When Jake isn't protecting lives and finding those responsible for taking them, Jake enjoys motorsports — particularly F1

Family: Mother, older sister, younger brother. His father died in a car accident when Jake was fifteen

Relationship Status: Currently in a relationship with Elizabeth Tanner, and he doesn't see that changing, ever

Career History: (2008-2009) Temporary Detective Constable at Croydon CID; (2009-2015) Detective Constable at Stratford CID; (2015-Present) Detective Constable with SO15

THE SO15 FILES

Jack Probyn's SO15 Files. Lightning-quick, fast-paced, edge-of-your-seat action from the first page to the last.

Designed to be read in one sitting — on the train, plane or automobile — each and every one is a 100% story-driven shot of pure entertainment, featuring characters from the DC Jake Tanner universe.

Join Jake and SO15, the Metropolitan Police's Counter Terrorism Command, as they battle invisible enemies, domestic terrorists, and an underground clandestine network.

The novellas in this series range from 20k-30k words, and can be read in any order.

ABOUT THE BOOK

THE WOLF

When Jake Tanner steps into the darkness, he comes face to face with… The Wolf

Jake Tanner is fighting to keep his job. Budget cuts within SO15, Counter Terrorism Command, are inbound. And everyone knows it's the last ones in that are first to go.

So when a crazed gunman sieges a popular cinema in the heart of London, Jake jumps at the opportunity.

And he soon learns that there's nothing more dangerous than a man who's willing to risk it all.

DARK CHRISTMAS

During the busy festive period, the body of a well-known and highly sought-after terrorist is discovered in the middle of a London street, his body still warm.

Jake Tanner and the Counter Terrorism Command team are called in to investigate.

Why was he there? Who killed him? And what does the note found in his possession have to do with a shopping centre?

The answers are as unsettling as they are surprising.

This Christmas is going to be one to forget.

* * *

THE EYE

When a deadly terrorist leaves a chilling warning before shooting dead two officers, Jake and the rest of Counter Terrorism Command must uncover the mystery:

One of London's greatest landmarks is next on the hit list.

Which one? And why?

And can they stop it in time?

THE WOLF

CHAPTER 1

As he stepped into the cinema, Phillip Bowden had come to terms with the fact it could be his last night on earth.

He wandered up to the desk, his large gym bag bashing against his leg, and collected his pre-ordered ticket to see this year's hottest movie – *Star Wars*. The regeneration of the dwindling saga that so many had once loved, and even more had come to despise. Yet grown men, women and children, dressed in various costumes of characters from across the series, hovered around the cinema entrance, anxiously waiting for the show to begin – their previous grievances forgotten. Phillip didn't know any of the characters surrounding him, but he kicked himself for missing a trick. With so many dressed in costume, he was the odd one out.

'You again?' the pretty young woman behind the popcorn counter asked. Her name badge read: Tara. 'Third time this week.'

'I've got a lot of films I need to catch up on.'

'It's a good thing you pre-ordered. We're completely

sold out.'

'It's my lucky day,' Phillip replied.

'I've been meaning to ask,' she started. 'You have a wonderful accent. Whereabouts are you from?'

'Nevada.'

'Like Las Vegas?'

'Yes. Like Las Vegas.'

'I've never been. What's it like?'

She couldn't have been older than her early twenties, late teens at least. A product of the social media generation that glamourised everything but struggled to find meaningful and fulfilling jobs. Phillip had seen her kind around the strip. Girls' holidays, hen dos – trips filled with frivolity and free-flowing alcohol, getting away for the week to forget the mundanity of life back home. And to make sure that it looked good enough for their Instagram pages.

'My view's compromised,' he said softly, 'considering I lived there for most of my life. I guess it's the same when people ask you about London. But I suppose it's all right, if you like that sort of thing.'

'Me and my friends were thinking of going. Some of my other mates went last year and said it was literally the best time of their lives.'

'Literally,' Phillip said, his sarcasm going way over her head.

A small machine printed his ticket, and Tara passed it to him.

'Did you want food and drink?'

Phillip shook his head. 'No, thank you. I've got some in here already.'

The young woman peered over her cash register and inspected the bag. Her expression changed. Perhaps she was taken aback by the fact he'd been so upfront about the food. Or perhaps it was the size of the bag that had shocked her.

'Is it all food in there?'

Phillip's hand involuntarily moved towards the soft, neoprene fabric. *You don't want to know what's really in here.*

Although she would find out soon enough.

'Yes. It is. All for me. What can I say? We Americans like our food.'

She let out an awkward chuckle. 'Don't we all. Enjoy the film.'

Phillip folded the film ticket in his hands and started off towards the screen without thanking Tara. It was 11:45 p.m., and there were still fifteen minutes until the midnight release took place. In the short time Phillip had been there, the ticket queue had more than doubled in size. And the queue for the bathroom was even longer.

For five minutes, Phillip stood patiently behind a row of men who'd decided amongst themselves, in an unspoken agreement, who was next in line for a cubicle. The Brits' natural ability to form a queue in the most unusual and obscene places continued to bewilder him, yet right now he didn't have a choice. He needed a cubicle – the privacy, the lock on the door that shut the rest of the world out. Phillip ignored the other men using the urinals and sinks as they brushed past him. He was more focused on something else. Something that was going to change his life forever. For better or worse. So long as his message was conveyed.

As the time ticked towards midnight, the anticipation for the film heightened, and some of the men in line slipped away towards the screening room, lest they miss out on the crucial opening credits.

Finally, the cubicle furthest to the right opened, and out stepped an overweight man with a shiny forehead wearing an Obi-Wan Kenobi costume two sizes too small. Phillip acknowledged the man with an awkward nod and then headed inside.

A pungent wave of nauseating excrement instantly hit him in the face, the smell making him gag as it abseiled down his throat.

Trying his best to ignore it and not to swallow, he lowered the toilet lid and then placed his bag atop it. Carefully, keeping the noise to a minimum, Phillip unzipped the bag. Inside, resting amongst an assortment of other equipment, was a dismantled M16 machine gun. The parts lay delicately at the top, wrapped neatly in a tea towel.

Phillip spent the next three minutes piecing the weapon together. Silently. Cautiously. Nobody, not even himself, could hear the pieces of the M16 coming together over the sound of flushing toilets and electric hand dryers whirring in the background.

And then it all went quiet. The last of the *Star Wars* superfans – or nerds as he liked to call them – had finished their ablutions and were on their way to the screen. By the time he was done with the gun, it was 12:02 a.m., and Phillip had missed the first two minutes of the showing. He was late.

No problem.

Still in the cubicle, Phillip removed his coat, revealing a brace he'd made himself. The brace comprised two leather straps that dangled over his shoulders and met in his chest to form a cross in the middle of his body. It was uncomfortable but necessary. In the centre of the cross was a magnet.

Phillip grabbed the M16 from the toilet seat, clipped the gun to the magnet and put his coat back on, concealing the weapon.

Then he reached into the bag again, removed a small Glock handgun and strapped it to his ankle. After zipping the bag and flushing the toilet for good measure – and partly as a force of habit – he was done.

Ready to begin.

Phillip had never been a fan of the *Star Wars* films, but he was fairly sure he was going to enjoy this one most of all.

CHAPTER 2

Jake Tanner, through no lack of trying, couldn't sleep. For the past few hours, his mind had remained awake, plagued with thoughts of work, the world and its woes. He lay there on his back, hands placed behind his head, staring into the black void of the ceiling. There was little light in the room, and now and then the darkness would move and shift and shape itself into something indiscernible, as if he was feeling the effects of a hallucinatory drug taking hold of his system.

Outside, the sound of cars fleeting past reminded him of the fact he was still at home, in the south of London. Safe. Next to him, his adoring wife, Elizabeth. Beautiful Elizabeth. The mother of his children. Her gentle snoring and steady breathing made him smile. Made him feel warm.

Jake gave her a kiss on the forehead, rolled out of bed and headed downstairs.

Their living room was full of Elizabeth's photography equipment – cameras, lenses, carry cases, tripods, lighting gear. She'd been in and out of clients' addresses so frequently there had been no time to unpack anything. Over the past few weeks, the gods had finally begun paying attention to her, and her freelance work had picked up tenfold. Now she was doing everything from wedding photography to portraits, editorial images to product photography. Building her brand and building her career. And she'd even had the courage to plunge herself back into the world of fashion photography – except this time on the other end of the camera, where she wanted to be, and where she felt safe.

The number of clients had grown, and naturally, so had her referrals. The website she'd spent many months over – and invested what little remaining money they had – was finally up and running, and she had a good business model in place. She might have been stretching herself too thin, but after what felt like decades of no results, she was finally seeing a positive return on her investment. And Jake couldn't have been any prouder and more accommodating. The mess in the living room was a welcome compromise, because it made her happy. For too long, she'd felt unfulfilled, and Jake was pleased to see a positive change in his wife's morale.

Happy wife, happy life.

He sat down on the sofa and grabbed the TV remote. Flicked through the channels. There was nothing on. Poker. Repeats of programmes from the noughties no one watched or cared about anymore. Music videos. Twenty-four-hour news. Enough to send any insomniac to sleep, but not him.

There was something weighing heavily on his mind. Something he couldn't bear to tell Elizabeth: earlier in the week, Jake had received an email telling him that, due to budget cuts and other such financial and political bullshit scapegoats, there would be a few redundancies made within SO15, otherwise known as Counter Terrorism Command, one of the Met's most elite policing branches. It was also Jake's new home, and had been for the past four months. The true impact the cuts would have on the department wasn't yet known, but he didn't want to get his hopes up. No one was safe. Especially him. He'd never experienced a redundancy before, but he knew that the newest members of the team were usually first to go.

Not to mention, the number of CID detectives across the service had dropped by nearly a tenth in as many months, *and* the number of police community support officers within London had been slashed by nearly five thousand. Good, hard-working, experienced men and women had lost their jobs thanks to a government that thought they could better spend the money elsewhere – on their own bonuses and handing out friendly contracts. And then, when they wondered why crime rates had soared as a result, they had the audacity to blame the good, hard-working, experienced men and women who were left doing the job for two.

No one was safe.

Jake stopped flicking through the channels on a film he'd somehow never seen all the way through before: *Die Hard*. He sat there and paid a minute amount of attention to it while his mind constantly thought of ways he could keep his job safe. And then, as the number of options gradually grew smaller and smaller, he began to think of the consequences of a redundancy. Elizabeth's income was hardly sustainable for the family – they had admitted that. So the only other option would be for him to find a new job. Perhaps he could go into psychology and put the degree he'd spent four years working on to use. Or perhaps he could go back to working behind a desk for the rest of his life, in a call centre, selling products and services over the phone, dealing with the malevolent and belligerent general public in a different way to the one he was used to. Or perhaps he could work his arse off and maintain job security for the future.

Jake preferred the last option.

On the screen, John McClane had just jumped from the top of the Nakatomi Plaza, secured by a hosepipe hundreds of feet in the air.

As he continued watching the rest of the film, he found his mind slowly drifting in and out of consciousness, the sound of gunfire and screams and explosions in the background soothing him into a slumber.

CHAPTER 3

The cinema was deathly silent, everyone inside fixated on the hundred and twenty foot screen in front of them, their eyes wide and their mouths agape, ready and waiting for the latest handful of popcorn.

Phillip was seated at the end of the back row, right at the mouth of the entrance. Easing back into his chair, he crossed his arms, feeling the gun underneath. Hard. Solid. Powerful. Deadly. It was his pride and joy. He'd first bought it twenty-five years ago at a car boot sale. Its previous owner, a former Vietnam veteran, had wanted to get rid of it for marital reasons and, Phillip had been assured, it had never fired a shot in its brief existence.

That didn't mean to say it couldn't, and after Phillip had taken it home and shown it to his wife, he'd cleaned it, repaired it, then taken it to a remote part of the desert and fired several rounds into an isolated and arbitrary piece of rock. Since then, it had been an important part of his life. A prized possession he carried with him everywhere. Same with the handgun on his ankle. He carried the latter everywhere, no matter how many security alarms he activated in shopping centres. It didn't bother him. Nobody would think to check his ankles every time he set an alarm off.

Yes, he was breaking the law. But only half so. Two years after he'd moved to the UK with his wife, a permit had come in the post, granting him permission to use a shotgun for a strict set of specific purposes. Neither the M16 nor the handgun were considered shotguns, but he took the term loosely: after all, they were both guns that fired shots.

Phillip felt something pressing into his bladder. It made him want to pee.

He lifted himself out of his chair, grabbed his duffel bag and started out of the auditorium. He was in no rush. The film had just finished the first act, and he wanted to savour every moment. A toilet break wouldn't harm anyone. And he didn't know how long it would be until his next opportunity.

Hours.

Days.

Idling along the corridor, Phillip absorbed the harsh, bright lights from the movie-poster screens that hung from the walls and paused to look at them for a moment, searching for any films he might like to see. They all looked over-expensive, over-hyped and over-reliant on CGI and green screens. There were no talented actors nowadays, no good movies – not like back in his day when they'd had meaning, purpose.

The toilets were empty. The sound of the movie played through cheap speakers overhead, yet it was unable to drown out the sound of running water. And nothing could mask the smell of ammonia and shit in the air. Phillip set the gym bag on the sink bench and relieved himself in the urinal before washing his hands and starting back towards the screen. At the doors, he checked his watch – 12:43 a.m.

Two minutes to showtime.

Gently, Phillip slipped through the door and into the auditorium. Crouching down in the shadows, he placed his bag on the floor, ripped the M16 from the magnets and—

The door beside him opened. Standing immediately in front of him was an IMAX employee, his name badge reflecting the light from the cinema screen. The teenage boy stood still and stared at Phillip, his eyes wide.

Phillip reacted quickest.

He grabbed the boy by the chest, threw him into the wall and pinned him against it. Using the same hand, he covered the boy's mouth and pressed the nose of the M16 into the boy's crotch.

Phillip felt the kid's breathing in his palm, warming it, making it sweat and lubricated and damp. He was sure he could smell piss as well.

Poor fella.

The worst was yet to come.

He leant in and whispered, 'Do not make a sound, OK?'

The boy nodded, his eyes growing wilder with every passing second.

Satisfied, Phillip bent down and reached into his bag, keeping the gun pressed against the boy's prized possessions. Seconds later, he removed a heavy-duty chain that was housed in a plastic casing to muffle the metal's clinking. It didn't work wonders, but it sufficed.

'Lock the doors,' Phillip whispered to the boy, while

darting his gaze down the alleyway, praying no one else needed a toilet break and would spoil his plan before it had even begun.

The boy followed orders without a word. Panicked, fearing for his life, he was too consumed with the fear that Phillip would shoot him if he didn't do what he was told. And, in some respects, the kid would have been right. But in others, not so much. If everything went according to plan, Phillip wouldn't need to shoot anyone.

And his hands would be kept clean.

The sound of something hitting the floor distracted him. The boy had dropped the chain. Phillip swore internally and hurried the boy along with a jab in the back.

'Make another sound and I will shoot your fucking face off,' he hissed.

Less than twenty seconds later, the doors were locked. But he wasn't finished there. He needed to make sure they were impenetrable. There was no knowing what defences the British government would send his way, so he needed to make sure they were well protected.

He bent down and retrieved a large tube of industrial-strength silicone sealant housed inside a plastic gun.

'Place it around the door edges,' he ordered. 'And hurry!'

The boy did as he was told, wary this time of the increased threat another fuck-up would cause to his crown jewels. And face.

After a short while, the door edges were covered in a white substance that solidified as soon as it was exposed to air. The barricade was complete. A lock and glue. Belt and braces.

Phillip gave a hard tug on the doors. They didn't move. They were sealed shut. No one in. No one out.

'There's a good little boy,' Phillip said, pushing the gun into the boy's back, moving him deeper into the cinema. 'Hurry!'

They stopped at the end of the alleyway, a few feet from the front-row seats. Phillip took a moment to breathe, control himself and adjust his thoughts. His life, and everyone in the country's, would change after tonight.

'Do as I say and nothing happens to you,' Phillip said. 'Understood?'

The boy nodded, keeping his gaze dead straight.

Saying nothing, Phillip pushed the kid in the back, sent him barrel-rolling onto the ground, then followed behind, gun raised, finger poised over the trigger.

'Ladies and gentlemen, may I have your attention please!' Phillip struggled to make his voice heard over the sound of the film.

But it would have made no difference if he shouted louder; the entire audience was captivated by the film, like brainwashed monkeys watching the flickering images, shovelling more and more food into their mouths.

Annoyed at the poor response from the crowd, Phillip was forced to commit the first act of the plan he'd wanted to avoid: he fired at the speakers. The deafening sound of bullets exploding ricocheted around the small enclosure, overpowering the noise of the speakers, and drowning out the sound of the film. It didn't take long for the speakers to stop working and for a moment of stunned silence to fall on the auditorium.

As the movie-goers gradually processed what was happening, the innate instinct of survival overwhelmed them. They rushed out of their seats, spilling popcorn and drinks onto the floor, and sprinted towards the exits. Stampeding, choosing their life over another's.

A group of them headed towards the fire exit on the other side of the room, his exposed flank.

A spray of bullets stopped them in their tracks.

Screams filled the air. High and low. In the background, images of heroes and villains lost in space continued to flicker on and off the screen.

Phillip sauntered into the centre of the cinema. Gun raised. The young boy in his grip.

'Everyone get back into your seats!' he said. 'Or I'll shoot the kid.'

And just as they'd been only a few moments earlier, the cinema-goers returned to their seats.

CHAPTER 4

Tara Han was wiping the surfaces with a cloth when she heard the sound of gunshots coming from screen fourteen. At first, she didn't register it – most films nowadays had guns and bullets and explosions in them, so she'd learnt to ignore them.

But when the petrified screams of horror and the sound of the cinema doors being pounded started, that was when she knew something was wrong. Very wrong.

'What the fuck was that?' Nathan, a small guy with pockmarked skin, asked. They had worked together for two months, and she'd still struggled to find the courage to ask him out.

'I... I don't know,' Tara said.

She surveyed her surroundings. Cinephiles had erupted from the other screens in the building and sprinted past her – streams of people racing towards the exit, their fear and paranoia tangible. She'd heard about things like this happening on the news. But she'd never thought it possible here. She'd never thought it could happen to her.

And neither had anyone else: owing to the stringent gun laws in the country, she and the rest of the team had received no training from head office on situations like this. They were left in the dark, with no idea how to respond or react.

'Fuck this,' Nathan said, throwing a box of popcorn to the ground, its contents spraying everywhere. 'I'm getting out of here.'

'No, wait! Nathan, come back!' Tara tried, but her efforts were in vain. He was gone, and shortly after, so was everyone else. Within seconds, the entire cinema had evacuated – as had her estimations of the boy she fancied – leaving her and a few other stragglers left behind. And all two hundred cinephiles in screen fourteen.

She didn't know what to do. Her body was prohibited by an invisible force holding her back, keeping her there. Fear. Flashbacks of being trapped inside the cave struck her. She'd been on a school trip in Gibraltar, visiting the caves within the giant rock, and then suddenly a piece of the cave had collapsed and crushed her friend, Vanessa, breaking her legs and paralysing her. Tara had run away in a panic, leaving her friend to suffer alone. And her world had been filled with darkness ever since.

Her friend had never forgiven her, and Tara could hardly blame her. They had always sworn to protect one another, and she'd failed. She'd betrayed her friend's trust.

The same as Nathan had betrayed her trust just now. The same way he'd left her, the most senior member of staff in the building, in charge.

Alone.

He'd made the selfish decision to look out for number one and save himself.

Tara wouldn't. She wouldn't stand by and let something awful happen to someone else. Not again.

No, she was going to stay and get help.

But where?

There were no phones allowed behind the cash desks; nor were the employees allowed their mobiles on their person. Their manager had strict personal rules on that and forced staff to keep them in the office.

It was a long way out the back, but it was the only place she could go.

She turned one-eighty, headed towards a dark blue door and weaved her way through a myriad of corridors, past the auditoriums where the films were shown, toilets, managerial offices and doors that led into the loading bay, until eventually she arrived at the staff room.

There, she found her locker, pulled out her iPhone and dialled 999. The dispatcher answered almost immediately.

'Hello? This is Tara Han. I'm in IMAX studios at Leicester Square, and I think there's been a shooting.'

Jake dipped in and out of consciousness. His eyes felt heavy, and every now and then, his head would loll forward, jolting him awake.

'This is ridiculous,' he said to himself.

Opening his eyes, he switched *Die Hard* off just as John McClane let the terrorist fall out of the window. He yawned. Stretched. Felt his body growing and his limbs becoming more supple. He propelled himself off the sofa and went into the kitchen to pour himself a drink.

The cold water felt welcoming down his throat. He was oddly thirsty.

After placing the empty glass in the sink, Jake sat at the dining-room table. His laptop was on there, closed. As it should be. He shouldn't open it, he knew, but he wanted to. Wanted to check his emails, find out if anything had been sent to him in the two hours since he'd last checked, despite the late hour. Or perhaps there was something on his to-do list he could accomplish – proper sleep still evaded him, so he might as well spend the time productively, even if his body and mind hated him for it in the morning.

Jake opened the laptop and logged in. His emails loaded on start-up, and so did Google Chrome.

After checking his inbox, he relaxed a little. There was nothing new in there. So that was something he could tick off his mental list.

He consulted it again.

Training. There was still some outstanding that he needed to complete. The world of counter terrorism, and all its ever-changing laws and regulations, was still alien to him. Do this, don't do that. Think this, don't think that. Behave like this, don't behave like that.

First on his list was terrorist negotiation. Hostages. Casualties. If there was one thing he was going to need to learn in order to develop his career and prove his worth, it was this.

Jake logged into the Metropolitan Police's external employee portal and started the training. Reading the words on the screen was making him more tired. Then his phone rang.

Unknown caller.

'Who's calling at this time?' he wondered aloud.

He answered and held it to his ear. 'Detective Tanner.'

'Jake, it's Lilly. Sorry to disturb you, but it's important. There's been reported gunshots at the IMAX cinema in Leicester Square.'

'OK.'

'There's a potential hostage situation taking place. We need you here. Mamadou wanted me to call you.'

'Is he already there?'

'As far as I'm aware, yes.'

Jake thanked Lilly and hung up.

Five minutes later, he was out the door, a note left by Elizabeth's head telling her where he was.

The training would have to wait.

CHAPTER 5

By the time Jake arrived, the entirety of Leicester Square and the surrounding area was deserted. Usually a thriving and excitable place, even in the early hours of the morning, the square was now a wasteland. Partygoers, diners and late-night revellers had now been replaced with an army of ambulances, police cars, fire engines and members of the Territorial Support Group, all positioned in what little space there was. Blue and white lights bounced off the buildings, as if creating a sombre and macabre disco for those brave enough to attend.

Jake eventually managed to find an empty space near Piccadilly Circus and hopped out. A cordon had been erected around the train station entrance, and members of the TSG were funnelling onlookers and curious members of the public away and into the Underground. At the cordon, Jake flashed his warrant card to the police constable standing guard, signed in, then dipped underneath it. As he crossed the road leading to Leicester Square, he rang Detective Chief

Superintendent Mamadou Kuhoba, his boss in SO15.

'Sir, I'm here. Where are you?'

'Front entrance. Two clicks to the right.'

'Right of what?'

'The doors, dickhead.'

'Sorry. It's late and I've had shit-all sleep.'

'You're about to get a lot less. Now hurry up and stop preaching to the choir.'

Jake hung up and wandered towards the IMAX, nodding courteously at other members of the force that recognised him. Ever since he'd helped uncover the identity of The Cabal – the owner and operator of a clandestine network of corrupt police individuals responsible for human and drug trafficking, as well as a host of other crimes – Jake had become somewhat infamous amongst the policing community. A hero that epitomised the work ethic and daily struggles of a police detective working in the heart of the city. And Jake both liked and disliked it. Rather, he'd grown accustomed to it. Sure, it felt good to be rewarded and appreciated for his efforts, but it also grew laborious having to explain the same story again and again. There were only so many times he could repeat it before he began hating the sound of his own voice.

As a result, he'd transferred to SO15 with an eye to putting that in the past. He wanted to move on, but he found it difficult when no one else seemed to want to let him.

One man who did, however, was Mamadou. The chief superintendent was aware of Jake's past successes, and it had been those that had impressed him and encouraged him to approach Jake. But The Cabal was in the past. And Mamadou was happy to keep it that way; if he wanted to remain a part of the team, Jake still needed to prove himself and do the work. There were no gimmes in Mamadou Kuhoba's team.

Tonight, the middle-aged man was dressed in a dark navy suit that looked as though it had been fished out of the washing basket, and was standing beside an unmarked Vauxhall Astra, talking to a police constable in a high-visibility jacket.

'What's this?' Jake asked, pointing at the Astra. 'Didn't think this was your taste?'

Mamadou turned, smiled at the sight of Jake and extended his hand. 'Shut up. It's not mine.'

'You're right – it's definitely not your colour.'

The two shook hands.

'Come on, let's go to The Hub.'

The Hub was how Mamadou referred to the bonnet of his unmarked BMW X5. It was the place he operated from and conducted most of his thinking. As senior investigating officer, Mamadou also held the responsibility of the operational commander. The man on the ground, constantly relaying information back to and following the instructions of the strategic commander, who was sitting behind a desk at New Scotland Yard somewhere.

'What's going down?' Jake asked, getting straight to the point.

'At approximately ten to one, gunshots were heard in one of the movie theatres. At the moment, there have been no sightings of anyone carrying a firearm, so we can only assume they're still in there.'

'Eyewitness reports?'

'Several civilians and patrons have fled the building. Some stayed long enough to be questioned when the first set of officers arrived. The others fucked off out of there.'

'Can we speak to them?'

'Sure.'

'And what about the person who called it in? Who are they, and where are they now?'

'Nineteen-year-old Tara Han. She's still inside.'

'Is she harmed?'

'No. She's hiding at the moment. She's our eyes and ears inside.'

'Is she safe?'

'As safe as she can be, considering.'

'Where are all the hostages?'

'Inside.'

'Which part?'

'Screen fourteen apparently. The new *Star Wars* midnight screening.'

'Jesus.' Jake shook his head, overcome by the immorality of what could force someone to such lengths. 'Have we got any casualties?'

'Unconfirmed still. We're working on feeding into the building's CCTV so we can ascertain who's in there, how many of them there are, where they're sat and, more importantly, who we're dealing with.'

'Makes sense. Any demands?'

'None yet. We're still awaiting contact to be made.'

Just as Mamadou finished speaking, a woman in a police vest – a member of the TSG – approached them.

'DCS Kuhoba,' she said, 'there's something I need to let you know.' The woman glanced at Jake and stopped speaking.

Jake recognised her but was unable to recollect where he might have known her from.

And then he remembered.

'Constable Penn?'

She stepped back, blushing a little, her face deepening a darker shade of red in the harsh artificial light.

'Nice to see you again, Detective Tanner,' she said.

'Likewise. Still policing – good to see.'

'Of course—'

'You two know each other?' Mamadou interrupted, his expression a combination of bemused and annoyed.

'PC Penn and I worked together when I was at Croydon CID.'

'Well, would you look at that? Small world. Now, if you'll forgive me, Constable, you had something to say. The two of you can catch up on your own time.'

'Oh. Yes. Sorry, sir. As I was saying, we've got the CCTV feed ready and waiting. If you'd like to follow me.'

Penn turned without saying anything more and led them to a large, conspicuous white van that looked as if it hadn't been serviced since its production in the late nineties.

They rounded the other side of the vehicle and stopped. The sliding door was open, and sitting inside was a man on a chair with a series of screens and flashing icons in front of him. Stood outside the van were four other members of the force, none of whom Jake recognised. The inside of the vehicle was like something out of a CIA spy movie, and it was unlike anything he'd ever seen before.

'This is The Hub,' Penn said.

The real Hub, Jake thought.

'This is where you'll find everything you need. You'll be in the capable hands of Inspector Carlton Hamilton.'

PC Penn left, and Jake watched her go, wondering

when – or if – he would see her again.

'Evening, gentlemen,' a nasally voice said, distracting Jake's attention back to the van. 'Or is it morning?'

'It doesn't matter,' Mamadou said abruptly.

Hamilton's face dropped; he'd just been given a full dose of what Jake liked to call Mamadou Malevolence. Tolerable in small doses; unbearable in more.

'Just get on with it. *Please.*'

It didn't matter who he was talking to, Mamadou would always greet them with the same contemptuous, short-tempered remarks. It was one reason he was one of the most feared and revered members not only of Counter Terrorism Command but also the entire Metropolitan Police Service. He was infamous for being the service's most belligerent arsehole. But it got results. And when it got results, no one in the upper echelons bothered to pay attention to anything else.

'Right,' Hamilton said, taken aback by Mamadou's abrasiveness. He swivelled round in his chair, typed into his computer and drew up the live CCTV feed on a screen. 'This is inside the cinema, looking out at the entrance.'

'Why are you showing us this?' Jake asked, looking at the empty foyer. 'We can see this from where we're standing right now. We don't need you to show us it.'

Jake couldn't help thinking that Mamadou's arrogance and snappiness were rubbing off on him.

'Give me a second, mate. And I'll find something for you – what is it you're looking for?'

'I want to see who was in here thirty minutes before the film started,' Mamadou said.

Hamilton agreed, told them to be patient while he

loaded the video to the correct time and, when he was finished, pressed play.

The three men watched the screen with intense scrutiny. Jake's eyes darted left and right, searching amongst the throng of people, trying to identify the person responsible.

'Could we play it at double speed?' suggested Mamadou.

Hamilton clicked a button and the individuals on the screen began moving frantically about the foyer, meandering, waiting, purchasing tickets, eating popcorn, entering the screening rooms.

And then, as the digits on the bottom-right of the screen rolled to 11:45 p.m., Jake said, 'Stop it right there.'

The image froze, and Jake pointed to a man wearing a large coat and carrying a gym bag by his side.

'There,' he said. 'There's our guy.'

'How do you know?' Mamadou asked.

'Look at him. Who else takes a gym bag *that* big to the cinema? Unless he's smuggling food and drink for the entire building. Have we got any other points we can view from inside the building?'

'Yes,' Hamilton said. 'Bear with me, mate.'

Jake didn't like being called "mate" at the end of almost every sentence. It was common, and it nibbled away at him. But he wasn't about to argue with someone senior than him right now. Not if he valued his job security.

Hamilton clicked a few more buttons and typed into his keyboard furiously until, a few seconds later, he loaded up the image of a long hallway where the different theatres sprouted off through dark double doors. It was busy – much busier than the foyer, with dense pockets of people lingering around the entrance to the screens. The playback speed increased, and everyone in the image disappeared.

Except for one person, arriving late.

The same man Jake had suspected moments before.

'Follow him,' he said, after the man in the video closed the cinema's double doors behind him.

'I can't. That's all we can get.'

'So there's no CCTV footage of inside the actual screen where they're showing the film?'

Hamilton turned to face Jake and shook his head. 'There is, but I can't access it. Something's prohibiting me. For now, this is all we've got. As for the rest, we're blind.'

CHAPTER 6

It had taken everyone a few minutes to eventually calm down, but now that they were finally paying attention to him, Phillip could begin. An icy chill seemed to filter through the air and swarm around his feet.

'Please, nobody do anything stupid because I will shoot you right after I've shot this kid in the head.' Phillip's deep American accent reverberated around the room. He pulled the boy's ear closer to his mouth and asked, 'What is your name?'

'J-J-J-Josh.'

'Very well, Josh. You're going to be my guinea pig for the evening.' Phillip turned his voice to the rest of the room. 'I hope none of you were planning to enjoy the film tonight?'

His question was met with yet another profound silence that seemed to beat with its own rhythm in his ears.

'If you were, then I suggest you pay attention. Because if you don't, then you won't ever get to see the end.'

He paused for dramatic effect. He could sense the palpable fear and dripping sweat in the air.

'Here's what I want to happen. Each and every one of you are to remain seated. I don't care if you get hungry or thirsty, or if you need a piss, or even if you need a shit – you are not allowed to leave here under any circumstances. Or unless I approve it. Is that understood?'

The light from the giant screen behind him illuminated everyone's faces, yet he remained in shadow, his features concealed.

The people in the front row slowly nodded. Cautious. Afraid. He kept a keen eye on them. Their lives would be the first to end if they did anything stupid. They were the closest to the fire exits. They would be the first to attempt an escape. It was simple logic.

'Now,' Phillip continued, 'does anyone have a mobile phone I could use please?'

The person on the other end of the call was named Amy. That was all Tara could remember about her. She was so caught up in the situation – in fear of losing her life – to store any other information correctly. Amy sounded sweet and soothing in her ear, but Tara was only just able to hear her over the sound of her pulsating heart.

'You need to get out of there as soon as possible,' Amy had said.

'No,' Tara had replied, peering through a small crack in the staff-room door. 'I'm staying.'

'Why?'

'So I can let you guys know what's happening. If I see anything, you'll be the first to know.'

'Then we need constant contact. Remain on the phone for the entire duration. Please, Tara,' Amy said. It wasn't a question, it was an order. And Tara knew it.

'How long's that going to take?'

'We don't know.' Amy hesitated. 'How much battery do you have left on your phone?'

Tara pulled the phone away from her ear. The screen illuminated, and she checked the percentage.

'Thirty-two.'

Shit.

'Is that going to be enough?' Amy asked.

'Probably not. It's been playing up recently. It just switches off whenever it wants.'

Amy exhaled deeply through the phone. No attempt was made to mask her uncertainty. 'Is there anyone else's phone you could use?'

'Potentially.' Tara looked around the room, casting her eyes over her colleagues' lockers; the possessions they'd left scattered around the room that wouldn't fit inside. Backpacks. Handbags. Shopping bags with Tesco meal deals left inside. Bottles of Coke and squash on the table. There wasn't a lot on offer, and if she knew the rest of her colleagues like she thought she did, then they would have ignored their manager's rule and had their phones on them during shift anyway. A price she would have to pay for being the only one who stuck to the rules. 'I'll have to look through their lockers.'

Tara set the phone down on the table in the middle of the staff room. Leftover tobacco adorned the surface. She twisted the handles and pulled on each of the lockers. Each of them was locked, except for her own and a few others that were unoccupied.

Shit.

'Do you know how to unlock them?' Amy asked.

'Not off the top of my head.'

'Do you have a hairpin you could use? Paper clip?'

Tara searched the room, until she finally found a paper clip atop the table, and grabbed it.

'Yes.'

'Put that in one of the locks, twist it around and try to pry it open. It works better if you can use two of them in tandem.'

'OK.' Tara inserted the paper clip in the lock. Hesitated. 'And if that doesn't work?'

'Then you come out of there. No arguments,' Amy said. Deadpan, assertive.

'No can do.'

She twisted and turned the paper clip inside the keyhole. After a few seconds of trying the clip and handle at the same time, the door eventually flew open. She reached inside and searched through the bag she found there.

Nothing.

Fuck you, Casey.

She moved to the next locker. Unlocked it successfully again and investigated the contents. But there was nothing inside except a water bottle and a change of uniform.

Tara swore out loud.

On the third attempt, the paper clip snapped in half. She slammed her fist on the door – her extreme force caused a dent in the metal. Her hand swelled and throbbed with pain.

'Tara, are you there? Can you hear me?'

Amy's voice echoing through the phone on the table

sounded distant, vacant.

Picking it up, Tara said, 'Yes. No luck. This is all I've got for now.' She looked at the percentage on her phone. 'I've got thirty left.'

'OK. There are emergency response units outside, with armed response teams on the way. They'll be there soon.'

'And what do I do in the meantime?'

'Sit tight. And wait.'

Jake watched Inspector Hamilton type on his keyboard in high anticipation. The image on the screen flickered on and off. After giving the side of the monitor a good smack, Hamilton managed to steady it.

'Sorry, lads,' he said. 'Tech's outdated, you know.'

'Yes. We know.'

'Now…' Jake said, leaning closer to the screen. 'Can you run facial recognition on this?'

A slightly pixelated image of a man frozen in time stared back at Jake. It was him, the man responsible. Jake was sure of it, and he committed the face to memory in case he needed it later.

'We're not that advanced, but we might be able to get a name from the financial details he used to pay for the tickets. It looks like he paid by card, so that should tell us something. I'll send it to the guys back at The Yard.'

'How long?' Mamadou asked sternly.

'Give me five minutes.'

'You've got three,' Mamadou said and pulled Jake away to return to his car.

CHAPTER 7

Precisely two minutes and twenty seconds later, Jake and Mamadou had their confirmation.

Detective Inspector Hamilton came running over to Jake, the tops of his loosened shirt bouncing up and down on his shoulders with every step.

'Guv!' he said. 'We've got it. Well, I say "we" – I actually mean the guys back at—'

'Get on with it,' Mamadou said, checking his watch.

'Right, sorry. The card details used to pay for the cinema tickets are registered to a Mr Phillip Bowden. Sixty-seven. Permanent address in Norfolk.'

'Norfolk?' Jake asked, confused.

Hamilton nodded.

'Long way from home. What's he doing in London?'

'Your guess is as good as mine. Mr Bowden is originally from Nevada, US of A.'

'An even longer way from home. Do we know how long he's been in the country?'

Hamilton shook his head.

'Find out everything you can about him. Get a

mobile number for him. Find out his social media – if he's on it. Find out what he does for a living, what he enjoys, where he spends his free time – all of it,' Mamadou ordered.

'Your wish is my command,' Hamilton said before turning and jogging back to his van.

'Christ, he's annoying,' Jake said.

The thought was supposed to remain in his head, but when he saw the sides of Mamadou's lips flicker slightly, he knew he was in good company.

'Preaching to the choir,' Mamadou replied. 'You're not the one who has to have regular meetings with him.'

Jake turned to face the cinema's fascia. 'What's the plan, guv?'

'We wait until he makes contact. There's nothing we can do in the meantime. Going in there armed would only cause us, him and everyone else in there a serious amount of harm. There's no knowing what he wants, nor what he's going to do, nor how he's going to react,' Mamadou explained, resting both arms on the open car door. 'And until we get a live feed of inside the screen, we've got no way of knowing how armed and dangerous he is. For now, we're fucked.'

'Royally,' Jake added. Not only were Mamadou's reactions rubbing off on him but also his vernacular. 'I don't like the girl being inside. It's too dangerous.'

'We'll have to wait until the CTSFOs get here before we can worry about her.'

'What's their ETA?'

'Let me find out. Hold on.'

Phillip Bowden wasn't sure if it was just his nerves, or whether it was someone on the outside messing with the system, but the air inside the auditorium felt cold. The hairs on the back of his neck stood on end, and a chill climbed up and down his body.

He extended his hand. A young girl was standing in front of him. She'd elected to give him her phone. Phillip inspected her. She looked defiant, early twenties, as if she didn't think anything was capable of hurting her and stopping her dead. Like an invincible alcoholic in a bar fight.

'Your phone please,' Phillip said, still pressing the gun into Josh's back. The smell of piss still continued to linger in his nostrils.

The woman reached into her back pocket and removed her phone, then handed it to him.

'Unlock it,' Phillip ordered, his voice neutral, plain, unassuming. 'And ensure it stays unlocked.'

The girl did as she was told and passed the phone back to him. As he held it in his hands, he cast his gaze over the rest of the room and smiled at the wall of grimacing faces staring back at him. No doubt every one of them was sending him their loathsome thoughts. Phillip didn't mind. He welcomed them.

'Cute background picture,' Phillip said. On the girl's home screen was an image of her and a blonde. Phillip presumed it to be a best friend. At most, a sister.

'Don't get too excited,' the girl said.

'Trust me, I won't. There are more interesting things to be getting on with.'

Before dialling 999, Phillip switched off the small electromagnetic pulse device he'd purchased online. At the press of a button, it emitted a signal just wide and powerful enough to disable and disconnect any phone or device with a radius of fifteen metres – perfect for using in the auditorium. At the press of another button, it stopped and allowed him to make a call.

The operator on the other end of the line answered on the second ring. '999, what's your emergency?'

'Good evening, this is Phillip Bowden – I'm currently calling from inside the IMAX cinema at Leicester Square. I'm holding approximately two hundred people hostage at gunpoint, and I would like to speak with the person in charge of this case. You have two minutes to find them and get them to call me on this mobile. Goodbye.'

CHAPTER 8

Chaos.

Night shifts in the dispatch room deep within the depths of a random building in a random part of London were usually quiet, devoid of any serious calls. *Serious* being the optimal word. Of course, there were serious incidents to respond to. Like a stabbing, or a shooting, or a missing person, or a house fire. But never *this* serious. None where there were hundreds of potential victims. A potential mass killing. A potential terrorist-hostage-negotiation situation.

And Naomi was the one dealing with it.

She raised the microphone on her headset, hovering it centimetres above her ear.

'Holy shit,' she whispered to herself, eyes fixed on the computer monitor in front of her.

Realising the seconds were counting down on an invisible clock over her head, Naomi jumped out of the chair and ran along the length of the room towards her manager.

'Gavin!' she said. 'I need your help. Quickly.'

Her manager looked up from his notepad and placed his pen down. 'What is it?'

Naomi explained.

'Oh, Christ,' Gavin replied. 'I'll find out who's handling it.' He reached for the phone on his desk and dialled. With the device held against his head, he asked, 'How long have we got?'

Naomi checked her watch. 'A minute,' she said, shrugging. The concept of time had completely flown out of the window.

'OK. Did you get the number noted—' Gavin began, but then stopped himself as he pressed the phone to his mouth and spoke. 'Hello? This is Gavin Myers. Dispatch. I need to speak to the senior investigating officer currently at the IMAX cinema hostage scene. Urgently.'

Naomi watched Gavin wait on the phone. They were both impatient; she tapped her feet on the floor, and he ran his hands through his hair.

Ten agonisingly slow and painful seconds passed.

'OK. Thank you. What's his number? OK. OK. Thank you.' Gavin scribbled a mobile number down then hung up without saying goodbye.

Gavin ripped the entire page from the notebook and handed it to Naomi. 'DCS Mamadou Kuhoba. Get him on the line and forward him on. You're running out of time. Go! Go!'

Naomi didn't need telling twice. She sprinted the short distance to her desk, wrapped the headset over her head and frantically dialled the numbers, her panicked fingers prodding the wrong buttons. A three for a two, a seven for an eight. The pressure was getting too much. How much time she had left, she didn't know. Worse, she didn't want to know. Unless she could get in contact with DCS Kuhoba in less than thirty seconds or so, the blood of everyone inside the cinema would be on her hands.

She couldn't afford that.

She composed herself. Breathed. In, out. In, out. Stared at the numbers on the phone, carefully pressed them, double checking, making sure it was the right mobile number and that she hadn't fucked it up again. Making sure she wouldn't be responsible for the merciless killing of innocent lives.

The phone rang, the dial tone sounding in her ear. Naomi exhaled deeply. All she could do now was wait. And pray.

Jake reached into the car and picked up Mamadou's phone.

'Hello?'

'DCS Kuhoba?'

'No. This is DC Jake Tanner. DCS Kuhoba has stepped away momentarily. Who is this? Can I take a message? He'll be back shortly.' Jake looked around him, scouting for Mamadou; his boss had decided to go to the bathroom at the most inappropriate moment and had left his mobile on the dashboard for Jake to use if necessary.

'My name is Naomi Taylor. Dispatch. I'm afraid it can't wait until DCS Kuhoba returns. We have received contact from Mr Phillip Bowden. Are you familiar with the situation?'

At the mention of the hostage taker's name, Jake froze.

'Hello? DC Tanner, are you there? This is important.

It's imperative you, or someone else who is senior and experienced enough, speak to him.'

'What…' Jake said, slowly coming to. 'What did he want?'

'He didn't say. But I have to pass you through to him now, or else there will be consequences.'

The line went dead.

At first, Jake panicked and thought he'd accidentally pressed the big red button at the bottom of the screen and ended the call. But before he was able to concern himself too much, the noise of heavy breathing sounded in his ear.

Then silence.

There was someone on the other end. Listening, waiting, playing the game of firsts: who would be first to speak, to make the first move?

Who would move the first piece on the board?

Jake looked around him once more. Mamadou was still out of sight, and the officers surrounding him were the same level as him, frantically hurrying from one side of the square to the next.

Fuck. What was he going to do? What was he going to say? How was he going to conduct himself? If only he'd had the time to finish going through that training less than an hour ago.

'Hello?' a voice said.

'Good… evening,' Jake responded, swallowing deeply to clear his throat. 'Or should I say, good morning?'

The voice on the other end chuckled. 'So I'm speaking to an intelligent man then?'

'It's been known that I passed an A-level examination back in my day.'

'And a funny guy as well. You're the whole

package, aren't you?'

'Jake Tanner. Detective Constable Jake Tanner,' he said, oozing with confidence now, 'if you want to get all James Bond about it.'

The voice chuckled again. 'Well, Jake Tanner, I hope you're the man in charge, and I also hope that you're capable of making things happen – because you're going to need to be.'

CHAPTER 9

'That's me,' Jake said. 'I'm qualified enough.'

He didn't think twice. The words burst out of his mouth. He was in a desperate situation and that was all he could think to do, to say. All he needed to be was a voice. The others surrounding him could be the ones to make things happen. He simply needed to relay the messages and pass the information on. And so long as he could do that efficiently, then he remained in good stead for keeping everyone alive, and for keeping his job.

It is with regret that we announce there will be some redundancies within the team…

'You and I have got some discussing to do,' Phillip said. His American accent sounded alien to Jake's ears; his only experience of such accents had been through TV and cinema, and he was surprised to hear a rawness to Phillip's voice, a pain that didn't make it through digital editing.

Like listening to his voice on vinyl.

'How can I help, Phillip?' Jake asked.

'You know my name?'

'We work fast.'

'Evidently.'

'What is it you want, Phillip?'

'First, before we begin all the pretence, I want you to be absolutely certain how serious I am about the lives of these lovely ladies and gentlemen here. And when I say "serious", I mean I hope you understand I will kill them if I need to – I am very much serious about *that*.'

The calmness in Phillip's voice solidified his seriousness. A man who was that calm about holding the lives of two hundred individuals in his hand was a terrifying and dangerous man indeed.

'Nobody needs to get hurt,' Jake replied. 'I'm sure it won't come to that.'

'You'd be surprised.'

'Sounds like you've done this sort of thing before?' Jake said, concerned. In the back of his mind, he tried to keep a running record of everything Phillip had said to learn all he could about the hostage taker.

'We're all experts in this field, one way or another. No matter who you are or which way you look at it. Copious amounts of crime drama on TV have prepared us for this.'

'Do you watch a lot of crime TV then?'

'I've been known to enjoy it now and then. But before we get into that, I have to show you something.'

'Oh, yes. Right. What?' Jake asked just as Mamadou returned. Finally.

'Who you talking to?' he asked.

Jake batted him away and gesticulated for him to be quiet.

Phillip continued. Quiet, reserved, articulate. 'In about two minutes' time,' he said, 'I will be sending out a young girl. Blonde. Pale complexion. Skinny face. Pretty. I'm sure you'd like—'

'Jake!' Mamadou said, clawing at the phone in his hand. 'Who are you talking to?'

For fuck's sake, Jake thought and rolled his eyes. He pulled the phone away from his mouth, covered the microphone with the palm of his hand and whispered, 'Phillip Bowden is on the phone.'

Mamadou's face dropped. He looked at Jake, perplexed, confused. The question *'Why is he talking to you?'* was written across his face.

For a brief moment, Jake returned the vacant stare, leaving Mamadou's silent question unanswered.

'Are you still there, Detective?' Phillip asked.

'Er… I, yes. We're still here.'

'*We*? Who else is part of the team?'

Shit. He'd dropped the ineptitude ball too early.

'My partner in crime, DCS Kuhoba,' Jake replied.

'DCS? Doesn't that make him your senior? I'm not that familiar with my British police rankings, but I'm fairly sure that's accurate.'

Jake hesitated. The hole he'd dug for himself was getting deeper and deeper. He stared at Mamadou, thankful he wasn't talking to Phillip on speakerphone.

'You'd be correct,' Jake said, feeling his palms turn sweaty. It was time to change the conversation. 'But anyway, you were saying? About a blonde girl coming our way?'

'I see you paid attention to the part you deemed most important. As I was saying – in one minute, a young lady will be exiting the cinema. She will be coming alone, but she will also have a bag of explosives strapped to her back.'

Phillip paused for a beat. There was an indistinct ruffling sound in the background, followed by some harsh whispers.

'She's just putting the final touches to her catwalk dress now, and I think she looks marvellous.'

'What's the point of this? What are you going to do?'

'I'm going to send her out.'

'I know. You've said that. But *why*?' Jake pressed, conscious of the fact that soon – very fucking soon, in fact – there would be a body of explosives heading directly towards half the city's law enforcement, and he'd failed to alert a single one.

'Because I want you to realise this is going to be a very dangerous and deadly night for everyone involved. That you are going to be dealing with someone who is very serious and passionate about protecting themselves. That you understand a change is going to be made tonight that will affect this country in ways it cannot imagine,' Phillip explained.

It scared Jake how calm and authoritative and intimidating and frightening Phillip's voice sounded.

He wasn't such a fan of vinyl anymore…

'Are you going to kill her?' Jake asked.

'Not unless you guys give me what I want.'

'What do you want?'

'To speak to your country's leader. I want to speak with the Prime Minister.'

Jake took a moment to catch his breath. The Prime Minister? What did Phillip want with her? And when was he going to tell Mamadou someone wearing an explosive vest would be shuffling towards them in less than a minute's time?

'I don't know if that will be possible.'

'You promised me you were the man who could make things happen. If they don't, the consequences will be fatal.'

Jesus Christ.

'She's on her way,' Phillip added. 'You have thirty seconds before she arrives, and a further ten to make your decision.'

Her name was Denise, and she was beginning to think her life would be over very shortly. The explosives weighed down on her shoulders, and she tried to walk slow and fast. To find the balance between getting out of there as soon as possible and also ensuring she didn't accidentally detonate as she did so. The sooner she got to help, the sooner they could rescue her. She didn't care about any of the others that were still trapped inside. Danny could stay behind, and if he survived, then she would let him know that she didn't want to see him anymore. That she'd been unsatisfied in their relationship for too long. She'd been given a chance to escape, and in life-or-death situations such as this, it was survival of the fittest.

Every man – or in this case, woman – for themselves.

The bright lights blinded her as she stepped out of the fire-exit door that Phillip had sent her through. It was the only way she, and everyone else stuck inside, could get out. The other entrance to the cinema screen had been sealed shut.

As she neared the cinema foyer, she saw the flashing

blue lights climbing the walls. The cars outside. The neon strips everywhere. The headlights. The men and women wandering around, and the other men and women standing together in knots, interspersed around the compound.

Denise's legs felt weak. Her body was consumed by adrenaline – and the reality that her life was going to be over unless she hurried the fuck up. Then her mind turned introspective and conjured images of her entire life. Her childhood. Her career. Her relationships. How each stage of her life had gone from bad to worse to miserable. Was this what it felt like to die? To have all your worst fears and truths come to you in a final moment of epiphany? To have all your regrets compound into one ball and remind you of the fact you'd wasted so much of it on unnecessary things and people?

If it was, she didn't like it.

She wanted it to stop. Now.

Phillip counted down in Jake's ear.

'Fifteen.'

'Fourteen.'

Jake joined him.

Thirteen.

Twelve.

On eleven, Jake saw the girl. There she was, tall, blonde, pretty. She reminded him of Elizabeth. And there it was, the two straps across her shoulders, undoubtedly part of the explosive device Phillip had mentioned.

Jake pulled the phone away from his ear, muted the

conversation and explained to Mamadou what was happening.

Ten.

Nine.

'Oh shit.' Mamadou shoved Jake out of the way, reached inside the car for the dashboard radio, and began commanding orders.

'Attention! X-ray approaching doors. Armed with explosives. DNF. I repeat, do not fire!' Mamadou slammed the radio down on the dash. Almost immediately afterwards, a flurry of authorised firearms officers swarmed the entrance, forming a semi-circle, guns raised. 'I'll take care of this. You take care of *him*.'

'What shall I say about the PM?' Jake asked.

'I don't know. Tell him she's on the way. Lie if you have to. Buy us some time.'

'And if she doesn't come?'

'She'll have to. It's all on her. Leave it up to me.'

Without saying anything else, Mamadou sprinted away as fast as his overweight body would allow. Jake relaxed a little; he felt safer knowing the situation was in somewhat more capable and reassuring hands.

'Three.'

Phillip's voice brought Jake back to reality.

'Two. Time's running out, Detective.'

'Wait!' Jake shouted. 'She'll be here. The Prime Minister's on her way.'

'Good. You've just saved this girl precious seconds of her life.'

'What do you—?'

Before Jake could finish, the line went dead.

'Hello! Phillip, are you still there?' he called, but it was no use.

Jake turned his immediate attention to the girl in the

foyer, behind the glass entrance to the cinema. Her hands were raised, and her body and face were contorted with fear.

The AFOs, dressed in Kevlar, with guns rested in the nooks of their shoulders, shouted at her to remain where she was.

'Do not come any closer!'

And then Mamadou stepped up. He held a large megaphone that made Jake think of school sports days. Jake didn't know where he'd acquired it so quickly, but he was glad he had.

'Hello,' Mamadou began, 'my name is DCS Kuhoba. Please remain where you are. The last thing we want is for you to get hurt. Can you hear me?'

The girl nodded slowly, like she was a puppet being controlled by a master somewhere.

'Is it possible for you to remove the device on your back?'

The girl shook her head. Jake swore inside. They were fighting against an invisible countdown, and nobody knew what was going to happen if they didn't dispose of the explosives in time.

Before anyone could decide on the best course of action, a figure emerged behind the woman, wearing an IMAX uniform, and at once Jake knew who it was.

Tara inched closer to the girl in front of her. From behind, she looked the same age. Young, inexperienced, naïve, optimistic about life. And yet, somehow, both of them had found themselves in this life-threatening situation. Where neither of them knew what the outcome would be.

Tara had heard the sound of a door opening in the still, quiet corridors, followed by the sound of whimpering and shuffled feet, and it had alerted her to someone's presence. She'd stalked along the walls, keeping herself hidden, well out of sight, and silent – until she realised who the person was and what was happening to them.

'Excuse me,' Tara said, five feet away from the girl. She kept her voice extremely low. 'Don't be alarmed. Don't make any sudden movements. My name's Tara. I'm going to help you, OK?'

The girl stayed facing forward. 'Who are you?'

'I work here. I think I sold you your ticket.'

'How can *you* help me?'

'I don't know. But you and I are going to work it out together, OK?'

Through sobs, the girl replied, 'Yes. Please help me. I don't want to die.'

Tara couldn't bring herself to lie and tell her everything was going to be all right because, in reality, she knew it wouldn't be. Nothing about tonight would ever be right again.

'Stop panicking. I just need to see what it is on your back.'

'It's… it's a bomb.'

Tara froze for a picosecond – a trillionth of a second – and stared at the girl's back, swallowing deeply. Both theirs lives were very much in her hands now.

'Hey,' Tara said, 'what's your name?'

'D-Denise.'

'Hi, Denise. I'm Tara.'

'Hey.'

Tara stopped inches from Denise's back and inspected the device. She couldn't bring herself to walk in front of Denise and introduce herself face to face.

'OK. I'll tell you what I can see, OK?'

'OK.'

'There's a lot of duct tape. It's black, and it's quite big. Is it heavy?'

'Yes.'

'OK. There's also another— Wait, is that…?' Tara paused.

On the device was a small piece of fabric that had been stuck to the outside. Hiding beneath it was a phone. Tara pulled at the fabric, trying to get the phone. As she did so, the bottom of the explosive device came into view. Attached to the phone's charging port was a small countdown timer.

'Oh my God.'

'What?'

The digits on the clock started to count down. In one rash, panicked movement, Tara had given herself five seconds to get the device from Denise's back and return her to safety.

'What is it? What's the matter?'

Tara ignored her. Grabbed the explosive. Pulled.

The duct tape sealing it all together extended and tore slightly.

Three.

She tried again. This time harder. And thankfully, the device dangled loosely from her lower back. With another tug, it came free.

Two.

Without thinking, Tara threw the explosive directly in front of her. Towards the exit. Towards security. Towards safety. Then she grabbed Denise's arm and yanked her backward.

'Run!' Tara screamed, her voice filling the nooks and

crannies around the cinema, reverberating in the distance.

They both made it as far as a set of sofas to the left-hand side of the foyer. Tara didn't know why she instinctively ran towards them, but perhaps it was because, if they were going to die, she knew it would at least be in a comfortable resting place.

One.

The sound of the explosion was ear-shattering. The force propelled Tara from her feet onto the hard concrete floor; she landed a few inches from the comfort of the sofa, an intense, searing red heat warming her skin.

Ears ringing, blood pulsing, she lifted herself onto her elbows, exhaled deeply and rested her back against the chair. Her eyes fell on the devastation the explosion had caused. The inside of the cinema was filled with acrid smoke that clung to her lungs and made her cough. The smell of decimated chemicals made her feel sick. And as she scanned the rest of the room, her eyes found Denise slumped to the floor. Small holes peppered her back, head and legs.

'Denise?' Tara asked, scrambling across the floor. 'Denise? Are you OK?'

As soon as she put weight on her left arm, Tara felt a stinging sensation shoot up through it. She looked down and saw a nail lodged in her forearm. The explosion and adrenaline had numbed the pain – and her entire body.

Ignoring it, Tara rushed to Denise's side, felt the metal pins buried in the woman's skin and rolled her over to check for a pulse. When she didn't find one, Tara collapsed onto the floor, smashing the back of her head against the concrete, and stared at the ceiling.

She'd failed to protect someone.

Again.

She'd let someone die.

We've had to amputate Vanessa's legs. The damage sustained was far too severe.

That sick son of a bitch had used a nail bomb to make sure there were a maximum number of casualties.

And Tara was going to make sure it didn't happen again.

CHAPTER 10

Phillip smiled. The sound of the explosion coming through the thick, near-soundproofed walls filled him with a tingling sensation that swarmed his skin. Almost like pins and needles. And it had been worth it. Months of researching, months of planning, trial and error, hurting himself in the process – it had all been to show them what he was capable of and the lengths he would go to.

Shooting someone wasn't enough; *destroying* them, on the other hand, was.

Phillip raised his hands, commanding silence in the auditorium.

'Please don't be upset,' he said. 'She killed herself. There was a small switch on the back of the device that would only be activated if a small strap was removed. So, whoever removed the strap is responsible for her death, not me. She was a necessary sacrifice.'

Phillip wandered up and down the length of the screen. He hoped it cast an ominous shadow over his face.

'You should let her death be a lesson to all of you. Nowadays, nobody wants to be the hero. So when the opportunity comes to protect ourselves and our loved ones, we simply stand back and allow merciless shit to happen to other people. Wouldn't you agree?'

Silence.

'Tough crowd, huh? Very well. Next orders: each and every one of you, on your feet – now.'

It took them a while, but eventually everyone in the room complied with the order.

'It's time to mix it up. I want you to separate yourself from the person or people you've come here with. Find yourself a new space somewhere in this room and sit in it. You have thirty seconds. Anyone without a seat gets shot.'

At first nobody moved, and he felt two hundred pairs of eyes staring at him. It wasn't until he raised the M16 that his prisoners reacted. Those at the front of the cinema leapt out of their seats and huddled up the stairs to the back. And within seconds, pushes and shoves broke out. A mass of bodies fighting against the tide of one another for safety and security. Safety and security that no one was willing to concede.

Phillip watched in amazement as families and groups of friends split up and became dismembered from one another.

Thirty seconds later, everyone had found a seat.

'That wasn't so hard, was it?' Phillip asked. 'Now you're all settled with your new friends and family, I want you to wait. That's all you have to do for the next hour. Wait, and nothing will happen to you. Kick up a fuss, and then we'll have a problem.'

Phillip gave one last look at the room, clarified everyone was in fact seated, and then dialled the last number in Denise's address book.

Detective Constable Jake Tanner. *The inexperienced one*. It was obvious how amateur Tanner was. He was going to enjoy making the detective and Prime Minister's life hell. *Especially if he lies to me.*

Phillip pressed the green button and waited for the call to be answered.

'Phillip?' Jake asked. There was a slight hint of apprehension in his voice.

'Hello again, Detective. Did you like the fireworks?'

'What *was* that? How did you detonate it?'

'I didn't. There was a switch on the back that could only be activated manually. One of *your* men initiated it. One of your men killed that young girl and probably multiple others. Were there other injuries? Did anyone else perish?'

Jake Tanner hesitated. The sound of shouts and screams and sirens echoed, filling Phillip with glee.

'None.'

'You're lying to me,' Phillip hissed.

'Why would I do that?'

'Because that's what you do. You lie, make promises you can't keep. You're all just politicians deep down, aren't you? After all, you are run by them. What they say goes.'

'There's greater autonomy nowadays than there ever has been.'

'True. But you're still not allowed to shoot anyone without someone's say so, are you?'

'Depends on the circumstances. Depends who's holding the gun. Depends whether or not they have a reasonable justification for it.'

'Would you say *this* is a reasonable justification, Detective? Would you say that shooting me is a reasonable justification?' Phillip kept his finger hovered over the trigger of his M16. It felt cold to the touch but also powerful, ethereal.

Jake scoffed in his ear. 'I'm not the one who has to make that decision. I'm not the one who has to reasonably justify it.'

'Well, let us say you did…'

'Why are you doing this, Phillip? What are your demands? What are *your* justifications?'

'How long have you got, Detective?'

'As long as you need. I'm not going anywhere.'

'Neither am I.'

'So then I think it's time you told me what you want out of this. And whether we can come to an amicable agreement. Your interests are our interests.'

'Cute.'

'So indulge me. Why are you doing this?'

Phillip inhaled deeply, filling his entire body with oxygen, and spoke. 'What are your opinions on guns, Detective?'

'Inasmuch as?'

'Inasmuch as defending yourself?'

'I don't think they're necessary. I think there are smarter, more appropriate means of protection. I think they're poison – like alcohol. Guns have the power to take a life instantly – no one should have that power. Ever.'

'Have you ever used one, Jake?'

Jake hesitated. The long stretch of silence was filled with a heavy sense of foreboding.

'No. But I've seen the devastation they can cause.'

'How?'

Another hesitation.

'A colleague of mine was shot in the head. I found

his body.'

'Did he deserve it, Jake?'

'There was a time where I thought he did. But now, no. Nobody does.'

'Why did he die?' Phillip asked.

'It's a long story.'

'I thought this was story time? I'm telling you mine. Now it's your turn to tell me yours.'

Jake sighed through the phone. 'He was corrupt. Got in deep with some dangerous people and betrayed them. It was my boss who shot him.'

'Sounds to me like he got what he deserved.'

'He made a mistake,' Jake said. 'We've all done it.'

Yes, yes, we all have.

Nobody felt that more than Phillip.

'Your colleague was eradicated because he'd done wrong. He was bad.'

'He wasn't a disease. He wasn't a virus you can just cure with a single shot.'

'You'll find that metaphor to be true on more than one level, Jake. What if he'd done something to your family? Would he still have not deserved it then?'

'That's a completely different matter.'

'Just answer the question, Detective.'

'It wouldn't have been my boss shooting him. It would have been me.'

'Why?'

'Because I'd do whatever I need to in order to protect my family.'

'And that's exactly what I did.'

Jake grunted through the phone. The noise he produced sounded as if he'd opened his mouth to speak but then closed it immediately afterwards. Phillip took it on himself to carry on.

'It was last year. After Christmas. The decorations were still up and there was leftover turkey in the fridge. It was my wife's idea to celebrate. I usually hate all that shit. It's boring, unnecessary and a waste of time. But this year was different. It was our twentieth wedding anniversary in the same month. So I compromised. And then it turned out to be the worst day of my life.'

'What happened?'

Phillip swallowed hard before continuing.

'It was the evening. My wife was cleaning up the dishes. I heard a knock at the door, so I answered it. As soon as the door swung open, three men charged in the house, shoved me to the ground, ransacked the entire place. My wife threatened them with a knife, but they snatched it off her and stabbed her in the stomach. She bled out on our kitchen floor while I was unable to save her. I couldn't do anything about it. I held her in my arms until the ambulance arrived.'

A moment of silence descended. They were taking their new bond to a different level. Phillip hadn't told that story to many people. It meant a lot to him. And he'd prepared himself to tell it tonight, but he hadn't believed it would affect him this much.

'I'm sorry to hear that,' Jake said, breaking Phillip out of his trance. 'That sounds horrible. It must have been very distressing for you.'

'It was.'

'Forgive me, but what does that have to do with guns, with tonight?'

'Because, Jake, if this were to happen in the United States – my home country, the place where I was born and raised proudly – I would have been able to defend myself. I would have been able to defend my wife. I would have been able to stop her death. And we would have been able to share the rest of our remaining years together. And your government took away that right. They stopped me from having my own gun in my own home, and I will never forgive them for that. Do you understand?'

Jake Tanner didn't say anything.

'And what's worse is that your laws and parliament think it's wrong for me to defend myself and inflict harm on those who enter my home without permission, meaning *I'm* the one who gets punished. Do you know how unjust that is?'

'I do.'

'So... Wait.' Phillip hesitated. Jake's blunt and honest response had taken him by surprise. 'So what can *you* do about it?'

'Nothing. I don't have that power for change.'

'But the Prime Minister does.'

'Correct.'

'And where is she?'

'She's on her way.'

Phillip checked his watch, using the blue light from the screen behind him to illuminate it.

'That's not good enough. She was supposed to be here eight minutes ago.'

'I understand. But she's coming from the outskirts of London. It might take a little more time.'

'How much longer?'

Jake began speaking, stopped, puffed through the phone, stopped again, and then spoke. 'I don't know.'

Phillip shook his head. 'That's still not good enough, Detective. Aren't you supposedly in charge? Surely you must know what's going on, or am I dealing with the wrong person here?'

'No, no! You're not! I promise.'

'Good. So let me make it abundantly clear what I want: the Prime Minister of the United Kingdom needs to be standing outside the cinema with you beside her. She needs to be here in thirty minutes and not a moment later. So go away and talk to your superiors or your inferiors to make it happen. And for every minute she's late, I will kill another hostage. I have more explosive devices and plenty of bullets in my bag. How does that sound? You have one minute to confirm what I need.'

CHAPTER 11

As soon as the line went dead, Jake rushed to find Mamadou. He was somewhere amidst the chaos and destruction. Dozens of officers and paramedics had swarmed the scene to attend to those affected. By now, the smoke had dissipated, but the stench that lingered in the air remained. Jake's pulse was through the roof as his internal body clock counted down the seconds.

He weaved his way in and out of the throng of people sprinting from left to right. It was like he was in an episode of *Total Wipeout*.

Jake stopped in the middle of it all. His eyes searched for Mamadou, bouncing between the heads and bodies and arms and legs and backpacks and helmets and vests, hoping he would find his senior before the time was up.

And there he was, talking to a police constable, gesticulating wildly in the man's face. Jake knew from experience Mamadou was shouting at the poor man.

Jake raced over, pulled Mamadou away by the arm, giving the police constable some breathing space, and told him what Phillip had demanded – and the consequences if those demands weren't met.

'She's not coming,' Mamadou explained.

His words felt like a wrecking ball had just hit Jake's lungs and knocked the wind from them.

'What do you mean?'

'She's not coming. It's as simple as that. It's too dangerous.'

'What are you talking about? She has to. Otherwise he's going to kill one hostage every minute, Mam.'

'I am very well aware, thank you. But she won't come. Something about COBRA. Why does he need her here anyway?'

Jake informed Mamadou of the motives behind Phillip's attack.

'Insane' was Mamadou's only response.

'Phillip wants to speak to the PM in person. There's no way she'll be able to do it behind a desk, behind her four walls, behind the big black door of number ten.'

Mamadou shook his head. Exhaled deeply. Rubbed his temples. 'Fine. Give me ten minutes. I can't make any promises, but I've got a few more buttons I can press.'

'And how long shall I tell Phillip it'll take for her to be here?'

'Twenty. And we better fucking hope she's no later than that.'

Jake nodded, returned to Mamadou's car and waited. He held the phone in his hands. Twirled it around using his thumb and index finger. Contemplated everything he and Phillip had discussed.

Drew Richmond, his old colleague.

Liam Greene, his old manager.

The shot. The bullet. Drew's body slouched against the chair. Blood and brain matter splattered against the wall.

His and Phillip's conversation had awoken a tirade of depression and turmoil he'd fought so hard to suppress.

The phone rang.

He answered.

'Phillip.'

'Time's up. When is she arriving?'

Jake checked his watch. The time was 2:12 a.m.

'She'll be here by two thirty.'

Eighteen minutes. Two minutes less than Mamadou had advised. A decision he was going to have to live with. He had to appease Phillip, even if it meant lying and risking the lives of everyone inside the cinema in the process. If the Prime Minister was late, it would be on her hands; she was already well aware of the situation, and had decided to dictate it from the safety and security of her office. There was no excusing cowardice, and everyone in the country would see that.

'Fine,' Phillip said. 'I'll be in touch. Until then, sit tight and pray there aren't going to be any more fireworks. We might even be able to catch the last of the film.'

Phillip rang off. Jake pocketed the phone and stood there for a moment. The sound of everything around him disorientated him, disturbed his thoughts. He needed peace. Quiet. Solace.

He hopped into the BMW X5 and closed the door, shutting out the outside world. He exhaled deeply, feeling the tension in his body release momentarily.

It was time to think. He and the rest of SO15 needed to have a plan – a way to save the hostages with as little collateral damage as possible. He tried to focus on a solution but couldn't. He was tired. Irate. And trying to combat the impending wall of guilt that he could feel rushing up to meet him ever since he'd mentioned Drew's name.

Think, for fuck's sake, Jake. Think!

He slammed his fist on the dashboard. Somehow, his other hand had pressed a button on the control that opened the boot. As it swung open, it gave Jake an idea.

A rear entrance.

Jake wandered to the back of the car, slammed it shut and returned to the driver's seat. There, he began to think. They needed to get in through the back of the cinema. To follow the same path as the poor girl currently lying dead on the floor in the foyer had. But they couldn't enter guns blazing. No, they needed to be inconspicuous, to see inside the cinema. They needed to see where Phillip was in relation to everyone else. But how? How would they be able to get a visual without drawing Phillip's attention?

Tara.

Yes, that might work. But it was a massive risk.

The other option was the fire exit.

And, with an idea formed in his mind, Jake exited the car in search of Mamadou.

He found him talking loudly into a phone.

'That's not the point. No. No, I didn't authorise that...'

Jake stepped into Mamadou's field of view. Mamadou's eyes widened as he looked at the phone in Jake's hand, then back to Jake.

'Could you bear with me one second please, Prime Minister? I just need to discuss something with my colleague.'

Mamadou muted the conversation. 'This better be worth the interruption.'

'I've got an idea.'

'What?'

'I'll tell you in a second.' Jake nodded to the phone in Mamadou's hand. 'What's she saying?'

'This is a threat to national security. She's staying well away.'

It is with regret…

The words of the email echoed in his mind.

Then: *And for every minute she's late, I will kill another hostage.*

'Give it here,' Jake said. 'Let me have a word.'

'No, you—'

Jake snatched the device from Mamadou's hands and scurried away before Mamadou could react.

It is with regret…

Jake stared at the small, brick-like phone. It had buttons on it and reminded him of something he'd had in the early 2000s when he was at university. Back then, it was the ultimate fashion statement and the height of technology. Now it was largely considered a piece of nostalgia.

Jake unmuted the conversation. 'Prime Minister?'

'Who is this?'

Jake introduced himself.

'What do you want, DC Tanner?'

'I want you to listen to me. I want you to pay attention to what I have to say because I would like you to be here by half past. I know you can do it. You're only down the road. You could walk it in time. Hell, you could even have a shower, some breakfast, coffee, do your hair and make-up and be here with a few minutes to spare.' Jake's mouth said the words before his brain had had a chance to approve them. Forty yards away, near Mamadou's X5, the Counter Terrorism Specialist Firearms Officers arrived in a blacked-out, unregistered van.

'Excuse me? How dare you talk to me like that—'

'I'll talk to you however I want. You're just another human, not much different from me. You've just been elected into a higher position, but that doesn't mean your moral compass should suffer as a result. There are people in there – *your people,* the people you're supposed to protect – and they need you. Now more than ever. Imagine the damage it will cause to your image and your reputation. I can see the headlines now: "PM allows dozens to die."'

'I don't know what to say, Detective. Your belligerent and abhorrent attitude bewilders me.'

'Stop using big words and just say you're pissed. Because I am as well. I'm really pissed. I'm not about to let dozens of people die because one person's ego is standing in the way. It's wrong, and I'm ashamed to think that I once believed in you. What are your reasons for not doing it? Are you scared?'

'No.'

'Then tell me why you're being a coward? Bring as many security and bodyguards as you want, but there is no way you will be harmed. The man responsible is hiding *inside.* If you can't bring yourself to face an almost invisible opponent, then what can you do?' Jake's chest heaved. His adrenaline was on a high. He'd just spoken down to one of the most powerful people in the country. And he didn't know if he was going to live to tell the tale.

It is with regret…

In his attempt to preserve his job, he may have just done the exact opposite.

A few painfully long seconds passed.

'I'll be there.'

The line went dead. Jake smiled and returned the phone to Mamadou, who'd finally caught up with him.

'And?' he asked.

'She's coming.'

Mamadou's expression changed. As if he'd just seen someone get slapped. 'Jesus, Jake,' he said. 'You've got bigger balls than me. I wouldn't dream of doing what you just did. So what's this plan of yours?'

Jake smirked. 'Follow me.'

CHAPTER 12

'Gentlemen,' Jake said as he and Mamadou approached the members SCO19, the Met's Specialist Firearm Command. They were dressed in black military gear from head to toe, and at once Jake felt intimidated. The majority of them were smaller than him, but they were all much more physically defined, even behind their uniform. Wider shoulders. Thicker arms. Legs as large as his waist. They were known as Counter Terrorism Specialist Firearms Officers, and were the highest trained firearms officers in the country. Kept on standby for twenty-four hours a day, the team of one sergeant and fifteen constables, could be called upon to storm buildings, planes, buses and even boats. And they were perfect for hostage negotiations.

Exactly what Jake, and the rest of the team, needed.

'All right?' the closest one to Jake answered. 'You the ones in charge here?'

Jake tried to place the accent but was unable to. Somewhere from up North, he presumed.

'He is,' Jake said, pointing to Mamadou.

'How can we help?'

'Who's your sergeant?' Mamadou asked. 'We need to speak with him.'

The man looked around at the rest of the men in black, stared at each of them for a second or two, and then said, 'That'd be me. Sergeant Marshall.'

Sergeant Marshall extended his hand, and Jake took it. His grip felt powerful, and Jake tried as hard as he could to match Marshall's strength.

He failed tremendously.

'Pleased to meet you. I'm DC Tanner, and this is DCS Kuhoba. I'm sure you're well aware of the situation?'

Marshall nodded. It was a soft, gentle nod, but there was something in the man's eyes, obscured beneath the helmet, that told Jake he knew even more than he was letting on. Jake wasn't sure if it was just his heightened sense of paranoia or whether there was some truth to it – but he hoped he wasn't right.

'Very well. What we need from you guys is to enter through the rear entrance of the cinema, insert a small, microscopic camera – or something similar – through the underside of the fire exit in screen fourteen. That way, we can spy on them and be ready to jump in when we need to. It'll also give us a clear visual on the target, so when the time comes, you'll know what you're shooting at,' Jake explained.

Marshall remained perfectly still for a moment. His expression didn't change. His intimidation level, however, multiplied.

'Interesting.'

'Can it be done?'

'Aye, it can. But we'll have to find the plans for the

rear entrance so we can plan our way in. And we also need that camera. Do you have one?'

Jake didn't. He hadn't even thought that far ahead. He'd simply assumed there would be one lying around. The lack of sleep was getting to him.

'Can you source one?' Jake asked, clinging to his last strand of optimism.

'I can,' Mamadou said energetically. 'Give me a few minutes. I'm sure there's somebody around here who knows what they're doing. If not, I'll call in a few favours.'

Mamadou left and disappeared almost completely, his helmet of silver hair acting like a beacon of light as he wandered away. If there was one thing Jake was learning about working for Mamadou and Counter Terrorism Command, it was that a lot of people owed Mamadou a lot of favours. Jake was certain he wanted to be on the right side of Mamadou's debt at all times.

'What more do you need?' he asked Marshall.

'The blueprints. A map. A vague idea of where we're going and what the inside of that place looks like. We won't be able to do anything unless we plan our escape route.'

Jake nodded. 'I'll see what I can do. Bear with me.'

Conscious of the fact he came across as inexperienced and amateur, Jake wandered over to Inspector Hamilton's van and asked him if he had any. Hamilton replied that he didn't, and then Jake asked him to find some – to print them out if he needed to – and bring them over to Jake when they were ready.

To Jake's immediate surprise, within thirty seconds, Hamilton brought up a PDF file of the buildings, and a smug smile on his face that said, 'I *am* useful for something.' Jake waited patiently while Hamilton printed the documents and handed them over. He returned to Sergeant Marshall with the pages in his hands.

'They're all yours,' Jake said.

'Thanks. Appreciate it.'

'How long do you need?'

'Just until you can get me that camera.'

'I'll hurry him along.'

'If you can find him,' Marshall said.

Jake started off but was held back by the sergeant's powerful grip. 'Before you go, there are a few more things I need to know. How armed is he? When will we have the instruction to advance and make a move?'

Jake realised he was the least qualified to answer, but if there was one thing he'd learnt tonight, it was that the more convincing and confident he came across in his performance, the more people seemed to believe and accept that he knew what he was talking about. The more they seemed to trust him.

'One thing at a time, Sergeant,' he said. 'There are lots of lives at stake, and we don't want to jeopardise them by charging in guns blazing. Both literally and figuratively.'

'I don't think you understand, Detective. We need to know the parameters around our attack. The dos and don'ts. So I'll ask again: who are we waiting for to give us what we need?'

Marshall stepped to within a foot of Jake's face, until the front tip of his helmet almost touched his forehead.

Jake swallowed. For the first time, someone had seen through his performance. Unless it was a test…

It is with regret…

'Me. You're waiting for me to tell you when to

advance. Understood?'

Marshall said nothing, just turned and walked away to the rest of his group, where he explained the situation.

They spent the next three minutes familiarising themselves with the blueprints, absorbing the information and digesting it.

'Jake!' a voice called from behind him.

Mamadou. The overweight man struggled over to Jake and came to a stop inches from him. His breathing was heavy, and he placed both palms on the bonnet to return the oxygen to his lungs.

'Are you all right?' Jake asked. 'There you were saying I needed to be in the gym more often.'

Mamadou flashed his middle finger.

Jake smirked. 'What have you got for us?'

'A special toy.'

Mamadou opened his other hand and revealed a small, tube-like device.

'What is it?'

'A camera, dickhead. What did you think it was? A sweet?'

Jake didn't retaliate. He took the camera from Mamadou's hand and inspected it.

'How does it work?' he asked.

'Like any other video camera. Switch on, press a button and *boom* – you've got yourself a live feed of whatever that little lens sees. Brilliant, isn't it?'

'Where's it linked up to?'

'This little thing.' Mamadou reached into his breast pocket and removed a small computer tablet. More robust and heavy duty than a typical Samsung or Apple tablet. Perfect for the requirements of the situation.

'So now we'll be able to see the inside of the cinema and know what's happening whenever Phillip isn't on the line,' Jake said, thinking aloud. 'This is brilliant.'

Before he could continue, Sergeant Marshall approached them both. 'Gentlemen, my men are briefed. They've just got to perform a few more checks.'

'This is yours.' Jake held the microscopic camera at arm's length, and Marshall took it.

'Appreciate it.'

'Oh and, Sergeant?' Mamadou started. 'If anything goes wrong, you know what the suspect looks like, right?'

Marshall nodded.

'Shoot to injure. Not to kill. As little collateral damage and civilian crossfire as possible please.'

'Certainly. On your orders, sir. Just give us the say-so.'

'There's one more thing we need to do first, but get yourselves in position in the meantime.'

As soon as Marshall and the rest of the CTSFOs were out of sight, Jake started away.

Mamadou called him back. 'Where the fuck are you going?'

'I need to make a call.'

CHAPTER 13

'How are you getting on?' Amy asked.

Tara was sitting with her back pressed against a wall, mountains of popcorn beside her, teetering on the precipice.

She'd run – crawled, in fact – to safety. She'd worked at the cinema for so long it had felt like a second home to her. But she'd never expected a bomb to destroy that second home. She'd never expected to see a dead girl, perforated with holes, lying next to her, bleeding out on the floor. So she'd done the first thing her mind had thought of: escape.

Tara had been inside the stockroom for the past ten minutes, staring vacantly at the opposite wall. Thinking nothing. Feeling nothing. Seeing *everything*. The girl. The blood. The nails. The smoke. The smell. The scorch marks on the floor. It made her feel sick; next to her was a pile of vomit she'd thrown up as soon as her mind had paused to acknowledge the situation.

'Tara, are you there? Can you hear me?'

Amy. Again, with her incessant questions. Tara

knew she meant well and that she was trying to do her job, but it was beginning to get on her fucking nerves.

'Yes,' Tara said, sighing heavily. 'I'm here. I'm fine. I just need… time.'

'OK. I understand, but that's the last thing you'll be able to have at the moment.'

'Why?'

'There's a detective on the line who would like to speak with you.'

'Me? Why?'

'I'll put you through to him now so he can explain. Don't worry – you're not in trouble.'

Even though it felt like she was.

The line went dead, then came the silence. Tara was sure she could hear something but wasn't brave enough to talk first.

'Hello?' a voice said. It sounded calm, soothing and deep. Like her dad's.

Tara felt compelled to answer. 'Hello?'

'Is that Tara?'

'Yes. Who is this?'

'Detective Jake Tanner. I work with Counter Terrorism Command. It's a part of the Metropolitan Police.'

'I know what it is.'

'Good.'

'What do you want? I'm not coming out of here. Not yet. Not until I've helped those people.' Tara felt as though she was actually talking to her dad, given the defiance in her voice; the teenage rebelliousness she'd not long grown out of.

'That's fine, Tara. I want you to stay in there.'

'Why?'

'Because you can be a real asset, Tara. You can make

a real difference to the outcome of this ordeal. You can be the reason these people live,' Detective Jake Tanner said.

She liked the name, and in her head she tried to imagine him but couldn't. Images of a tall, dark and handsome man in a polo shirt and chinos, leaning against a Mercedes convertible jumped out at her. But knowing her luck with men – if Nathan was anything to go by – he would be more like the sweaty overweight car dealer trying to sell the Mercedes.

'How?' she asked, trying to force the image from her mind.

'I need you to help us. Of course, you can say no if you wish, and we won't judge you. The final decision is yours.'

'What do I have to do?'

'Do you have access to the room the current showing of *Star Wars* is being transmitted from?'

'The projection room?'

'Yes! That's the one. Do you have access to it? Can you get to it safely and securely?'

'I don't see why it would be an issue. I might need a key but that's about it. I can find that easily anyway.'

Tara rose to her feet. She could already begin to decipher what Jake Tanner was asking of her.

'Excellent. What I need you to do is enter the room, peer through the hole into the auditorium and report back what you see. You don't have to do anything else. Just look in there once and leave if you feel uncomfortable. The last thing we want is for you to be put in any other sort of harm – we can pull you out as soon as you need us to,' Jake explained.

Tara opened the door a fraction, peering through the small sliver. There was no one on the other side.

Nothing except for the fear and guilt of Denise's death stuck in the forefront of her mind.

Tara swallowed deeply. 'It's fine. I'll do it. I'll give you a call when I'm there.'

'We'd prefer if you stayed on the line please. Just in case something happens to you.' Jake sounded concerned, and it made Tara feel a little warm inside.

She looked down at the battery level. Fifteen per cent. Dangerously low.

'I know the fastest way there,' she said. 'I can call you back in two minutes, I promise.'

There was a pause on the end of the line.

In the end, he said, 'Don't make promises you can't keep.'

Jake hung up the phone. Looked around him. The CTSFOs were pooled together in the distance. All of them standing powerful, authoritative, commanding, oozing charisma. Mamadou was next to them, discussing, advising, pretending as if he knew what he was doing. Mamadou was the far more experienced of the two, yet Jake knew his manager and friend had never found himself in charge of a situation like this. They were both as out of their depth as one another.

But Jake needed to make sure his plan worked. His job security was riding on it.

He checked his watch – 2:26 a.m. *Four minutes left.* And still no sign of the Prime Minister. Jake was beginning to think he'd made a terrible decision in forcing her to come – and in lying to Phillip about her imminent arrival.

Jake started off towards Mamadou when a large

convoy of blacked-out Range Rovers rolled up to the outskirts of Leicester Square. Jake watched them intently. Out stepped the Prime Minister. Tall, defiant, and carrying an air of dismissiveness and control about her.

The most powerful person in the country had entered the conversation.

Jake watched her glide across the square until she came to a stop in the centre, a few yards from where he was standing. Mamadou was the first to acknowledge her and shake her hand, followed by the several members of staff behind her. Jake was the last to arrive. He stood on the edge of the small knot of people and observed.

'Thank you for coming, Prime Minister,' Mamadou began. 'The situation is currently under as much control as we can reasonably believe it to be.'

'Sounds convincing,' the PM said sarcastically. She stepped forward into the knot of people. 'Where is a Mr Jake Tanner?'

Jake lowered his head. Kept himself shielded behind one of the soldiers. What was she going to do? What was she going to say?

There's only one way to find out.

'I'm here,' he said, stepping into view.

What was left of the Prime Minister's smile vanished. 'So am I, as you wished. But I don't have long. What is it you need me to do?'

'Answer a phone call. Answer a few questions. Pray nobody else gets killed.' Jake then informed the PM of Phillip's motives. How he wanted an upheaval of the UK's gun laws. How he wanted to be able to defend himself rightfully in his own home.

'My team and I have worked on something to say to

him. What will happen in the meantime?'

'That's where we'll be stepping in, ma'am,' Sergeant Marshall said. 'We'll be entering round the back and inserting a small camera into the auditorium so we can see and hear everything that goes on inside.'

'Why hasn't this been done already? Those hostages have been trapped in there for a substantial amount of time now.'

Jake wanted to roll his eyes at that comment but knew he would be seen and that it wouldn't be worth the dismissal.

'These things take time, ma'am,' Mamadou said.

'Fine. How long until this phone call?'

Jake and everyone else around him checked their watches.

'One minute.'

Then, almost as if on cue, the phone Jake had been using all evening vibrated. He watched the screen light up. The mobile number flashed at the top. He imagined Phillip on the other end, holding the phone to his ear, gun in the other hand, waiting, listening, paying attention to the dial tone…

Jake answered. 'You're calling early.'

'I know. It felt like such a long time ago since we last spoke.'

'Which vaguely translates into a lack of trust,' Jake said.

'That's both true and not true, Jake.'

'This is only going to work if you do trust me. I can't help you if you don't.'

'Whatever you say.' Phillip chuckled. 'Is *she* there?'

Jake looked over to the Prime Minister. Their eyes locked.

'Yes. She is. She's right in front of me.'

'Pass her over.' Phillip's voice dropped. Whatever excitable tone it had held, no matter how minimal, had completely disappeared.

Jake wandered towards the Prime Minister. It was the first time they'd met, and he realised it couldn't have been under worse circumstances.

'I'm passing you to her now.'

Jake handed the phone over. As soon as the baton had been passed, Jake felt a wave of relief lift from his shoulders; it was in her hands now.

'Hello. You are speaking to the Prime Minister of the United Kingdom on an unsecured line. Please be informed that we are taking this situation very seriously, and that we would like all the hostages under your duress returned home to their families safely.'

CHAPTER 14

The corridors were empty.

It felt surreal, that something usually so densely populated was so deserted. Even when there were multiple viewings taking place at once, it still seemed *busy*. Still, Tara wandered through them on high alert. She didn't know what was round the corner. Nor did she know if someone would erupt from the auditoriums and startle her – or, worse, attack. Nor did she know if one of the screening rooms or the toilets were going to blow up and kill her in the process.

Her irrational imagination ignited sparks of paranoia and dread in her mind.

Tara stopped at a set of double doors. Gently, she pushed them open and, upon seeing the corridor on the other side was empty, stepped through. Feeling a little safer, she dropped her shoulders and relaxed. Then she wandered through another set of doors and eventually arrived at the projection room.

Carefully, she opened the door, paying particular attention to the sound that the rusty door hinges made, lest they alerted anyone to her presence.

Once inside, Tara crept towards the small square in the wall that separated the projection room from the auditorium. Resting her back against the wall, she slid to the ground. Composed herself. And listened.

The auditorium was deathly silent. Eerily silent. So much so that the hairs on her forearms rose and her skin turned to gooseflesh. No sound of movement, no sound of breathing, life.

Were they all dead?

Tara didn't want to think about it but then realised she didn't have a choice. She needed to find out.

The police were asking her to.

Jake Tanner was asking her to.

With his Mercedes and handsomeness.

Crawling on her hands and knees, Tara positioned herself under the square in the wall and rose. She peered over the lip in the small window, keeping her head out of the camera's projection; if she got in the way, she would cause a shadow on the screen which even the most non-observant person would notice.

The auditorium was pitch-black, save for the light bouncing off the screen. Standing before it was a man holding a gun. Beside him was... *Josh! Oh my God, Josh!* His face, lit by the flickering images projected from behind Tara, filled her with both excitement and guilt. Dozens of questions raced through her mind. Was he OK? Why was he being held at gunpoint? How had he got himself involved in this mess? How had either of them?

'Hello?' a voice rang out from inside the auditorium, and Tara frantically ducked under the window.

'Prime Minister,' the terrorist continued, 'what an

occasion this is, eh? I didn't think you'd actually turn up… Everyone's safe. For now… That depends how you respond to my demands, I'm afraid.'

Intrigued, Tara rose carefully above the lip and peered through again to see the terrorist was holding a phone to his ear. She waited and listened, keeping one eye on him and one eye on the sea of hostages. She needed to get in touch with Jake Tanner. That's what he'd told her to do. As soon as she was in there and safe, she was supposed to call him and let him know what was going on. But she'd been so caught up in the situation, her adrenaline had prohibited her from doing so.

Tara dialled the last number in her address book. It took her straight through to a switchboard.

'Hello?'

Tara jumped down from the window and rested her back against the wall. In front of her, the enormous machine playing the rolling film droned on, creating a soft hum in the room.

'Hello? This is Tara. I need to speak to a Detective Jake Tanner,' Tara whispered.

'Pardon? Who is this? What are you talking about?'

Fuck. Wrong number.

Tara hung up and did all she could think to do: dial 999.

As soon as the call connected, she explained the situation.

'Of course – one moment please,' the person on the other end told her.

As she waited on the line, Tara held the phone away from her ear. Keeping herself out of sight, she strained to hear the terrorist's conversation.

'Introduce a new gun law, Prime Minister, similar to

that of the United States, and everyone, including me, gets to walk out of here alive. It's as simple as that… I understand what this will take, but it is what is necessary to improve the security of this country. Imagine if these people here had guns and an attacker wandered in – the attacker wouldn't stand a chance. So far, nobody has died at the hand of a bullet, and tonight you have witnessed the dangers of explosives. If a suicide bomber were to wander along the street in this country, he would have every right to stroll up to someone and detonate himself in front of them. But if you arm every man, woman and child in this country, then you can stop that attack from happening. You can save lives, Prime Minister. People are only safe when they've got a 9mm in their hand.'

Tara's attention was distracted by a noise coming from her mobile.

'Excuse me, Miss? Are you still there?'

'Yes. Hello. I'm still here.'

'OK. Thank you for your patience. Unfortunately, I am unable to contact Mr Tanner at the moment. It seems his line is busy. I'll keep trying.'

Tara shook her head. 'Would you be able to pass me to Amy? She works in your team somewhere. She knows the situation. I'm sorry – I don't know her surname.'

'Certainly.' The person on the other end pressed a button, and the line went dead for a moment.

'Hello?' a familiar voice said a few seconds later.

'Amy, thank God it's you.'

'Tara – I'm glad to hear your voice. Are you OK?'

'As OK as I can be.'

'Where are you now?'

'Inside the projection room. The man with the gun is

on the phone at the moment. I think he's talking to the Prime Minister.'

'Are you safe?'

'I was told to come here. I need to get in touch with Detective Jake Tanner. He told me to report back to him.'

'OK. What can you see?'

'Not a lot. Mostly darkness. He's standing at the front with Josh.'

'Josh? Who's Josh?'

Just as Tara was about to respond, the projection-room door burst open. Nathan, the colleague who had originally abandoned her, entered the room.

Panicked, Tara screamed. Her high-pitched squeal penetrated the almost-silent air, taking Nathan by surprise.

'What are you doing here?' she whispered harshly.

'I came looking for you,' Nathan replied.

But before she could respond, a gunshot sounded from the auditorium, and a bullet soared through the small window and buried itself in the ceiling.

'Whoever is in there, do not fucking move,' the shooter said.

Tara froze with fear.

She'd failed. Given herself away. She could hear Amy calling her name in the background, pleading for them to answer. Nathan dropped to the floor, protecting his head from the raining plasterboard and dust.

'Slowly, I want you to reveal yourself with your hands up,' came the calm, authoritative voice from within the auditorium.

Chest heaving, Tara gave one last look at Nathan, whispered the word 'go' and then rose to her feet, peering through the small window in the wall. There, she looked straight down the barrel of a gun.

CHAPTER 15

The gunshot, unsurprisingly, induced panic in the square. Upon Jake and the Prime Minister's instructions, the members of SCO19 grabbed their equipment, regrouped and sprinted off towards the rear entrance to the cinema. Jake stood firmly rooted to the spot, cemented in place by apprehension, as he watched them surge past him in a well-drilled, regimented manner. Their movements were fluid, as if they were a moving convoy and each of them was a wheel. A true force to be reckoned with.

Once they were out of sight, Jake's thoughts instantly turned to Tara. How he'd put her life in jeopardy. How, if anything happened to her, it would be on his head, his shoulders, his chest – and his career.

He just hoped she was OK.

Alive…

'What do we do now?' Jake asked Mamadou.

'Nothing,' he replied. 'We need to wait for the CTSFOs to plant the camera. After they've done that, we'll regroup and rethink. Fuck!' Mamadou slammed his fist on the side of the blacked-out van in frustration.

Blocking out those around him, Jake moved away and dialled the last number that had called him. It should have taken him directly to Tara, but the phone kept ringing and ringing. After ten seconds or so, Jake hung up; if she'd been apprehended by Phillip and he noticed her phone was ringing, all contact with her would be lost for sure.

All he could do now was wait. And pray she, and everyone else inside the auditorium, was safe.

Alive.

Sergeant Marshall led the squadron into the building as he'd done many times before. Swiftly, efficiently, silently. Like one body, communicating telepathically, breathing as one.

The back door to the building, their first obstacle, wasn't much of an adversary; a powerful kick buckled it inwards, and the team charged through. They had all committed the layout of the cinema to memory, so each of them could find their way to the correct location without assistance. Even if one of them got lost and split up from the rest of the pack, their internal compass would direct them towards their destination. Years and years of training had hardwired that ability into their brains.

The silent and deadly killing machine wandered through the desolate and quiet corridors. Marshall's breathing was steady as he kept his eye trained down the barrel of his gun. Finger poised over the trigger. Ready. His body finely tuned and alert for the unexpected.

He came to a stop at a set of double doors, raised his hand in the air, fingers spread open, then closed them into a fist. The rest of the platoon stopped dead behind him.

Marshall pushed the door. The hinges squeaked.

He peered through, opened it a little further. Further still. Pausing each time it made a sound.

The fire exit to screen fourteen, an inconspicuous set of doors, was in sight.

Before crossing the threshold, Marshall did a recce of the corridor. Deeming it safe to continue, he released his fist, fanned his fingers and eased through the door, skipping across the hallway. He came to a stop on the left-hand side of the fire exit.

One by one, each of his men joined him, altering the sides of the door they went to. In the end, seven were on the left; eight were on the right.

Once they were all in position, Marshall nodded to the soldier immediately opposite him and reached inside his wrist pocket, removed the camera and inspected it. Then he inspected the door. Despite their preparation, the camera was the one piece of the puzzle he didn't feel comfortable with. If he couldn't find a secure place to leave it, the mission would have been unsuccessful. How he would do it, he didn't know. But he hoped his second in command would. He looked at the pair of deep blue eyes behind the mask and helmet, and they exchanged a knowing look – neither of them had a suggestion.

Instead, Marshall turned his attention to the auditorium. He pressed his ear against the door and waited, listened.

The sound of whimpering and screams sounded distant through the thin cracks in the door. Then someone on the other side of it spoke. Marshall presumed it to be the man responsible for this entire ordeal. The man who wanted guns to be commonplace so that he, and the rest of the population, could defend themselves. *I'd love to see how he defends himself against this,* Marshall thought as he looked down at his Heckler & Koch MP5, and stroked the trigger.

Breathing calmly through his nose, Sergeant Marshall began to push the left-hand door ajar. Mercifully, this time the hinges made no sound. He stopped as soon as there was a thin gap, wide enough for the camera lens to fit through, and left it there, suspended in place by the two doors opposing one another.

It was the best he could do.

Then Marshall took a step back and held a finger to his ear.

'Camera in place. Confirm visuals,' he whispered.

'Roger that, Sergeant. Visuals confirmed. Turn round and exit.'

'No,' he replied. 'We're staying. If he fires a single shot, we're going in.'

CHAPTER 16

The stupid bitch from the front desk struggled in his arms. She was small, thin and nimble, but there was a ferocity in her that Phillip admired – like she could retaliate if necessary. She hit him across the face as he grabbed her arm. The first and only one to defend themselves, and in less than five seconds.

This is exactly what the country needs, he thought. *Except with guns. Heroes who are able to stand up for what is right and wrong, and willing enough to stop acts of extreme violence and murder.*

'Get your hands off me!' she shouted at him.

Around them, other women whimpered and gasped.

'As you wish,' Phillip said, releasing the girl. 'What's your name?'

'Louise.'

'Don't lie to me. What's your name?'

'Tara.'

'Tara,' Phillip repeated. Now he remembered. 'What were you doing up there?'

Tara didn't reply – she just stared coolly into his eyes.

'Who told you to be up there?'

'Nobody.'

'So you just wandered up there by coincidence?'

She shrugged.

'How old are you, Tara?'

'Does it matter?'

'It does if you want to live.'

'Nineteen.'

'A child. You've still a lot to learn.'

Tara scoffed. 'Like what? How *not* to shoot people?'

'Not quite. I think you need to listen and learn how to respect others and pay attention, and to do what you're told – and to answer me truthfully when I ask you something.' Phillip hesitated. 'Who sent you up there to spy on me?'

'I don't know their name.'

'Was it the police?' Phillip reached down to his ankle, removed the 9mm he'd holstered there and aimed it at Tara's forehead, between her eyebrows. 'Give me the name. Who sent you to spy on me?'

Tara's eyes widened as the cold metal touched her forehead. 'Tanner.'

'Ah, Detective Constable Jake Tanner. The hero.' Phillip's lips flickered. 'Perhaps you and I should make a call.'

He returned the 9mm to his ankle, removed his mobile and dialled.

Jake Tanner answered on the first ring. 'Bowden?'

'Tanner. I think there's someone who would like to speak with you.'

Phillip held the phone against Tara's head. She stared back at him defiantly, probably deciding whether she should say anything. In the end, she conceded defeat.

'Jake, it's me. Tara... Yes, I'm OK. No, not yet. I... I will—'

Phillip cut their conversation short by pulling the phone away from her face.

'Touching. Do the two of you know each other?'

'Don't hurt her, Phillip,' Jake said in his ear. 'Your issues are not with her. They're with me. The government. The Prime Minister. She's just an innocent civilian.'

Phillip shook his head. 'You still don't understand, do you? My wife was an innocent civilian, and look what happened to her. Crime doesn't care if you're the wealthiest or the most powerful person on the planet. It will attack you from anywhere. It's a cruel bitch, and fire should be met with fire.'

'It still doesn't give you the right to shoot people and hold them against their will, Phillip. Please don't hurt her. She's done nothing wrong.'

'Did my neighbour do anything wrong when he was beaten into a hospital bed when his home was broken into? Did my friend do anything wrong when he was mugged in an underpass? No, he didn't. But that didn't stop the cunts from doing it to him. And now he's afraid to leave his home without any protection. Do you know what he does now?' Phillip purposely hesitated, drawing an unwilling answer from Jake.

'No. What does he do?'

'He carries a knife with him. In all his fifty-three years on this earth, he has never been so frightened to wander the streets of his own country. I'm a foreigner and even I feel afraid, and I've grown up around criminals. Imagine how everyone else in this godforsaken place feels.'

Phillip stared into Tara's eyes as he spoke. A small part of her reminded him of his wife. The other part reminded him of the youth of today. The defiance. The arrogance. The belligerence. The naïveté. The ignorance. The belief that the world owed them everything. That they didn't have to work a day in their life and someone – something – should give them it all for nothing. She was the part of youth and society he hated.

'What's your friend's name, Phillip?' Jake asked.

'I won't give it to you. You're not arresting him – not when there are worse people out there.'

'That's the last thing I want to do. We'll be able to help him. Relocate him. Make sure he feels protected. Maybe even increase police presence in his area.'

'And who's going to pay for it? You and I both know there's not enough budget to do all the things we want. If there was, you and I wouldn't be in this position. And who's the one responsible for that, Tanner?' Phillip hesitated. 'I think you know who; she's fucking standing right next to you.'

'You've highlighted one of the many things wrong with the country, Phillip. But there's very little I can do about it. So what do we do now?'

Phillip took a moment to absorb his surroundings. He glanced around the auditorium. At the plethora of shocked and fearful faces staring back at him. They were all wary, afraid of Phillip's next move. He could sense it. In the time he'd taken them hostage, he hoped he'd shown his underrated volatility; they could tell it was there, sensed it even. Sure, he'd strapped explosives to someone's back and been responsible for their death. But as to how far he was willing to go, they hadn't seen that yet. They hadn't seen his real purpose for being there.

It was time to change that.

'I'll tell you what's going to happen, Tanner. Remove your men stationed around the building and send them home. And I promise no one will get hurt. Then I'm going to disappear.'

'How?'

'Into the darkness.'

'How?'

'It's what I do. That's why they used to call me The Wolf.'

Jake muttered something inaudible over the phone. Was that a chuckle?

'There's no way out for you,' he said eventually. 'Even if we remove all the officers, there's only one place for you to go.'

'Which is?'

'Prison.'

'Interesting.' Phillip paused. 'As for my final demand: you, Detective Jake Tanner, hero of the night, will enter the cinema and save your little friend here.'

Phillip stroked Tara's cheek. She flinched. Closed her eyes. Phillip could sense her skin crawl.

Maria. Oh, Maria.

'What can I receive in—'

Phillip shut off the call before Jake could finish. He pocketed the phone and gazed into Tara's youthful eyes.

'Move,' he said, gesticulating with the M16. 'You and I are going to take a seat.'

The two of them climbed the stairs until Tara stopped at row F. There were two seats available at the end of the row. Phillip perched himself on the second seat, while Tara sat next to him on the aisle.

Now we wait.

CHAPTER 17

Jake blocked the world out. He needed to think. And he needed to do so quickly. He was faltering. So far he'd failed at the hostage negotiation, and soon the damage he would inevitably be held accountable for would be irrevocable. If he was going to resolve this, he needed to mix things up, give the people above him a reason to keep him in the job, and not cut him loose like a stray strand of hair dangling from their fringe.

To do that, he needed space. *Time*. But in the square he had neither. Instead, he was surrounded by a temporal and spatial doom. And to make matters worse, he had the head of the country next to him, scrutinising his every move.

Mamadou prodded him in the chest. He hadn't realised it, but the phone was still in his hand, held against his ear, and it looked as if he was still talking.

'What did he say?'

Jake repeated everything Phillip had told him. The Prime Minister hovered to Jake's left, and he sensed her listening in as he spoke.

'What do we do now then, Detective?' she asked.

'I need to speak with him more. Learn from him. Get inside his head.'

'Fuck that,' Mamadou said. 'We don't have time.'

'I'm starting to think you're the wrong person for this job, Tanner,' the Prime Minister said.

Her words cut him deep.

'We'll have to find someone else who can rectify this situation.'

'No!' Jake exclaimed. 'That won't be necessary.'

The Prime Minister folded her arms across her chest. 'Come up with a solution, otherwise I will have wasted a journey down here, and put me and the rest of my team in extreme danger – all for nothing.'

Fighting the urge to roll his eyes at her, Jake started off towards Hamilton, plucking up the courage to shoot her one last defiant look before he went, however. Like a child who'd just received a pep talk, he strolled through the throng of people with a renewed sense of determination and purpose.

'Hamilton, what have you got for me regarding Phillip Bowden?' Jake asked, slamming his fist on the inside of the van.

Hamilton jumped out of his seat. 'Jake! Sorry, mate. Didn't see you there. You surprised me.' He hesitated, looked Jake in the eyes and frantically searched his makeshift desk. 'Right. Information. Let me see.'

'It's here,' a female officer with short dark hair said to Jake. In her hand, she held a document. She passed it to him. 'Everything you need to know about Phillip Bowden is in there.'

'Where was this an hour ago when I needed it?'

The officer looked taken aback. 'It's the early hours of the morning, Detective. Personnel are sparse.

Everywhere is stretched at the moment. You know how it is.'

'I don't care. It's not an excuse.'

Jake stopped himself before he said anything else he was going to regret. He hadn't meant to shout at these people. They were his colleagues, and in his career he'd already learnt that it was far more difficult to mend bridges than build them.

'I'm sorry,' he said, attempting a half-smile. 'Thank you. I appreciate it.'

With that, he turned and started back towards Mamadou, skimming through the most important information as he went.

Phillip Bowden was sixty-seven, born and raised in Nevada, and was a gun enthusiast. Moved to the United Kingdom twelve years ago. Wife – deceased. Two kids, a boy and a girl – still living in America. After years of trying, he'd eventually obtained a gun licence. For hunting purposes only. Lastly, he owned and operated a fully functioning small business: a weapon and armour museum in the east of England.

Underneath the text on the page was a small photograph of Phillip standing proudly outside his museum.

The last point interested Jake the most. In particular, Phillip's obsession and fascination with guns.

Jake turned the page over and continued reading.

And then he had his answer.

Phillip Bowden had served in the US army during the Vietnam War. As soon as he'd turned eighteen, he'd become a private. Had gone AWOL after a mission went wrong.

That's why they used to call me The Wolf.

Jake stopped beside Mamadou, interrupting his

conversation with the Prime Minister. Another gentleman was beside them. Jake didn't recognise him.

'OK,' he started. 'Here's what's going to happen—'

'Not so fast,' Mamadou said, pointing to the tablet the man accompanying them held in his hands.

Jake stared at the screen. The image was split in two down the middle. The left was illuminated, with images flickering on and off. The right was dark. Jake recognised it as the cinema auditorium. The live feed Sergeant Marshall and his team had managed to place through the fire exit.

'What am I looking at?'

'Phillip Bowden.'

'Where is he?' Jake squinted closer at the screen.

'Exactly. He's fucking gone!'

CHAPTER 18

Jake stared at himself in the almost pitch-black of the screen. Where had Phillip gone? How had he managed to deceive Jake and the rest of the police force and slip through the exit of the cinema unnoticed, escaping the wrath of the regiment? Jake didn't think it was possible.

'He's still in there,' he said defiantly. 'He's got to be. Too much is riding on this for him. He's putting his entire life and beliefs on the line. He's not about to slip away just yet.'

'How can you be so sure?' Mamadou asked.

'I can't. But something's telling me he's still in there.'

Jake's intuition, instinct – whatever it was – was on high alert and signalling loudly in the pit of his stomach.

'I'm sorry but we can't be relying on your spidey senses, Constable,' the Prime Minister added. 'We're going to need something a little more concrete than that.'

'The footage,' Jake said, and turned his attention to the screen. 'What's happened in the last five minutes?'

The man holding the tablet appeared flustered and almost dropped the device in surprise. 'I… We…'

Jake snatched the device from him and rewound the playback. After watching the past five minutes unravel on the screen, Jake thrust the device back into the man's hands.

'Well?' Mamadou asked.

'He's still in there. He's got Tara, and he's sitting in the seating area somewhere.' He turned to the man. 'If you'd been paying attention, you would have seen him hoist her from the projection window and make her sit down with him.'

The man hung his head in shame. Rightfully so too. His mistake could have led to serious casualties.

'Excellent,' the Prime Minister said sarcastically. 'What now?'

'I need to go in,' Jake replied.

'Don't be a knob,' Mamadou said, deadpan.

'I'm not.'

'You are. You're putting yourself in a potentially dangerous situation. For nothing. You're too valuable for us to let anything happen to you. There are people who are paid to risk their lives in situations like this. It's what they want to do; it's what they signed up for; they jack off to it. So sit back and let them do it.'

'I can't.'

'Why not?'

Jake rolled his eyes. 'Because he wants me to go in. Me, and me alone. It was the last thing he said to me.'

'Don't lie to me, Jake.'

'I wish I was.'

'I don't like it. It's too dangerous, too much is at

risk. We don't know what this asshole's really like. Just because he's not shot anyone yet doesn't mean to say you won't be the first.'

'And what about Tara? I risked her life by sending her in there. If anything happens to her…'

'You don't need to be a hero, Jake.'

He'd heard that before. Several times, in fact. And each time he'd failed to heed the advice. And each time he'd come out the other end alive, safe and well.

He wasn't a mathematician, but even he could work out he had a one hundred per cent success rate to uphold.

He took a moment to stop and think about his actions. What he was doing. And why he was doing it. The end result was always the same: his family. They were the driving force behind all of his decisions. Their safety, their future. If he could help build a world for them with one less terrorist, one less criminal, one less extremist, then he would do everything in his power to make that a reality. And he wasn't going to let anyone stand in the way of that.

Jake pulled Mamadou to the side so their discussion was out of earshot.

'What's going on here, Mam? Why are you being like this?' he asked.

Mamadou looked at the ground sheepishly. Then, after a second which had felt like a minute, he returned his gaze back to Jake. 'I've been worried about you. You've been overworking yourself recently, and it's had a detrimental effect on everything. You've lost weight. You constantly look tired, and pumping yourself with coffee every hour isn't going to help. I know you want to impress, but sometimes you need to learn when to take a step back and relax. You can't save everyone.'

I can, Jake thought. *And will.*

'We don't have a choice.'

'I don't like it,' Mamadou said.

'I'm not asking you to. You just have to respect my decision. I'm doing my job, Mam. Those people could die in there if I don't. I'm not ready for their blood to be on my hands.'

Mamadou and Jake stared at one another for a beat. Jake respected and adored the man opposite him – his boss, his friend, his mentor. They had grown close over the months since Jake had joined CTC, and in that short space of time, they had dissipated the manager–employee divide. They saw one another as equals, even if the status and pay cheque at the end of the month said otherwise. After all, they both shared the same goal: eradicating the streets of extremism, one step at a time. It was one of the reasons everyone else in the office was jealous of their relationship.

Mamadou said nothing.

Jake nodded, hesitated and turned away.

'Where do you think you're going?' Mamadou asked.

'Boss, we—'

'Not without protection, you're not. You need a bulletproof vest.'

Five minutes later, suited with a vest, helmet, earpiece and a stun gun, Jake started off towards the mouth of the cinema. His heart pounded furiously in his ears; his skin vibrated with every pulsating throb. The harsh light blinded him as his eyes attempted to readjust to his surroundings. Inside the foyer, men and women dressed in white plastic overalls, with gloves, goggles and face masks, were on their hands and knees, attending to the debris that had been left as a result of the earlier explosion. Jake tiptoed around them, avoided the evidence markers on the ground, apologised for disturbing the scene and continued through.

He ignored the dead body on the floor. Not because it had been covered with something that reminded him of a white bedsheet, but because he didn't want the vivid images to haunt his mind for the next few minutes. He'd seen a dead body before, and he would see one again. Over the years, he'd trained his brain to box those images up and compartmentalise them in the deep recesses of his mind. That way, he couldn't find them, unearth them and obsess over them.

After a few more steps, he stopped. He was on the precipice. A line ran across the floor in front of him where solid flooring met carpet. It felt as if he was about to step into the void of the unknown. He swallowed hard, made a quick mental note of the way he needed to go and stepped forward.

No turning back now.

As he reached the popcorn counter, he made a left turn and headed into the darkened corridor, heedless of the movie posters hanging from the walls. It was a long time since he'd last been to the cinema.

Eventually he arrived outside screen fourteen. Paused. Breathed. Controlled himself. Attempted to relax. Stared at the red door. To the left. To the right. The corridor was empty. There was no sign of Phillip waiting for him, lurking in the shadows, ready to pounce from behind. Jake swallowed and pushed the door.

It wouldn't budge. Stuck, as if someone was leaning into it on the other side.

He tried again. This time more forcefully.

Still nothing.

Then, almost instinctively – at least, he presumed it was instinct – he knocked on the door. The sound echoed up and down the corridor, and Jake felt his heart pause momentarily as he awaited a response. A sign. A signal. A cough. A scream. A cry for help. Something that would let him know someone was on the other side of the door, safe.

The phone in his pocket vibrated.

'Hello?' Jake answered.

'Is that you knocking on my door?' Phillip Bowden asked.

'Yes.'

'Sorry. We don't like cold callers. You'll have to come round the back. It's much more private round there.'

'I'll be round as fast as I can.'

'Do you know the way?'

'I'm sure I can work it out. I'm a big boy.'

Jake started off towards the set of double doors at the end of the corridor. As he walked past the toilet room on his left, Jake remembered the images he'd seen of Phillip disappearing and reappearing moments before he'd taken the cinema hostage.

'A big boy like you can get lost sometimes. Even the biggest boys can.'

'What about you?' Jake asked. 'Did you get lost?'

Silence.

'Have you ever been lost, Phillip? What about in Vietnam? Ever been lost there? Why did they call you

The Wolf, Phillip?'

Silence.

Then: 'You don't know what you're talking about. Just hurry the fuck up. Let's end this.'

The line went dead.

Jake lowered his arm, phone still in hand. His palms were sweaty, and he rolled the phone around in his fingers like it was a stress ball. He continued through the double doors, made a right turn, headed through another corridor, recalled the blueprints of the cinema he'd seen only briefly earlier and stopped at another door. Cautiously, he opened it. As soon as it swung open, he heard the unmistakable sound of a gun cocking. A figure, dressed in black, pointed a Heckler & Koch MP5 directly at Jake's face. His body froze with fear and then gradually eased up as he realised who it was.

'Jesus Christ,' Jake whispered loudly, his hand on his chest, his beating heart pounding against his ribs. 'What the fuck are you doing?'

'Watching and monitoring,' the man replied. His words were muffled behind the balaclava.

'And?' Jake asked. 'Have you seen anyone?'

'Like who?'

'The guy we're looking for?'

The man stuttered, looked around him, clueless.

Frustrated, Jake peered over the soldier's shoulder at the rest of the unit. By now, some of them had noticed his presence and were heading towards him.

'Detective,' one of them said. Jake recognised him as Sergeant Marshall. 'What are you doing here?'

'I'm here to speak with the target. Have you seen him leave the premises?'

Marshall shook his head.

'As far as I'm aware, he's still in there.'

'With the girl?'

Marshall nodded. 'To the best of my knowledge.'

OK, Jake thought. *They're still in there. Nobody knows where, but they're still in there. It's going to be fine.* You're *going to be fine.*

Jake's face must have gone blank, because Sergeant Marshall shot him a confused look. 'You all right, Detective?'

'What? Yes. I'm fine.' Jake advanced towards the door. 'I'm going in.'

To his surprise, Marshall allowed him past. It wasn't until Jake was a few paces ahead that Marshall grabbed him.

'Hey – take this.' In his hands he held a Glock 17. 'You might need it. Keep it in your waistband.'

Jake accepted the small handgun, checked the ammunition magazine, closed it, then placed it against the small of his back. He nodded as a sign of appreciation before turning and heading towards the door.

As he arrived, Jake's mindset changed. Minutes earlier, when he'd wandered through the front entrance, he'd been afraid. Petrified. Vulnerable. But now – he felt confident. Invincible.

Armed, Jake opened the door and stepped into the darkness. The movie had finished and the only source of illumination was the small square hole in the wall by the projection room. Which meant Jake couldn't see any of the faces in front of him clearly. He felt like a deer in headlights.

He stopped in the middle of the auditorium.

'At long last,' a voice said. *Phillip*. 'How nice of you to join us.'

CHAPTER 19

It was so intimate and so acoustic and claustrophobic in the auditorium, the voice sounded as if it had come from inside Jake's head.

'Where are you?'

'Guess.'

'How?'

'Use the sound of my voice.'

Jake tried to scan the overflowing room in search of Phillip, but he couldn't see anything; his eyes were still adjusting to his surroundings.

'And what happens when I find you?'

'We talk.'

'What about Tara? Are you there, Tara?'

'Yes,' she replied without a moment's hesitation. 'I'm fine.'

Her voice sounded as though she was sitting on the opposite side of the room to Phillip. This wasn't going to be easy.

'Why did you call me here, Phillip? Why did you want *me* personally?'

'Because I like you. I sympathise with you. And you sympathise with me. Even if you won't admit it to yourself. I'm sure there are probably many similarities that you and I—'

'From what I've seen so far, I'm not so sure.'

A beat of complete silence.

'And what have you seen?'

'Vietnam. Prisoner of war. Gun enthusiast. Weapons museum owner. You know, the basics.'

'And do you think you know me?'

'Of course not. How could I? They're just words on a page. There's a lot more to anyone's life than the biography they leave on Facebook. There's a lot more to someone's life than the ones left in a military report as well. They could never reveal the true nature of someone's life, and I wouldn't even want to begin attempting it – and I've got a psychology degree for crying out loud.' Jake's mouth was doing all the talking, while his brain played catch-up. Despite not having finished the training guide on hostage negotiation, he was pretty certain antagonising the hostage taker wasn't recommended.

'Maybe you should do an evaluation of me. Diagnose me with an insane mind.'

'Do you think you have an insane mind?'

'That would be for you to find out.'

'It's been a long time since I last got involved with any of that. The less I know, the better,' Jake explained.

'Some detective you are.'

'It helps me dissociate myself from everything. Helps take my mind off the possibilities.'

'Possibilities of what?'

'Things that may happen to my family in the future.'

'I hope you never have to suffer the same experiences as me, Detective.'

'Me too.'

Jake hesitated. An awkward moment lingered in the air.

'Come on, Phillip. What's going on here? What are we *really* talking about?'

'Did the Prime Minister come to a decision about my request?' Phillip asked.

Jake was no closer to pinpointing the man's location.

'She did.'

'And?'

'It's a no go, I'm afraid,' Jake lied. He hadn't remembered to ask the Prime Minister about Phillip's demands to change the UK gun laws, but he sensed the answer would be no anyway. 'This country's had those laws for decades. They're not just going to change overnight.'

'Crazier things have happened.'

Jake decided to stop probing. Instead, he needed to get Tara and the rest of the hostages out of there as fast and as safely as possible.

'Phillip – what do you say about the two of us letting some of these people out of here?'

'What do you mean?'

'Gradually, a group at a time. They've been stuck inside here, worrying for their lives. And some of them probably need the toilet. How does that sound?'

Jake scanned the auditorium again, this time hoping he could see a slight adjustment in one of the floating heads. But the space was just too great, and there were too many people, the margin for error too wide. In his mind, he tried to come up with a plan. He collated everything he knew about Phillip and rolled it into one ball of information.

Phillip was an old man. Alone. Afraid. Resentful. A war hero. A prisoner of war. Which meant he was volatile. Which he'd already shown with the bomb. Which meant he would be susceptible to another outburst of mayhem and destruction. But there was one thing Jake hadn't managed to ascertain: whether Phillip had any more explosives on him, as he'd claimed.

'No,' Phillip said, breaking Jake out of his meandering thoughts. 'That doesn't sit well with me. Either we all go at once or none of us go at all. We can stay here as long as I like. And if anyone thinks about leaving – including you – I'll shoot you.'

Jake considered this for a moment. He had two options. He liked the first best.

'Fine,' he said. 'We all leave. But I don't want anyone to be harmed.'

'Depends how accurate your guys are at aiming,' Phillip said.

Did he know about the unit of highly trained firearms officers stationed outside the fire exit? Had he known all this time and was just using Jake as some sort of bargaining tool – a bargain for escape?

No. Tara's the insurance package he needs.

'They won't make the first move unless you do, Phillip. You're very much in the driver's seat,' Jake said loudly. He hoped Marshall was able to hear.

'Good boy,' Phillip replied. 'Now, everyone up on their feet please.'

It took a while, but the entire room stood, different groups of people rising sporadically, making it infinitely more difficult for Jake to identify Phillip amongst the crowd. All he had to go on in terms of a visual ID was a pixelated CCTV image. And as for Tara… well, he didn't even know what she looked like. It was going to be like finding a needle in a very small, and very well armed, haystack.

The sound of discussion and general excitement at their imminent salvation gradually echoed around the room.

'Detective Tanner!' Tara called suddenly.

He recognised her voice almost instantly. Everyone else in the room paused.

'You have to go first. Phillip's orders. Please don't do anything stupid, he says, otherwise he's going to hurt me.'

Tara's words were laced with emotion – raw, deep.

'Of course,' Jake called back to his invisible tormentor. Then he started towards the fire exit, opened it, paused.

Immediately in front of him was Marshall and the rest of SCO19. Jake ordered them to retreat to the building's front entrance and watched them slowly leave, keeping their weapons trained on Jake and the auditorium behind him. As soon as they were out of sight, Jake continued forward. The mass of people followed behind, as if he was the leader of a football firm on their way to the next fight. The only difference was everyone in the firm was nervous and afraid for their own safety.

Walking beside him was a small child dressed in a C-3PO costume. Next to him was his father. The sight made Jake smile. He reached into his pocket, removed his phone and dialled, then passed the phone to the little boy and told him what to say.

'He won't see *you* ringing the good guys,' Jake said.

'But he'll see me, and we don't want that, do we?'

The little boy shook his head.

Almost immediately after he'd finished, the young boy began speaking, telling Mamadou that everyone inside the cinema was on their way out, and that, on Jake's command, they were all going to run left or right of the cinema entrance.

The little boy hung up and handed the phone back to Jake. He hoped Mamadou understood what he meant; Jake had to be careful not to tell the little boy too much, for his own sake.

Like a tide, they swept along the carpets, rolling through the corridors, past the screen entrances and movie posters, and made a right turn into the cinema's foyer. It was oddly cold; the blasted windows now allowed a bitter wind to blow through. In his excited state, Jake hadn't noticed the cold before. Glass and other bits of debris were still scattered across the floor, and the forensics teams had disappeared with the victim's body. No effort had been made to clean the blood, however.

On the other side of the floor-to-ceiling windows were the flashing blue lights of the city's police. Ready and waiting.

As Jake and the rest of the crowd reached the thin black line that ran across the floor, Jake looked at the little boy and said, 'You ready, buddy?'

The little boy nodded.

'Good. You and your daddy just keep running, OK? Make sure you get someone in a police vest to look after you.'

'OK,' the boy said and grabbed for his father's hand.

This is it, Jake thought as he gave one last look to the

cinema's entrance before whispering at the child on his right, and the two women on his left, to run. They acknowledged their instruction with a nod, the little boy's face beaming as he became caught in the excitement of it.

Then Jake stopped mid-flow and turned to face the crowd.

'Go! Go! Go!' he whispered.

The crowd didn't need telling twice. As soon as the words left his lips, they sprinted either side of him towards the exits. In his head, it had been a good plan. But not a well-thought-out one. Spur of the moment. Acting on instinct. He didn't know how Phillip would react. Whether he would be too shocked and surprised to pull the trigger. Or whether his muscle memory from years of training in Vietnam would return. It was a massive gamble, and Jake had taken it.

It worked.

As the mass of bodies rapidly filtered out and the crowd thinned, Jake could discern Phillip hovering at the rear, gun in hand, Tara pressed tightly against his body. Their eyes locked for a long moment.

Then something knocked into Jake's shoulder and an overweight, sweaty man dressed as R2-D2 sent him flying to the floor. He landed hard, white pain descending over his field of vision. A liquid sensation spread across the back of his skull, making it tingle slightly, before his head began to throb.

Trapped on the floor, a stampede of bodies trampled over him in a mad frenzy of escape. He shielded himself using his arms and legs, but it did little to soften the impact on his ribs and sternum.

A few seconds later, after the stampede had subsided, Jake regained himself.

Reaching into his waistband and finding the Glock, he rose to his feet as the few remaining stragglers rapidly exited the foyer.

Phillip and Tara were opposite him. Fifteen yards away. Phillip held a handgun to Tara's head with one hand and a machine gun aimed at Jake in the other. Two against one. Odds Jake didn't like.

'Put the guns down, Phillip,' Jake said, aiming the Glock at Phillip's head.

'I will if you do.'

'Let Tara go.'

'You know I can't do that.' Phillip pressed the nose of the gun against Tara's temple; she squirmed in his arms, tears forming in her eyes.

At that moment, an image popped into his head. Drew Richmond. Liam Greene.

The room changed, and he was transported back to Drew's kitchen.

Night turned to day.

He was back there again, reliving the nightmare.

'You all right, Tanner?' Phillip asked. 'Not having any flashbacks, are you?'

'Perfectly fine,' Jake replied, his anger and frustration boiling. 'Now put the weapons down and let Tara go,' he said through gritted teeth.

'Why don't you put your gun down?'

'What will happen if I do?'

'You let me walk out of here a free man.'

'And if I don't?'

'She dies. Then you.'

'That's not a wise decision, Phillip. There are dozens of armed officers stationed outside this building. You won't make it out alive.'

'And neither will you. So if you want to live, I

suggest you put down your fucking gun and step aside.'

For a long moment, Jake stood there, considering his options. He wasn't going to do what Phillip wished, but he was willing to meet the man in the middle.

'OK,' he said, placing the gun on the floor and kicking it to the side. 'Now let's talk.'

CHAPTER 20

'What about?'

'Why I think you should lower the gun.'

'Does your wife complain about all your talking?' Phillip asked.

Jake smiled. 'She's worse than me.'

'Christ. Must take some doing.'

'It does. And the kids are just as bad.'

Jake waited for a response, but it didn't come.

'Don't do this, Phillip. What would *your* kids say? How will they react when they find out what you've done? I don't think they'll believe it. They won't want to believe the man who raised them, the man who gave them everything he ever earnt, was capable of such wrongdoing. They won't want their image of you as their hero to be tarnished with this, will they?'

Phillip didn't reply.

'And then when they realise that it's the truth, what will they do then? The psychological repercussions of your actions may force them to do drastic things. You don't want to harm them, do you? Because that's who you're going to be affecting most, Phillip. Your children. Your grandchildren. And as for your wife – if she were here now, what would she be saying?'

Now Jake waited until Phillip answered. For the first time, he looked down at the ground, pensive.

'She'd... She'd tell me to... stop being a tool.' Phillip's voice was hoarse. 'She'd tell me I've become everything I said I've ever hated. And that I was a weak human being for doing so.'

'You're not weak,' Jake said.

'I am. I am. I'm *weak*. Weaker than I've ever been. I'm just as bad as those cunts who robbed my house. Killed my wife. Tortured me. Mentally. Physically. This has all been a mistake. I... I never... I...'

Phillip stopped speaking.

And then it happened.

His eyes widened at first. Then he stared into the ground just in front of Jake's feet.

Then he shoved Tara to the ground and dropped the machine gun to the floor.

Then he aimed the handgun at his head.

No.

He buried the nose of the gun in his mouth.

'No!' Jake screamed.

But it was too late.

Phillip pulled the trigger, and his body collapsed to the floor.

CHAPTER 21

For a very brief moment, Jake was in shock. And then he realised where he was and realised that he had to act, even if it meant doing so on autopilot.

He sprinted towards Tara, lifted her to her feet and moved her aside. She was crying and hysterical. She clung to him with both arms, digging her nails deep into the soft parts of his body.

An army of armed officers burst into the foyer behind him and swarmed Phillip, who was lying on the ground, a large puddle of blood spreading around his head.

'Are you OK?' Jake asked Tara. He wanted to see Phillip, but he couldn't leave her.

Before she could answer, a paramedic rushed over and made to carry her away to safety.

'I'll find you,' he told her before she disappeared. 'I'll find you later. I promise.'

Once she was gone, Jake clawed his way through the sea of police officers and paramedics. He stopped as Phillip came into view. The man was lying on his back, eyes wide open – even wider than they'd been in the moments before he'd shot himself. Flecks of blood and saliva dribbled out of his mouth as he tried to speak. Jake didn't know what had happened, but he could take a guess: Phillip's bullet had travelled through the back of his mouth and not through his brain. Which meant he was choking on his own blood while trying to speak. And if the paramedics didn't get him to a hospital quickly, he was going to drown.

Their eyes met.

Phillip continued to babble inaudibly. Jake bent down to his ear.

'S-S-S—' was all Phillip could manage. The rest of his words were drowned out.

'It's OK,' Jake said. 'You're going to be all right. We'll get you to a hospital. They'll look after you.'

Phillip didn't say anything more as he slipped deeper and deeper into unconsciousness. And for the next few minutes, while the emergency response team prepared his body for the back of an ambulance, Jake looked at the old man and felt sorry for him. Here was a man who had witnessed horrifying and mortifying things that nobody should ever have to see. Here was a man who was defending his right to stand up for what he believed in. Here was a man broken, battered and beaten by life. Trying to make a change in the world, even if his motives and methods were misguided. Jake couldn't help but think that somewhere along the way the system had failed him. The vessels for change – those currently sleeping in their beds, locked behind protected doors – had failed him. The injustices and barriers in the world had caused Phillip's wife to die, and that had, in turn, produced a knock-on effect.

Without those injustices, there would be no crime,

and without that crime there would be no more Phillip Bowdens.

DARK CHRISTMAS

CHAPTER 1

It wasn't every morning the Metropolitan Police Service discovered a dead body on the streets of East London. Especially when that morning was in the early hours of Christmas Eve.

PC Arthur Maxwell had been driving along the cold and empty roads of Stratford for forty minutes. It was 3 a.m., and he was still on shift. Making sure the streets were free of troublesome individuals wasn't going to be too much of an issue – not when one of the busiest days in the Christian calendar was right round the corner. In his fifteen years experience, it seemed like the city's criminals postponed their illegal activities until *after* Christmas. After all, those big boxes of TVs, games consoles, computers, and other pieces of state-of-the-art technology were all brilliant signposts for petty thieves and the criminal underworld. A veritable shopping list of this year's hottest items, and the hottest places to find them. For free.

What irked Maxwell the most, however, wasn't the crime itself. It was the hordes of victims who marched towards the station and complained that they'd been robbed. When confronted with the fact they'd advertised their Christmas presents on the front doorstep, they didn't want to know about it. It was somehow his fault. His colleagues' fault.

Everyone else's but their own.

Each year it was the same. Same arguments, same complaints.

'Well, not this year,' PC Maxwell said to himself as he tapped his fingers on the steering wheel absent-mindedly to the beat of the radio. He looked at the small hula girl bobblehead on the dash, his only companion on his late-night rides. 'One more shift and we've got the entire month off, haven't we?'

As he said it, the pool car dipped in and out of a small pothole, and the figurine on the dash bobbled from side to side. Maxwell smiled. It was the little things in life that entertained him. It was lonely sometimes on shift. Sometimes he needed the company. And Hannah the Hula Girl was his only option. Not to mention she was the most attractive out of all the men and women back at the station.

Maxwell eased the car to a stop at a red light. The road was empty. There was no one around him – not even any opposing traffic making full use of their green light. It was times like this he wished he could just switch on the blue lights and not have to worry about the consequences. Sure, he could just pretend he had a call of some sort to attend. An attempted robbery somewhere. A drunken boyfriend getting too aggressive after his girlfriend had kicked him out for the nineteenth time. The possibilities were endless. But that wasn't him – that wasn't his way. He had been entrusted to uphold the law, and by God that's exactly what he would do.

After what felt like an eternity, the traffic lights eventually turned green, and Maxwell accelerated, lowering the pedal to the floor slowly. There was no point going anywhere any time fast. He still had a few hours to kill, and with any luck, he'd be able to complete his shift without encountering any trouble.

He was wrong.

As he swung a right onto a small, poorly lit road, something on the pavement caught his eye. At first, he thought it was a carefully laid out pile of rubbish. Then his mind perceived it to be a homeless person resting on the concrete, attempting to get a good night's sleep despite the almost-Arctic temperatures outside. Maxwell looked at his dash. Two degrees above zero. *Bloody freezing,* in his books. A moment of compassion came over him.

Maxwell swerved the car to the side of the road just in front of the homeless man and switched off the engine. Heaving himself out of the car – and raising his heartbeat tenfold in the process – Maxwell pulled out a flashlight and beamed it at the person on the floor. His breath plumed in a white cloud as he walked closer to the body. The glare from the flashlight was harsh on his eyes, so he aimed it at his feet, illuminating the surrounding area.

And then he stopped, the last wisps of smoke dissolving in the air as he held his breath.

There was no homeless person lying there. Sure, there *was* a person, but they hadn't been wrapped tightly in a sleeping bag like he'd originally thought. Instead, whoever was lying on the floor was dressed casually. A thick, padded coat, navy in colour, protected the person from the harsh elements.

Maxwell bent down, ignoring the signs of ageing in his knees and lower back.

In front of him was a man whose skin was as incandescent as the moon that shone brightly overhead. The dark brown eyes buried deep within the man's skull were open and staring vacantly into the void above. A fine layer of hair decorated the man's face. Stylish, it looked as though it had been recently shaved but offered nothing in the way of protection from the elements.

Maxwell shifted his feet into a more comfortable position and observed the rest of the body. The man wore a pair of white Nike trainers that shone almost as brilliantly as his skin and a pair of loose corduroy jeans that had slid halfway down his hips. The next thing Maxwell did was feel for a pulse, placing his fingers on the man's neck, even though he already knew it was a pointless endeavour.

'Jesus,' he whispered as he surveyed the area for any signs of life. The man was dead, very dead, but given the conditions, it was difficult to say how long that had been the case.

Once satisfied he wouldn't wake up, Maxwell moved his search towards the man's coat. There were no obvious causes of death. No bullet wound. No pool of blood surrounding the body. Not even a stab wound, which surprised him, as this area of East London was particularly prolific for that sort of stuff.

Maxwell eased the zip open. The teeth rolled down the length of the man's body, revealing something he never thought he would see.

Strapped around the man's waist was an improvised explosive device. Six separate packages of indiscernible content were connected via a network of wires and duct tape across the victim's chest. The man was carrying a suicide vest.

'Jesus fucking Christ!' Maxwell stumbled back as the synapses in his brain began to work in the cold and piece the information together.

He rushed over to his car, jumped inside and radioed it in. He spoke too fast for the receiver to comprehend and so was forced to repeat himself, aggrieved at the call handler's ineptitude. His pulse raced; this was the first time he'd ever seen a dead body in such a position as this. And this was the first time he'd ever seen explosives strapped to anyone. He'd learnt about this type of thing during training but had never imagined it would one day become a reality.

'The bomb disposal team are on their way, as are CID,' the woman on the other end replied. 'Is there anyone else you would like to be at the scene?'

'Yes,' Maxwell replied, the name already at the forefront of his mind. 'SO15, Counter Terrorism Command.'

CHAPTER 2

Detective Constable Jake Tanner's phone vibrated on the bedside table, inches away from his head. The device moved furiously each time it rang, sending it on a spiralling journey towards the edge of the table. The harsh and abrasive sound brought him abruptly from his light sleep.

Alert, panicked, he glanced at the time before checking the caller ID – 3:30 a.m. Either a prank call from someone in the office trying to wake him up on Christmas Eve, one of the very few days he had off this year, or something serious. Much more serious.

And in his experience, he knew that there were never any good 3 a.m. calls.

He blinked a few times and glanced at the caller ID. It was Detective Chief Superintendent Mamadou Kuhoba, the man in charge of SO15, the counter terrorism branch of the Metropolitan Police. Jake had recently joined the team following a successful period in CID and had found himself settled quickly. In the short space of time Jake had been there – seven months

– he and Mamadou had overcome the employer/employee divide and considered one another friends.

'Hello?' Jake answered quietly. His voice was hoarse, the sound of sleep still trembling in the last syllable.

'Tanner!' Mamadou yelled, sounding too excitable for this time of the morning. 'Merry Christmas. Or should I say Merry Christmas Eve? Anyway, up you get. There's been an incident. I need you to come to West Ham straight away.'

Jake rubbed his temples and then his eyes, rousing the cogs of his mind into action. He pulled the duvet from his body and grabbed his clothes. Fortunately, his wife Elizabeth had cleaned all his dirty work clothes the previous evening so they were out of the way in advance of the post-Christmas washing-basket dump.

As he stepped outside onto the landing, so as not to disturb her sleep, Jake asked, 'What's the situation?'

Mamadou laughed, his deep voice unsettling. 'Abraham Al Bakir,' was all he offered.

In his half-delirious state, Jake struggled to attach the name to any relevant meaning. 'What about him?'

'Well, he's currently lying dead in the middle of a pavement in West Ham.'

'OK,' Jake said, still confused. 'I'm assuming this is a good thing?'

'You'd think, but sadly no. Young Abraham was found dead on the street with six kilograms of explosives strapped to his chest.'

That caught his attention. His mind no longer had any time to gradually wake up of its own accord – it needed to be on high alert as soon as he left the house and remain that way until the moment he returned. Counter Terrorism Command had been following

Abraham Al Bakir and his terrorist cell for months, way before Jake's time. Through a series of undercover surveillance operations and intelligence gathering, they had built a profile on Abraham and a comprehensive network of his underlings. Abraham was the head of the cell, the top dog, the man in charge.

And now he was dead.

'Jake?' Mamadou murmured. 'Jake, you there?'

It took a moment for him to break from his reverie. 'Yes, boss,' he said. 'Text me the address and I'll be there as soon as I can.'

Jake hung up the phone and leant against the bannister on his landing. Why was Abraham dead? Why did he have explosives strapped to his chest? And what the fuck had he been planning?

In Jake's admittedly limited experience, he knew the answers to those questions were never going to be easy to stomach, nor would they be easy to find.

He went back into his bedroom, woke Elizabeth and explained to her the situation.

'Really?' she murmured softly, still partly caught in the clutches of sleep. 'It's Christmas Eve.'

'I know,' Jake said. 'But something's come up, and I need to go in. I'm sorry.'

'Be careful please.'

'Always,' Jake replied and gave her a kiss on the forehead.

CHAPTER 3

A few minutes later, Jake was in his Austin Mini Cooper, revving the little 900cc engine as quietly as he could. On the way to the crime scene, he ate a banana and a breakfast bar he'd brought with him. He didn't know when he would next be able to eat. With any luck, it would be lunchtime. But after several years in the job, he'd trained his stomach to withstand long passages of time without food or water. And when he did finally eat, it was usually a takeaway or some other form of heart-attack-inducing fast food. Such was the nature of the job that he didn't have much choice in the matter. If he didn't like it, there were always several permanently open doors from which he could leave.

Just after 4:30 a.m., Jake pulled up to the crime scene, a little over forty-five minutes after he'd left. The traffic had been quiet, given that most of the Christmas Eve's Eve partygoers had gone home for the night – although a few clusters of drunken men, women and teenagers, who could handle their hangover on Christmas Eve morning, had remained, singing and dancing long into the night.

Abraham Al Bakir's crime scene was positioned on the corner of a residential street, right outside an off-licence. Beside it was a telephone box and a row of waste bins. A police cordon had been set up fifty yards from the body. Blue and white lights flashed intermittently, illuminating the surroundings and bouncing off the buildings in a macabre disco. The street and surrounding area were littered with members from several branches of law enforcement. Some he recognised, some he didn't. Police constables, SO15, CID, bomb disposal, scenes of crime officers.

Jake stepped out of the car and was greeted by an overweight man who introduced himself as PC Arthur Maxwell.

'You SO15?' he asked.

'Yes.'

'Course you are. You look the part. I was just doing the rounds, you know. And then I saw this body on the ground, so I pulled over and got out. At first I thought he was just a homeless man who couldn't find anywhere to stay for the night. But when I walked up to the body, I realised it was a dead bloke on the side of the road. But it wasn't just anyone. There was something stuck to him, so I called it in. I thought to myself, *Jesus Christ, I'm way out of my depth with this one*.'

'Thanks,' Jake replied. 'You did good.'

He didn't want to come across as short, but his tired mind could only tolerate a minimal amount of small talk this early in the morning.

The man's face illuminated with a warm smile, and Jake reckoned that was the first time in a long while Maxwell had received praise.

'Tanner!' DCS Mamadou Kuhoba interrupted. The balding, middle-aged man looked tired. His cheeks had sagged considerably since Jake had last seen him, and dark crescent moons dangled loosely underneath his eyes. They shook hands. 'About time you showed up.'

'Sorry, Mam,' Jake said. He looked over Mamadou's shoulder. A silhouette, like a fashion-store mannequin, lay on the ground. 'You know how I am on early mornings. When do I get to see him?'

'Now.'

'Already?'

Mamadou nodded. 'Bomb squad disarmed the device and cleared the area about ten minutes ago. SOCO are combing through the evidence now. We've got uniform and some PCSOs doing the house-to-house, seeing if anyone knows or saw anything.'

'Can't imagine they did. Everyone's tucked up for Christmas.'

'Not everyone.' Mamadou pointed to a group of plainclothes officers on the other side of the cordon. 'Your old mates at MIT are here, but I can't see them spending much longer.'

Jake's old mates at the Major Investigation Team consisted of his old detective chief inspector, Darryl Hughes, and detective constable Ashley Rivers. The rest of the team had either died, been sent to prison, medically retired or resigned. Jake had been a successful member of Stratford CID for the better part of four years and had given everything to the role – and to the fight against The Cabal, the leader of a clandestine network of corrupt police and government officials. He'd received death threats, had his career tarnished and had almost died on several occasions, all in the fight against evil. He'd seen colleagues die, colleagues betray him and colleagues turn a blind eye to the true nature of the underside of the Metropolitan Police Service, and it was a part of his career that he was keen to put behind him.

But sometimes the past just had a way of creeping up on you.

'What are they doing here?' Jake asked.

'Under the circumstances, the last thing anyone wants is a murder investigation on the eve of Christmas, but I think they felt obliged to attend on a professional level, given the fact that he's dead. And quite possibly been murdered. Either that or they *really* need the work.'

Jake chuckled. 'Ever the cynic, aren't you?'

'Or it's because they know we're absolutely decimated thanks to the holidays and fancied helping us out for a change. I've done the rounds and you're the first to turn up.'

'I'll wear that honour with pride, sir.'

And it was with pride that he scurried away to a white van, found himself a crime scene forensic suit and then hurried back to Mamadou. The two of them, dressed in white-and-blue scrubs, shuffled towards the body, the sound of chafing material disturbing the solemn and sombre air. A group of SOCOs surrounded Abraham's body, cameras in hand, searching for any evidence and clues that might shine a light on Abraham's death.

'Are we certain it's him?' Jake asked.

Before answering, Mamadou whistled for someone named Jenkins. A tall man with big teeth came hurtling over, seemingly unsteady on his giraffe legs. In his hands he held a zip-locked bag. Inside was a wallet and a loose driver's licence. Jake searched through the bag and understood there was no doubt.

'Where's Chris?' Jake asked.

'No idea. Not picking up his phone. Jenna's trying to contact him now.'

Chris Bates was the detective inspector in charge of Green Team, the small unit of detectives running Operation Montague, among other things. Through a series of surveillance operations and intelligence gathering, Operation Montague was the investigation that had been looking into and cataloguing Abraham Al Bakir's terrorist cell. Chris and his team were responsible for knowing everything there was to know about the head of the group. It was little help if the expert wasn't there to divulge any information.

'And what about Tyler?' Jake asked, searching for his friend.

'On the razz, it would appear. When I called him, I think he was about six pints down and about six inches deep.'

'Lovely.'

'But he should be here first thing in the morning, I've been reliably informed.'

Tyler Stuart was of similar age to Jake, with a similar upbringing, yet the two couldn't be any more different. One was happily married with a family and mortgage; the other was a misogynist who always took the 'work hard, play hard' mantra too literally. But Tyler had been the only one, along with Mamadou, to welcome Jake into the team and nourish him. The three of them had become close, especially he and Tyler, and so Jake had been willing to put aside their cultural and moral differences, and now he considered him one of his closest friends.

Turning his attention to the investigation, Jake bent down beside Abraham's body, pulled the plastic sheet from him and looked at his stomach. As soon as he saw the IED, he said, 'Jesus Christ. There's enough explosive here to blow this entire street up. Is it all homemade?'

Jake looked to Mamadou, who looked to one of the SOCOs opposite.

'We suspect so,' a woman wearing a set of oversized glasses behind a face mask said. 'Bomb disposal took some samples and they reckon it's hydrogen peroxide. And lots of it.'

'Enough to send us all to Timbuktu,' Mamadou added, tapping Jake on the shoulder.

'Is that what killed him?' he asked.

'From what I can tell, yes.'

Now it was the turn of the pathologist to speak. Jake hadn't recognised her at first, but as soon as she spoke, the voice registered in his mind. He glanced into her eyes to confirm.

The woman opposite him was Poojah Singh, the forensic pathologist who had frequented Jake's crime scenes during his tenure with the Major Investigation Team. The two hadn't always seen eye to eye, but they possessed a deep bond hidden a few layers beneath the surface very few knew about. Since joining SO15, Jake hadn't found the time to catch up, but he felt as though there was no love lost over their gentle drifting apart. It was life, human nature, and these things happened. Maintaining contact with everyone he'd ever had a relationship with would not only be exhausting but leave little to no time for him to focus on himself and his family.

'Good to see you again, Jake,' she started, crouching

down beside Abraham's head. 'I've done some preliminary observations, and from what I can see so far, I think he may have ingested some of the hydrogen peroxide – enough to make him extremely sick, at least. But I won't know the full extent of it until I've done my bits. Until I've cut him open and done a thorough examination, I can only guess.'

Jake and Mamadou thanked her for the information and allowed her to carry on with her work.

Over the next couple of minutes, Jake continued to look through Abraham's possessions. His pockets. His clothes. His shoes. All in search of a clue – anything that might tell them exactly what he'd had planned.

And then he found it. It was so simple that it had been completely overlooked by everyone else who had studied the body.

Hiding inside one of Abraham Al Bakir's socks was a piece of paper. So thin that it barely stuck out against his leg. But somehow, by some miracle, Jake had seen it.

He thumbed the sock away from the man's hairy leg and removed the folded piece of paper. The words on the page confused him, and he swore aloud.

Then he said, 'Mamadou, I think you need to see this.'

CHAPTER 4

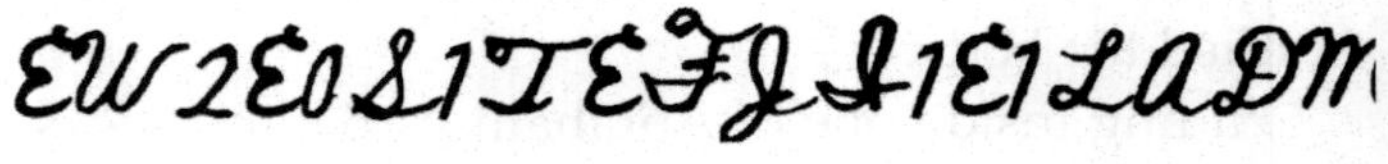

The scrawling on the note was barely legible. The ones, Is and Ls all looked the same, as did the A and D. And for the past few minutes, Jake and Mamadou had been standing there trying to decipher it, scratching their heads.

'Is it Arabic?' Mamadou asked, and as he tried to lean in for a closer look, he reached for the note in Jake's hand.

Jake swatted him away. 'Look with your eyes, not your hands. Didn't your mum ever teach you that?'

'My mum was never one for verbal guidance. A quick slap usually fixed me up all right. You learn quicker that way.'

If that was his belief, then Jake feared for any child that might one day come into Mamadou's life.

They were getting distracted. Before either of them

could further contaminate the piece of evidence, it needed to be contained. Jake summoned a SOCO, who placed it into an evidence bag and catalogued it with the logger.

'What do you think it means?' Mamadou asked after snatching the evidence bag back from the SOCO.

'I think it might explain why he died. He clearly didn't want anyone to find it if he was keeping it in his sock. The only question remains what he's doing out here in the middle of the night, just before Christmas, strapped to the heavens, with a coded note hidden on him.'

'Only he can answer that.'

'And the person who killed him.'

Mamadou looked at him in mild disbelief. 'Murder?'

'Why else would he have ingested hydrogen peroxide? It's not something you drink by accident, like picking up the salt rather than the sugar.'

'So you think it's part of something bigger?'

Jake nodded. He did. The little switch that said 'intuition' in the back of his brain had been niggling away ever since he'd heard the news. From the little he knew about Abraham and his cell, they were based in Barking, not far from where they were now, and they had several sites around the East London area that they used to meet, discuss, and prepare their training and attacks. It was happening every day, right in front of these Londoners' eyes, and they didn't even know it. In fact, it was happening all over the city. All over the world. The network was considerably extensive, which meant there were egos, opinions, and personalities for Abraham to manage and control. And if the scales of mutiny became too lopsided, there was only one outcome.

'I think we need to be prepared for something bigger coming our way, yes. Because right now, none of this is making any sense.'

With a wave of his arm, Mamadou flagged down the crime scene manager, who came shuffling over. He thrust the bagged note into her hand. 'We need this analysed for fingerprints and all the other stuff immediately. Who can you spare?'

The crime scene manager hesitated a moment. 'Ian's probably the best guy.'

'Mr Sutcliffe?'

'Yeah.'

'My old friend. He's probably still in bed now.'

'Half the city is,' she said. 'Would you like me to call him, sir?'

'No that's quite all right,' Mamadou replied. 'Leave it with me. Ian's like a honey badger – if you piss him off too much, he gets very angry.'

Jake didn't understand the reference but went along with a chuckle anyway. Sometimes it helped to massage the boss's ego.

'I'll keep the note for now too,' Mamadou added, taking it back from her. 'We'll hand it over to him ourselves.'

A brief moment of respite was broken by the sound of heavy boots stampeding towards them. A few seconds later, a uniformed police constable careened to a stop a few metres away from them.

'Sorry to interrupt, guv, but I think you need to come with me.' The man was out of breath and visibly nervous at speaking with someone of Mamadou's rank and seniority.

'What is it, Constable?'

'The off-licence, sir. I was doing the house-to-house and thought I'd check in on the flat upstairs, but the door's been left wide open and I can smell a lot of bleach.'

CHAPTER 5

Careful deliberation had been made as to who would enter the flat first: the bomb disposal team or the armed response unit who'd arrived at the scene only moments before the PC's interruption. In the end, as senior investigating officer, Mamadou had chosen the armed response unit. Not only because they had firearms and the ability to dispose of any threats with the pull of a trigger, but because he saw the threat to life significantly reduced with Abraham outside the flat.

Fortunately, Mamadou's suspicions had been correct, and the property had been found empty. As a result, both the bomb disposal and armed response units were in and out within minutes.

Now it was Jake and Mamadou's turn.

They climbed the steps tentatively, each of their footsteps creating a symphony on the creaking floorboards. The walls in the stairwell were laden with damp, and the smell of it was caught in a battle with the stench of chemicals and explosive material, fighting for superiority in the air and in Jake's throat. He gagged and choked behind the face mask until he was forced to remove it momentarily to catch his breath. It was almost as bad as the rotting stench of a six-week-old carcass that had been left to decompose in the summer heat.

The stairwell opened onto the living room, which wasn't much of a living room at all. The only feature of the room that suggested any form of living had taken place was the small, battered leather sofa pressed against the wall, buried beneath the detritus of takeaway boxes and energy drinks. Immediately in front of it was a glass coffee table, servant to a mountain of explosive gear – chemicals, scales, nails and other drug-dealing paraphernalia. Over the back of the sofa, hanging from the wall, was an ISIS flag. On the opposite side of the room was a desk, equally cluttered and overloaded with chemicals of destruction.

This was Jake's first ever terrorist bomb factory, and he was appalled at what he saw. An entire room, an entire flat, dedicated to the purpose of senseless killing.

Jake wandered about the flat, his gaze searching the minutiae of the room, surveying for evidence that would indicate why and how Abraham had died. Behind him, the remaining SOCOs began filtering into the room, readying to conduct searches of their own.

Jake waded his way through the dust and dirt on the carpet into the kitchen. There, he found an empty bottle of hair dye capsized on the kitchen counter. He opened his mouth to speak, but Mamadou beat him to it.

'Come here,' he called.

Jake did so, following the low din of his manager's

voice all the way into the bedroom.

It was a skeleton of a room; a single mattress lying on the floor, with a thin brown sheet draped over the top of it, was the only thing that resembled a bed. It wasn't much of a luxury, but at least it had two pillows, Jake thought as he entered. As for a wardrobe, that was over in the corner: a pile of clothes dumped atop one another, no discernible distinction between clean and dirty.

Mamadou crouched on the other side of the mattress. In his hands he held a notebook with even more of Abraham's illegible scrawlings over it. Except that wasn't what intrigued Jake. What caught his eye was the torn corner of the page on the bottom right.

'Is that what I think it is?'

Mamadou pulled the evidence bag containing the note from behind the book and hovered it in place. The note married perfectly with the missing page in the book. Jake felt like they were in a movie – *Indiana Jones and The Secrets of the Off-Licence Flat*.

'What else is in there?' Jake asked, gesturing towards the notebook, hoping to find other treasures inside.

'Nothing, from what I can tell. It's all in a different language. We'll need it analysed.'

'All of it's in a different language?'

'Yes.'

'All of it except for this note?'

'Yes.'

'Curious,' Jake said. 'Why do you think that is?'

'Not sure. Any ideas?'

Jake cleared his throat and readjusted his face mask over his nose. 'I think he's trying to tell us something. He knew he was dying – whether it was slowly or quickly – and he needed to show us somehow.'

'Elaborate...'

'The note, for starters. I think it's a clue about an imminent attack. And I think the vest he was wearing details how it's going to happen. Even if he was murdered, it would make no sense for him to be wearing it unless he was planning on detonating it tonight.'

Mamadou nodded his understanding then turned his attention back to the books on the floor. Jake joined him. Together they burrowed through the sheets of paper and notebooks. Jake picked one up to inspect it but quickly put it down as soon as he realised it was in a language he didn't understand. The rest of the book contained mathematical equations and measurements, the evidence of which was sitting on the glass coffee table in the living room. Beside the notebooks was a pile of leaflets that had been posted through the letter box and dropped in a heap. Jake had a pile of his own at home and paid little attention as he flicked through them.

After ten minutes of searching, Jake and Mamadou returned to the outdoor crime scene. Waiting for them on the other side of the cordon was DI Chris Bates. He was dressed in a thick coat to protect against the cold, and his hair looked freshly washed. Unlike many of the other staff members in attendance, he wasn't sporting a case of bed head. In his hands, he held a cup of coffee.

'Morning,' he said. 'Or is it evening?'

'Neither,' Mamadou responded, unimpressed. 'It's put-a-forensic-suit-on-and-have-a-look-at-this time.'

Sighing, Chris did as he was asked, and a minute later, the three of them were hovering over Abraham's body.

'Fucking hell,' Chris said. 'I take it the cold didn't kill him.'

Jake chose not to respond.

'He never was much of a looker.'

'I'm advising you to stop talking and take this seriously, Chris,' Mamadou said. 'You're part of Operation Montague... what can you tell us about this?'

'I wish I knew. Our intelligence on him and his cell's dried up recently.'

Before any of them could continue, a police constable carrying Craig's disposable cup of coffee dipped beneath the cordon and threw it into the bin beside them.

Mamadou leapt to his feet. 'What the fuck do you think you're doing?'

'Sorry, sir, I—'

'You know you're not supposed to be behind the tape without the correct gear!'

Listening to Mamadou lambast the constable, Jake turned his attention back to Chris and saw the man searching Abraham's feet. They locked eyes.

'And what are *you* doing?' he asked the inspector.

'I assume you've done this already, right?'

'First thing we did,' Jake responded.

He was about to let Chris know about the note when a violent scream pierced the air.

'Smoke!'

Jake snapped his head towards Mamadou.

A stream of smoke poured through the hole in the bin, and panic enveloped the street.

Jake didn't think – he reacted.

He jumped to his feet and sprinted in the opposite direction.

Wherever his legs would take him.

CHAPTER 6

'What the fuck do you think you're doing?'

This time Mamadou launched his tirade at Chris. The three of them were standing on the other side of Jake's car, several feet away from the smoking bin, while they waited for the bomb disposal unit to clear the area.

The heightened and tense situation had done nothing to abate Mamadou's frustration towards Chris.

Nor Jake's.

'I don't know what you mean, guv,' he replied.

'That coffee, it was yours. You shouldn't be drinking anywhere near a crime scene. And why are you giving your mess to police constables? You're a big boy – you should be able to tidy up after yourself.'

'Guv, I can explain.'

'First you don't answer my calls. Then you turn up late – but that's all right, so long as you're looking freshly washed and clean-shaven. And you even had time to get a coffee on your way in!'

'I'm here, aren't I?'

Uh oh. Big mistake. The first rule of dealing with Mamadou Kuhoba, if he was already incensed with you, was to bite your lip at all times, and refrain from saying what was truly on your mind. The privilege of arguing with him and not backing down was reserved for those Mamadou respected. Jake liked to think he was a part of that list.

'Excuse me?'

'I'm here, aren't I? More than can be said for everyone else on the team.'

'Don't worry about them. They're not here to receive their bollocking. As soon as I see them, they're all going to get it. But for now, you're getting the brunt of it. Not only do you represent us and the team to our colleagues but also to the general public. So don't make us look like a bunch of bellends in front of everyone.'

Jake enjoyed being a fly on the wall in these situations. Less so when he was in Chris's position. But this time Mamadou's attitude and response had been completely warranted. Chris's behaviour since arriving at the crime scene had been nothing short of unprofessional.

After a moment of calm and quiet, Chris lifted his head sheepishly and apologised.

'*Prove* you're sorry to me, Inspector. And then we'll see how you get on.'

'Yes, guv. Sorry, guv.' He dropped his head like a small child and then looked back up at Mamadou imploringly. 'What would you like us to do next?'

'I'd like *you* to answer my question. You're the one in charge of Operation Montague. Tell me everything you know. What intelligence do we have regarding an imminent attack?'

'None, sir. I've not received anything from any of

my team, or in any of MI5's intelligence reports. We've been following Abraham and his cell for weeks, but there doesn't appear to be any out-of-the-ordinary behaviour.'

'We need the names of Abraham's associates. I want them arrested and interviewed now. We need absolute discretion in this situation, gentlemen. If a terrorist attack is imminent, then I don't want a word of this getting out at all, not until we know more. Can you get the names across to the team and I'll arrange their arrest?'

'Of course, sir,' Chris answered. 'Anything else?'

'Yes. Your informant.'

'What about him?'

'We need to have a chat with him.'

Chris hesitated a moment. 'I dunno, sir. I haven't dealt with Farsaid for months. Last I heard, he'd denounced himself from the group.'

'Tough. I want to see him.'

Jake, feeling slightly left out of the conversation, stepped forward and asked, 'What about me, guv? What do you need me to do?'

'Get back to The Room. Analyse the note and try to decode it, if you can. After we've coordinated the arrests, I want you on the interviewing team. We've got a skeleton crew, so we're all going to have to muck in and do other jobs around the place.'

CHAPTER 7

Room 1430, or The Room as it was colloquially known, was the name given to the headquarters of SO15, Counter Terrorism Command. It had originally been appointed the moniker in the eighties, thanks to the room number printed on the original door. Since then, the room had changed, the door had changed, and the team had expanded to over fifty individuals, but the name had stayed the same. It had become a part of the fabric of the identity of SO15 and had become synonymous with the work they did behind closed doors.

Jake arrived at an empty Room 1430 just after 5 a.m. On the drive back, he'd quickly stopped at a twenty-four-hour petrol station to grab a ready-made sandwich for himself. By the time he got to his desk, it was still pitch-black outside, with only the artificial lights of the office to keep him company. When he returned to The Room, he placed the food in his top drawer and then headed to the forensic laboratory in the back of the building.

Evidence collected at a crime scene was typically examined in-house before being sent to a private company for further external examination. The lab at the bottom of the building was designated for urgent cases. The note found in Abraham's possession was one such case.

After signing in his attendance, Jake prowled along the corridors in search of Ian Sutcliffe. Even on a busy day, the building was considered quiet. But now, as he stalked through the halls in the early hours of the morning, he found them eerily quiet. Like someone was behind his shoulder, breathing down his neck, disappearing every time he turned to face them. A jump scare waiting to happen.

Eventually, Jake arrived at the last door in the corridor. The name Ian Sutcliffe was printed in the centre, and Jake was reminded of his conversation with Mamadou before leaving the crime scene.

'What's this Ian Sutcliffe character like?' Jake had asked.

'One of the most anal and irascible guys you will ever meet, but he's an absolute whizz in the lab. Fortunately, he's nothing like the other Sutcliffe you're thinking of. Although he does have a tendency to... *snap*.'

Jake hoped he didn't get on the wrong side of his new acquaintance.

He knocked and was very quickly granted permission to enter.

Ian Sutcliffe's office was smaller than Jake had expected. It was almost the same size as a bathroom, and there was barely enough space to contain Ian's possessions: papers, notebooks, folders, everything a lab technician needed. And then there were the items to Jake's left that concerned him. Small, macabre and terrifying trophies collected from previous cases that had been handed back to him once the investigation had finished in court. A blood-stained sock, a piece of chipped bone and a clump of hair all stood out to Jake. He stared at them for a long while before he stepped into the office.

'Hello?' Ian began, bringing Jake back into the room. Ian Sutcliffe was an elderly gentleman, with a set of bifocals dangling from the tip of his nose. They were too big for his face, and every few seconds he spent speaking, he had to readjust them higher on their perch. Jake found him sitting at the business end of his desk.

Business, Jake thought. *Time to get back to business.*

'Thank you for agreeing to come in at such a ridiculous time,' he said, stepping forward to shake Ian's hand.

'And on Christmas Eve.'

'Yes.'

'And at five o'clock in the bloody morning.'

'Yes. We wouldn't have asked you unless it was absolutely necessary.'

'Why else would I be here?' Ian pushed the glasses further up his nose.

Jake fished inside his blazer pocket and produced the evidence bag. 'We found this on a dead terrorist about an hour ago. Can you tell us what it means and whether there are any traces on it that can lead us to any other potential suspects?' Jake asked in the politest tone he'd ever heard come out of his own mouth.

Ian didn't respond. Instead, he lifted the glasses from his nose and placed them on his forehead. At that moment, Jake realised the man's eyes bulged from his skull like a fish with popeye disease.

'Has this been contaminated?'

Jake hesitated before speaking. 'Well... Unfortunately, the problem with that is...'

Ian sighed, rolled his eyes and begrudgingly took the bag from Jake. He shuffled round the corner of his desk and slipped through a door Jake hadn't noticed before. The door led into a small laboratory, twice the size of the office, and was devoid of paper and trophies. Ian moved towards the nearest counter and set to work. Jake hovered over his shoulder, hands in pockets, trying not to feel like a discarded toy.

'Please don't stand and watch,' Ian told him. 'Nothing pisses me off more.'

Jake smirked.

One of the most anal and irascible guys you will ever meet, but he's an absolute whizz in the lab.

Mamadou had been right about the first part. Jake just hoped he was about the second too.

Jake thanked the man again then left.

When he returned to The Room, he found it teeming with his colleagues from Green Team, many of whom he hadn't seen in the last few hours.

'You finally made it then,' Jake said to the open room.

'Just in time,' DS Carla Harding said. 'The first of Abraham Al Bakir's associates has been brought in. And he's ready for interview.'

CHAPTER 8

Mamadou switched off the engine, the air around them silent and stagnant. The bitter morning chill graced the window, and the sky was still pitch-black, making the cones of light from his headlights more ominous. They were stationed outside Farsaid Dali's last known address. Chris had given it to him before they entered the car and directed them here. According to the information, Farsaid Dali lived in a small, semi-detached one-bedroom house that was in a row of neat, little houses that all bore the same architectural laziness. They were almost identical. But that didn't mean to say cheap either. Especially if Mamadou's tiny one-bedroom flat in Watford was anything to go by. Whether it was the illegal gains of terrorist funding that had enabled Farsaid to purchase the house, or whether it had been the discreet payments he'd received as an informant, Mamadou didn't know. But right now, it was low down on the list of priorities. One to check out in the future.

'Wait here,' Chris said. 'I'll speak to him first.'

'If he's home,' Mamadou replied.

Chris glared at him. 'If he's still there, I'll speak to him, let him know what's happening. It's been a long time since we last saw each other. He might react badly if he sees both of us appearing on his doorstep unannounced in the middle of the night on Christmas Eve. He'll think he's getting arrested.'

'Should he be?'

Chris didn't say anything, just looked down into the footwell then started out of the car.

Before he left, Mamadou grabbed him by the sleeve and said, 'No funny business.'

Chris nodded and closed the door gently, so as not to disturb the quaint street.

For a few moments, Mamadou did nothing except watch in complete silence as Chris wandered up the road, vanished behind a row of cars and then reappeared as he approached Farsaid Dali's last known address.

CHAPTER 9

The first of Abraham Al Bakir's associates was a twenty-one-year-old called Hasan Qasim. He was sitting opposite Jake in one of the interview rooms in the bowels of the building, and beside him was his solicitor. This morning, Jake was conducting the interview alone. Usually, he would have had a colleague beside him to ask any of the questions he may have missed, but with the staff levels during peak season at a record low, he was forced to go it alone. No problem though. He felt confident that in the seven months he'd been a part of the team, he had sufficient experience to sit face-to-face with a terror suspect.

Before he began, Jake tried to analyse Hasan. The young man was only a few years younger than himself, and he tried to remember what he'd been doing at that age: fresh out of university, armed with a psychology degree, filled with an abundance of aspiration and hope.

An abundance of aspiration and hope that had landed him a job in a call centre in South London.

From the information Jake had scanned prior to the meeting, he'd learnt that he and Hasan had quite similar backgrounds. Both born and raised in South London. Both the middle child to two siblings. Both university educated, both intelligent.

Yet their paths could not have been at further ends of the spectrum.

Jake sought to understand where it had all gone wrong.

'A few hours ago,' he began, 'the body of a man under our close surveillance was found dead on the pavement outside his home. That man's name was Abraham Al Bakir. Does that name mean anything to you?'

'No comment.'

Great, Jake thought. *Off to a brilliant start already.*

He continued. 'Do you know Abraham Al Bakir?'

'No comment.'

'Have you ever met him?'

'No comment.'

'Have you ever worked for him?'

'No comment.'

Jake sifted through the pile of papers in front of him and slid across a coloured photograph. The image taken from one of Green Team's directed surveillance operations showed Hasan and Abraham conversing outside a building.

'This suggests to me you do know one another. What are you talking about here? For reference, this photo was taken last month.'

Hasan remained stern in the face of Jake's questioning, his lips tight. The photo made no difference to his expression or his answers.

'We know that Abraham Al Bakir is the head of a

terrorist cell here in London. We've been surveying him and the members of his group for a while. We believe that you're a member of that group. We've since arrested all of your colleagues, and they're currently being interviewed in this very building. Did Abraham recruit you into the group?'

'No comment.'

Jake sighed inwardly, making an effort to ensure his displeasure didn't reach his face.

'How long have you been working for Abraham?'

'No comment.'

'We found this on his body,' Jake said as he removed a photocopy of the note collected from the crime scene.

He slid it across the table, half-expecting Hasan to disregard it the same way he had the photograph. Except this time, the young man leant forward, his eyes fixated on the letters on the note. Then he turned to his solicitor and whispered in the man's ear.

Jake waited.

And waited.

And waited.

'No comment,' Hasan replied.

Immediately, Jake's hopes came crashing back down.

'Do you recognise this note?' he continued.

'No comment.'

'What about the letters and numbers – do they mean anything to you?'

'No comment.'

'We know about the attack, Hasan. We know you're implicated in it. We just want to know how deeply. Help us to help you by telling us what we want to know.'

This seemed to give Hasan cause to consider. He

hesitated, his face contorting as an internal battle raged. Speak or stay silent. Confess or hide.

In the end, he did exactly what Jake expected him to.

'No comment.'

'Very well.' Jake snatched at the documents on the table and returned them to his folder. 'Tell me about university, Hasan.'

'What?'

At last, a response other than 'no comment'. A battle won in a war of many defeats. A minor victory.

'Your education. You went to university, right? Studied chemistry at UCL. Professor Bryden was your lecturer in your final year. You graduated with a first-class honours – congratulations. Your accommodation was paid for in cash, although you don't have any living relatives left in this country. You received the maximum student loan maintenance fee. And shortly after you graduated, you worked in a shopping centre, called…' Jake leafed through the pages until he found the name. 'Westfield – and you still work there.'

He paused to look up at Hasan. The man's shock-stricken face satisfied him. 'You see, we know everything there is to know about you. We know that you have no family who can support you. We know that you have no friends from university that you keep in touch with. We know that Abraham recruited you into his group this time last year.'

Hasan shifted uncomfortably in his seat.

'What I think happened was that after university, you felt lost, lonely. After all, you had this fantastic degree, and you had the world at your feet. You were young, invincible. But when you realised you couldn't get a job, you suffered mentally. You found yourself going to pubs and clubs and the rest of it, trying to drink your sorrows and pain away. And then Abraham found you… You didn't find him, did you? He was the one who found you. And do you know why that is? Because he's a predator. He's a man who preys on innocent and vulnerable young men like yourself. You're not the suspect here – you're not the problem. Abraham was. And now he's dead – which means that someone else is to blame. And we're trying to find out who. And we want to know more about this attack so we can put a stop to it, so more innocent and vulnerable people aren't hurt. Do you think you could help us with that, Hasan?'

Jake let out a long, steady breath as he waited for Hasan to respond.

For a moment, the young man retreated into his mind and battled with himself again. Good versus bad. Wrong versus right. Both elements of morality fighting for superiority. His face contorted and his breathing increased. He began fiddling with his hands, rubbing his fingers against one another, picking at his fingernails and the mess beneath them. Until eventually he looked up at Jake and said: 'It wasn't my fault. Abraham lured me in. He manipulated me. He… he-he lied to me.'

'I know.'

'He made me do things I didn't want to do. Lots of things.'

'You can tell me all about them later. But right now, I need to know who killed him and more about the attack.'

Time was sensitive. And he was running out of it.

'I don't know who killed him. I'm sorry I can't help you with that. But I can with the attack.' Hasan pointed at Jake's folder. 'Can I see the note again?'

Jake was more than happy to oblige. Hasan inspected the note carefully.

'It's the location of the attack. Do you have a pen?'

Jake's intrigue piqued, and his excitement brewed so much that he almost didn't hear Hasan. He handed a pen across, and Hasan started writing the letters and numbers in a line at the bottom of the page.

EW2EOS1TEF3I1E1LADM

Then he moved deeper through the layers of the code.

E201E311AMWESTFIELD

Jake watched in amazement as the code unravelled and the answer became clear to him.

Hasan completed it and pushed it back.

WESTFIELD

E20 1E3

11 A.M.

'The attack's taking place at Westfield this morning?' Jake asked.

'Yes,' Hasan replied. 'But by now you're already too late.'

CHAPTER 10

Chris was taking a long time. An abnormally long time.

Four agonisingly slow minutes had passed since he'd wandered up to the house and knocked on the door. From his seat, Mamadou was able to see the patio light casting a deep shadow over a figure in the doorway.

Somebody was standing there, talking to him.

Somebody was home.

An invisible clock of danger counted down inside Mamadou's head. Right now, they didn't know what was going to happen, nor when. And the more time they spent dawdling, the less time they had to act.

'Fuck it,' Mamadou whispered to himself.

Just as he was about to climb out of the car, his phone rang. He pulled his leg back in and answered the call.

'What have you got for me, Jake?'

'Westfield, sir.'

'Excuse me?'

'Westfield, sir. The attack. It's on Westfield. This morning. At eleven when the shopping centre opens.'

Mamadou let the words fall over him, absorbing them into his body. Westfield shopping centre was a highlight of the Stratford area, a popular destination for tourists and residents. Mamadou didn't know the exact visiting figures, but he'd heard they were in the tens of thousands.

Daily.

Add that number to the busy holiday season with a deluge of last-minute purchases and you've got yourself a hotspot for casualties and death.

At 11 a.m.

Approximately four hours away.

'Sir, you there?'

'I'm here,' he confirmed, although not completely. His mind was thinking two hours in advance, planning what stage they needed to be at, pre-empting the people he needed to alert. 'How certain are you, Jake? Has this information been verified?'

'I heard it from the horse's mouth. One of Abraham's associates told me. And it's been confirmed on the note we found in his possession. It was the letters of the location, postcode and time of the attack jumbled up in reverse.'

Mamadou switched his brain back to work mode. 'How many have we arrested?'

'Four, sir. I'm told they tried to arrest the fifth, but he's missing.'

'Then I think it's safe to assume the attack's going to go ahead. And possibly with this MisPer in charge of it. I want Superintendent Thompson as deputy SIO. He's in charge while I'm out. Tell him he needs to arrange Red Team to intercept all media communication from

Abraham's associates. Tell him they need to find out whether anyone else is behind this attack. Then I want Green Team managing the CCTV from the centre itself – and outside the flat, if there's any. If you really think that Abraham's signposting this attack to us, then we need to search every bin receptacle within a five-hundred-metre radius. Lastly, I want Thompson and the rest of you to rally everyone we can find and have them ready on standby. In the meantime, their main priority is to find that missing associate. Pass those messages on, and leave it up to Thompson. If you have any questions or issues, you address him.'

'Yes, sir. Understood.'

Mamadou hung up, and feeling the adrenaline bubble beneath the surface, he hurried towards Farsaid Dali's house.

'Chris,' he said as he arrived at the doorstop. 'Everything all right?'

The man standing behind the doorway was smaller than Mamadou had perceived him to be from the car. His hair was dishevelled, a reminder that he'd just been woken up by Chris, and a dark beard adorned his chin. It was trimmed, thin, stylish, understated, yet overstated. As if he'd spent multiple hours and paid ten times the cost of a pint of beer just to sit in a chair and have someone style it for him. He didn't seem to flinch at the sight of Mamadou.

Chris, on the other hand…

'What are you doing here?' he asked, surprised. 'I thought I told you to stay where you were.'

'And I thought I told you no funny business.'

'This isn't funny business.'

'You sure? Then what have you been doing all this time?'

'Talking to Farsaid.'

Chris looked at the man in the doorway. Farsaid Dali nodded curtly, his expression blank.

'Mr Dali,' Mamadou said, 'may we come in? There's something important we need to discuss with you.'

'Yeah. You got five minutes.'

Farsaid Dali's living room was small. It possessed a beige carpet, two sofas, a coffee table in the middle, and a fifty-inch flatscreen TV hanging from the wall. Underneath it was a Sky box, PlayStation 4, Xbox One and a Nintendo Wii. Positioned either side of the TV were Bose surround-sound speakers. The perfect setup for parties and downtime with mates.

Or the perfect setup to discuss terrorist activity.

For a man who, as far as Mamadou was aware, had no job or steady form of income, he was doing all right for himself. A thought that set the alarm bells ringing.

Farsaid sat on one of the sofas and reclined the seat, as though he was the poster boy for relaxation.

'What's this about?'

'Mr Dali, we need to ask you a few questions about Abraham Al Bakir.'

'Am I under arrest?'

'No.'

'Am I going to be if I tell you something?'

Mamadou shook his head. 'You're still a registered informant. This would fall under that blanket. And for now, this is strictly off the record.'

'How come?'

'We're under a tight deadline.'

'Tut-tut,' Farsaid said. 'What have the police come

to? First you send this wanker to my house in the early hours of the morning.' Farsaid pointed to Chris, who looked taken aback by the personal verbal attack. 'And then reinforcements show up, asking unwarranted questions about a man I haven't seen in months.'

'How many months exactly?' Mamadou asked.

'Ten or so. Maybe a year. It's been a long time.'

'And you've had no contact with Abraham since then?'

Farsaid Dali shook his head.

'OK. How were you affiliated with him?'

'Shouldn't you be asking Chris these questions? Surely he's told you all of this already?'

'We prefer for it to come from the horse's mouth,' Mamadou said, his voice deep and stern. Intimidating. He stood tall with his wide shoulders tensed.

'If you say so.' Farsaid shifted in his chair. 'He was a terrorist, as you know. Working for an organisation from Turkey. Underground, deep beneath the depths of anything imaginable. Creating horror on an incomprehensible scale. I was a part of their outfit originally. Joined when I was nineteen, served there for five years. But then I started hearing these horror stories. Saying that they'd take you to these training camps where they'd torture you, feed you chemicals to make you behave the way they wanted you to. Abraham went to one. Said it was the best thing he'd ever done, and that he was going to send me. After I heard that, I got cold feet and left. I was lucky to get out. They were recruiting so many teenagers, adolescents – young men who didn't know any better, who didn't know what they were getting into and what would happen to them.'

'How many did Abraham recruit?'

'Dozens at least. That was while I was there though. As I say, it's been almost a year now, so that number has most likely multiplied. But people were getting moved about a lot. Shipped to different parts of the country. I never saw many of the same faces twice.'

Mamadou's thoughts turned to teenage boys who had been lured into a denigrated life of violence and extremism and hatred. They were young, naïve and with no one in their lives to guide them on the right path. Countless men were at risk.

'Think back to the time you were last working for Abraham – can you remember anything the cell may have been working on? Anything they were organising?'

Farsaid nodded. 'Lots. So many operations I lost track. I couldn't even count them on my fingers three times over.'

'What were they?'

'Some of them were small. You know, exploding petrol stations, HGVs on the motorway. And some of them were big. Blowing up Harrods, pharmaceutical companies, Canary Wharf. But they never went very far.'

'Why not?'

Farsaid shrugged, nonchalant. 'Disagreements. There were a lot of egos in the room. Some of the men didn't want to listen to Abraham, thought that he'd had his day and that he was going senile in his old age. It was all those chemicals, fuzzing his brain up.'

'And what did you think when *you* were working for him?'

'Excuse me?'

'What did *you* think? I'm assuming you had an ego. I'm assuming you had your opinions.'

'Of course I did. But I was never listened to, so I stopped trying. I was only a foot soldier, one of the lowest in the group. They were never going to listen to me.'

'Did that influence your decision to leave?'

Farsaid nodded. 'A little. Ain't nice not being heard.'

Mamadou concluded he'd heard enough so far and decided to play his trump card.

'This morning, a few hours ago, Abraham's body was found dead outside what we believe to be his place of residence. Do you know anything about that?'

Farsaid's expression dropped. His eyes widened and his lips parted, the look of surprise stretching across his face. 'No! I know nothing about that. My God.'

'You sound concerned about his death?'

'Well, you know, I worked with him for five years. I got to know him. Yeah, he was a bad person who wanted to hurt a lot of people, but when you've been on the other side of the fence, you learn to look at people differently.'

'He was found with a vest of explosives strapped round his chest,' Mamadou said, hoping the shock tactic might unearth some information from Farsaid.

'Is that what killed him?'

'No. We believe he ingested chemicals. We're trying to find his killer now. But he left us a clue.'

'Oh?'

'A note,' Chris chipped in. His sudden intrusion into the conversation took Mamadou by surprise. 'We're trying to decipher it at the moment.'

Mamadou removed his phone from his pocket and flashed an image of the note he'd taken at the crime scene. 'Mean anything to you?'

Farsaid leant forward and scrutinised the note, his eyes lingering over the letters. Then he shook his head.

'This is the first I've ever seen anything like this. We never had notes of this description in the past. I'm sorry, but I wish I could help.'

As Mamadou had expected.

Farsaid Dali was a black hole of information. Someone who, over the years, had absorbed everything he'd ever seen or heard. Information that would never see the light of day again, lost for an eternity.

'Do you have a phone, Mr Dali?'

'Like most people, yes.'

'Is it all right if we take some contact details for yourself?'

Farsaid opened his mouth to protest but quickly stopped himself.

Once they had his details, Mamadou and Chris made to leave. The now visible and looming countdown of 11 a.m. was at the forefront of Mamadou's mind. Slowly ticking down, growing ever larger, ever closer.

For now, Mamadou didn't think it was possible to arrest Farsaid. As far as the evidence against him went, there was none. Chris had assured him that his information on Abraham's associates was accurate and up to date, and that arresting Farsaid would have been seen as a form of harassment. For now, all they could do was take his details and station a surveillance officer – one of the very few they had to spare – outside the house. Watching, waiting, praying for him to make a mistake and reveal his true role in the organisation.

CHAPTER 11

When Mamadou and Chris returned to Room 1430, the effects of Operation Chestnut, the name appointed by Mamadou, were in full swing. Jake had passed on the instructions to the deputy SIO, and Graham Thompson had carried them out swiftly and efficiently. Green Team, positioned in the far corner of the room, were investigating the CCTV footage of the shopping centre. Beside them, Red Team were monitoring all of Abraham's associates' historical media communication, spreading the net of their investigation into the underworld. Finally, Yellow Team, stationed in their own room, were handling the frontline response on the ground. Jake had heard through the grapevine that over a hundred officers, uniformed and plainclothes, had been called in to Stratford, prepared for a large-scale event.

It was 10 a.m., and they were nearing the endgame. A final decision as to the management of the situation had yet to be made however, and time was running out.

Something which they were all painfully aware of.

If they left it too late, they risked endangering the lives of countless individuals. If they acted too soon, and alerted the missing associate to their presence, then they also risked endangering the lives of countless individuals.

A lose-lose.

A catch-22.

Jake was at his desk, staring at the note that Hasan had helped decipher when he felt a hand on his shoulder. It was Poojah, the look of fear shining in her eyes.

'Where's Mamadou?' she asked.

Jake pointed to a small office in the corner of the room. 'In there.'

Poojah left without saying anything and, intrigue getting the better of him, Jake decided to follow. She knocked on the door and entered before Mamadou declared it acceptable.

'I didn't realise my closed door was an invitation to walk in like this is a fourth-century brothel,' Mamadou retorted. 'So this better be good, Poojah. What have you got for me?'

'A murder, sir.'

'A murder, you say? Sounds like the start of an Agatha Christie novel.'

'Sadly, this one's much more serious than that.'

'Pray, do tell.'

'Your victim, Abraham Al Bakir, was murdered, sir. How? Hydrogen peroxide ingestion. And a lot of it. Someone forced it down his throat. There were legions on the inside of his throat. I did the PM as fast as I could.'

'And you're a hundred per cent?'

'Like I said, I did it quickly. Like you asked.'

'Of course, of course. Well, that still doesn't help us much.'

He turned his attention to Jake. 'What are you doing here, Tanner?'

'Being nosy, sir.'

'Right. Get back to work then. I'm holding a brief in five minutes. I need everyone there. Make the announcement please.'

The major incident room, or MIR, filled within minutes of Jake's announcement, and every one of the thirty-two staff members were already waiting for Mamadou to enter exactly five minutes later.

'I don't need to give you all a recap,' he started, commanding the attention of the entire floor. 'You all know the situation. You all know what's going on. What I want to know is what we're doing to prevent it.'

A forest of hands shot into the air. Mamadou picked his first victim.

A member of Red Team.

'Following Jake's intel, sir, and the idea that Abraham Al Bakir was leaving behind clues, we looked into the CCTV footage of Westfield Shopping Centre over the past couple of nights. Paying particular attention to the bins inside the premises.'

Jake sensed where this was headed immediately. And he didn't like what was coming next.

'We have footage from two nights ago showing someone we believe to be Hasan Qasim placing explosives inside the bins along the main thoroughfare. We checked and he's a member of the cleaning staff at the centre. So far, we've counted fifteen IED packages.'

'Fuck a duck,' Mamadou said before catching himself. 'Has the centre been warned?'

'Yes, sir,' added another member of Red Team. 'Centre management has been informed, and they've let bomb squad in already. The team are diffusing the explosives as we speak.'

'Do we have any information on how they work? Are they similar to the one found in the bin and on Abraham?'

'Virtually identical, sir. So I'm told.'

That meant Jake had been right. Abraham had been signalling the plan to them all along. A terrorist trying to redeem himself? Jake thought it would take a lot more than that.

'Where's the missing man?' Mamadou asked. 'Have we got a trace on his phone?'

Nobody in the room was brave enough to answer.

Until the deputy SIO cleared his throat. 'We're struggling at the moment, Mam. He's disappeared. He wasn't at his home address; nor was he at any of the addresses DI Bates and his team have identified. He doesn't have a mobile phone registered in his name, so we're assuming that he's working on burners. And any phone that we've traced back to him in the past is now defunct.'

'What about Farsaid Dali?'

'We're monitoring him as well. So far, nothing.'

Mamadou paced from side to side, deep in thought. Then he came to a stop, scratching the top of his ear.

'We need to monitor all mobile phones within a five-hundred-metre radius of the shopping centre. If our missing man is going to come waltzing into the centre, strapped to the heavens, we need to make sure we find him before he can detonate.'

'You think he's going to be there, sir?' Jake asked.

Mamadou nodded. 'He's on a mission. Right now I'm guessing he's panicked, freaking out that the rest of his mates have been arrested, and so he's going to do what he's been told – he's going to see this through to the end. In addition, Abraham was murdered. We mustn't forget that. His killer's still out there somewhere, and I believe that this person's still orchestrating the attack – they're the ones giving the orders.'

With that said, the conversation moved on to difficult terrain, the question of whether the team should keep the centre closed, or allow them to open for customers.

It was a question of life or death, where lives hung in the balance. A monumental decision that Jake was glad he didn't have to make.

That onus lay with Mamadou.

'At this moment in time,' he started, 'I think we need to keep the centre closed. We have no way of knowing how many more explosives there are hiding in the bins or in other various parts of the building. And all it takes is one phone call – one phone call and the whole thing goes up. I can't allow that. Too many lives will be caught in the crossfire.'

'But if you close the centre, you risk doing the same thing, sir,' a member of Green Team stated.

'Explain, Tariq.'

'Imagine it for a second. You've got hundreds, maybe thousands of people, flocking towards the centre within the next hour. When they find out it's closed, they're going to hang around. Especially if they see the bomb squad inside. A cordon's going to do very little to deter them, and that will be the prime spot for him to detonate. In the middle of that mass of people, and we won't be able to get to him in time.'

The argument was sound, but Jake disagreed.

'You're forgetting that trying to find him in the centre, where there are hundreds of moving parts and even more hiding places, is drastically more difficult,' he said. 'Plus, we have no way of knowing whether there are any more explosives inside. There could be fifty bombs hidden inside the shops' bins, or the toilets, or anywhere else. And by the time we find out, it'll be too late.'

The room fell silent, each member of the team locked inside their head with their own thoughts.

'Either way,' somebody in the room said, 'he's a dead man walking.'

Yes, Jake thought. *He is.*

And how the hell do you stop one of those?

CHAPTER 12

Eventually, after careful consideration and much deliberation, the decision had been made to close the shopping centre, and the enormous monument was to remain closed until the New Year. The busiest period of the shopping calendar was more or less over. And Jake saw an impending upheaval on their hands.

A police cordon had been placed around the perimeter of the building, and over a hundred uniformed constables, along with detectives from local CID and SO15 outfits, were stationed around the cordon. The Territorial Support Group, a specialist unit of the Met trained in dispersing large and aggressive crowds – among other roles – were on standby a block away.

For the past two hours, the bomb disposal unit had been inside the premises, silently and efficiently diffusing the bombs in the bins. So far they had diffused seventeen. The building was on complete lockdown until all IEDs had been removed, and a thorough sweep of the premises conducted.

Jake, meanwhile, was standing on the outskirts of the crowd outside, wrapped tightly against the cold in his coat. Fog misted in front of his face with every breath, and he shivered almost uncontrollably. The adrenaline of the situation did little to allay the effects of winter on his skin. He and many other plainclothes officers were strategically positioned around the perimeter, conducting surveillance work. Each of them had committed the missing associate's face to memory, and they were actively trying to seek him out.

Like they were playing a life-sized version of Where's Wally?

Jake checked his watch – 10:45 a.m.

Fifteen minutes until scheduled opening time.

Fifteen minutes until the associate showed his face.

And already the crowds of eager, last-minute shoppers were beginning to form, swelling like a furious tide.

Jake didn't want to think how long it would take for their fury to spill out. Having worked in a fashion shop to pay for his university accommodation – and an unhealthy dose of alcohol on the weekends – he was fully aware that shoppers were notoriously volatile and prone to shouting matches and aggression when they didn't get what they wanted. In fact, they were more like the honey badgers Mamadou had referred to earlier. And he didn't want to get on the wrong side of them. Closing Westfield shopping centre was an event that could trigger a civil war.

Jake pressed his finger to his ear, pushing his earpiece into a more comfortable position. Each plainclothes officer had been fitted with one, and they were an alien sensation to him. Despite being seven months into the job, he still hadn't got used to wearing them. And it didn't help that the earbud was too small for his annoyingly large ear holes.

'Jake,' came Mamadou's voice over the speaker. 'Provide an update on your location.'

For this part of the investigation, the most pivotal part, Mamadou was as far away from the situation as the upper echelons of the Met wanted him to be. He was the strategic commander, responsible for feeding information, intelligence and strategy into the operational commander, who was the eyes and ears on the ground. The OC, Superintendent Thompson, had positioned Jake outside a small coffee shop a hundred feet from Westfield's entrance.

'Nothing yet, guv,' he said, his eyes scanning as inconspicuously as he could manage. 'No signs of disturbed activity.'

A young woman, walking with a pram and a toddler by her side, strolled past him. The sight reminded him of Elizabeth, of his daughters Ellie and Maisie. Of how it could be them, waltzing into danger without even realising it. The thought made Jake sick.

What worsened the sensation was that Mamadou and the deputy assistant commissioner had been happy to keep the situation from the general public, away from the news outlets, and away from social media in any form. The theory was that by keeping it hidden, the suicide bomber wouldn't know anything was amiss, and so the team had a greater chance of finding him amongst the crowd. Whereas if they had plastered the news all over the TV, there was no knowing where and when he might detonate, if at all.

The dead man walking…

It was a risky move, one that Jake didn't agree with. Leaving this many people out in the open was a recipe for catastrophe.

He checked the time – 10:55 a.m.

Five minutes.

With each minute, he felt the palpable tension in the air – and in the depths of his chest – increase. In five minutes' time, he could be hearing the explosion. In five minutes' time, he could be seeing the explosion. In five minutes' time, he could be on top of the explosion. In five minutes' time, there might be no explosion at all.

The various images of each scenario flashed through his head several times until a call came in over the radio.

'One minute to opening. Repeat, one minute to opening.'

Jake gradually rose from his chair outside the coffee house and ambled towards the shopping centre. Towards danger. His palms turned sweaty, and his ears switched to a different level; now he was able to hear everything. The sound of his own pulse, his breathing, the footsteps of the woman behind him, the man on the other side of the street sneezing, the music emanating from a teenager's headphones.

Everything except the voices in his ear communicating with him.

Those noises were muffled, distant.

When he'd been in a high-pressured situation before, his body and mind had been on full alert. Now, it was like he was in a coma, only vaguely aware of his immediate surroundings.

'Eleven o'clock,' a voice said. 'I repeat, eleven o'clock. All officers be on high alert for the target. Any suspicious activity must be recorded and dealt with immediately. Be safe out there.'

It took Jake five seconds to realise the voice was Mamadou's.

Be safe out there.

Like a general giving the final orders to his men before they went over the top.

CHAPTER 13

Ten minutes passed. Nothing.

And with each passing minute, the knot in Jake's stomach drew tighter and tighter, denser and denser. It was the waiting that killed him. The constant waiting for the explosion, the waiting for the activity. The paranoia seeping through every synapse in his brain. Posing the question *what if?* over a million times and conjuring images of every possible scenario. Like waiting for a cancer prognosis.

Ten minutes quickly turned into twenty.

And in that time, a sea of people had formed outside each of the entrance points to the centre. Shouting and accosting the uniformed constables standing guard on the other side of the blue-and-white tape. Meanwhile, the conversations continued in his ear as the strategy was adapted and altered to suit the ever-changing dynamic.

'If nothing happens by midday, we're letting everyone into the building,' Mamadou addressed everyone tuned in to the channel. 'We've got to draw him out eventually. And I've just received word that bomb squad has disarmed all the IEDs inside. They found one more lurking in one of the bathroom stalls. The fucker was set to blow as soon as someone lifted the lid.'

Such an insidious device made Jake's skin crawl. He'd never be able to look at a toilet seat the same way.

He was walking around the outskirts of the building when someone caught his eye – DI Chris Bates speaking on his phone, pacing from side to side. Jake was about to approach him when a fight broke out in the crowd.

Two uniformed police constables reacted quickest and were on the scene within seconds, breaking the affray and dispersing the crowd in a matter of moments. It wasn't much, just a simple disagreement between two frustrated and paranoid consumers, but it was enough for Jake's heart to tighten with fear. He'd once been a bobby on the beat, a uniformed constable, and there had been a time when he would have thrown himself into a situation like that, but now, with his responsibilities and his kids, something had paralysed him, frozen him to the spot.

He found a wall nearby and leant against it to catch his breath.

Twenty minutes turned into thirty. Thirty into forty. Forty into fifty. And by the time it neared 11:51 a.m., Jake had fully recovered and continued his patrol of the area he'd been designated. He ambled along the pavement, studying the faces of everyone he saw.

'All units, remain on high alert,' Mamadou's voice echoed through his head. 'Remember your training.'

Jake did and began to recite the checklist in his head. Someone had once told him suicide bombers were easy to spot – you just needed to know what to look out for.

The first sign was paranoia. Erratic behaviour, eyes darting left and right.

The second was sweat.

The third was their clothing. Big coats. Large rucksacks. Anything that would conceal what they had strapped to their body.

The fourth: no sudden movements. Even the slightest jolt could set the explosives off.

The fifth: holding their stomach as if they had bad cramps. Protecting the bomb was just as vital as setting it off.

The sixth: staring straight ahead. A terrorist's eyes would be fixed on something directly in front of them. Or perhaps nothing at all. Nobody knew why, but it was always the case. Jake supposed it was because, at the moment they were about to blow themselves into oblivion, they contemplated every decision they had ever made. Whether they were good or bad. Whether killing themselves for some form of political or religious belief was *really* worth it. Nine times out of ten, they were too afraid to walk away, lest their manipulators and agitators punish them afterwards. Farsaid's description of the organisation, which Mamadou had shared with them, had confirmed those suspicions.

Finally, the seventh point on the list was mumbling. The majority of the time, according to his training, bombers would mumble words of prayer. To some higher form of deity. Some god that was going to accept them with open arms for having killed themselves and dozens of other people. But sometimes, eyewitnesses had reported that bombers often sent their prayers and wishes to loved ones, family members, friends, begging for respect and mercy for committing an act they knew to be wrong.

It was the list Jake tried to create in his head. Another thing the special operations division had told him.

And then, no sooner than he'd finished, he noticed it.

A figure, dressed in jogging bottoms and a puffy black coat that made him look twice his size. The perfect hiding spot for a suicide vest. On his head, the man wore a beanie, pulled low over his ears and forehead. But it did nothing to conceal the face of the man they were searching for.

Amir Khalid.

Al Bakir's final associate.

The only problem was, Amir was heading in a completely different direction.

Not wanting to raise false alarm and panic, Jake pursued him, his mind working a mile a minute. He maintained his distance and kept his eye on the figure at all times as he followed him away from the shopping centre and towards the underground car park.

The car park.

Those two words concerned Jake.

But why he couldn't say.

And then an image popped into his head, and he was transported back to Abraham Al Bakir's flat, flicking through the pile of leaflets on the floor. One of them had been emblazoned with an artist's impression of the shopping centre. Beneath it had been detailed drawings and descriptions of the car park.

Five thousand spaces. Three separate car parks.

Eleven sections.

And then it all made sense to him.

The note, the code.

The last piece of the clue hadn't referred to the time of the attack at all – 11AM referred to the location of the detonation.

Section 11. Car Park A. Midday.

Jake glanced down at his watch.

It was 11:53 a.m.

CHAPTER 14

Jake tapped the microphone in his ear to activate it as he followed the dead man walking into the car park.

'This is Jake. I've got eyes on a suspect heading towards car park A. Armed units approach. I repeat, armed units approach. Suspect is holding a mobile phone.'

There was a brief pause in his ear, and for a heart-stopping moment Jake thought he'd lost signal beneath the massive concrete structure.

'Anyone copy?'

'Yes. We heard you,' a voice responded. 'Approaching now. Standby. Update for further location.'

The inside of the car park was cold, as if the chilled air had crept through the avenues and wide spaces in search of a good place to rest. Jake lowered his voice, lest it echo off the walls and alert the bomber to his presence.

'I've got a plan,' he said, the confidence in his voice belying the way he felt.

'No, Jake,' Mamadou insisted. 'Wait for armed support to arrive.'

Jake didn't like the sound of that. By then it could be too late.

'I need to get that phone before he detonates himself.'

'If you get too close, then you—'

'Here's what I want to happen,' Jake said, aware that he was ignoring his boss's direct orders. 'I'll go for the phone. Distract him. Apologise profusely. Then the guys come charging in, armed, pinning him to the ground.'

'Jake—' Mamadou started but was interrupted by the operation firearms commander bleating over the radio. 'AFOs are in the building. En route now. Where are you, Jake?'

Amir Khalid came to a slow stop in front of a lift. Jake quickened the pace and raced towards him while explaining his exact location to the armed officers.

Ten yards separated them.

Jake touched his ear, fished inside for the earpiece and threw it inside his pocket. He didn't want Amir Khalid to spot it inside his ear.

Seven yards.

Picking up the pace a little, Jake reached inside his other jacket pocket.

Six.

Grabbed his phone and held it to his ear.

Five.

'No, you were supposed to order that,' he started.

Four.

'It was on the purchase order.'

Three.

'How can you be so stupid? What am I paying you

for?'

Two.

'You've got twenty minutes to send me the corrected—'

One.

Jake's knee collided with the terrorist's hand, knocking the phone from the man's grip onto the ground. Jake had been looking down, feigning arrogance and ignorance. He looked at the mobile on the marble ground and watched it slide to the edge of the kerb.

'Oh my God!' Jake yelled. 'I am *so* sorry. Here – let me get it for you.'

Amir looked bewildered. Stunned. Dazed.

Element of surprise.

Jake bent down to pick up the phone, dropped his in the process on purpose and fumbled for both of them. Acting clumsily, Jake knocked Amir's burner phone over the small kerb and onto the tarmac beyond.

'I am so sorry. Please forgive me,' he said.

But before Khalid could respond or do anything else, half a dozen armed officers swarmed them both, yelling, screaming, shouting for the terrorist to get down on his hands and knees.

Amir didn't flinch. Not even an eyelash. He remained calm, relaxed, cool-headed, almost as if he'd expected it.

The armed officers inched closer. Guns raised. Faces covered.

'Raise your hands in the air!' one of the men screamed.

Amir Khalid did as he was told – slowly and composed.

As he lifted his arms, his coat parted down the

middle. Jake hadn't noticed it, but when his back had been turned, Amir had undone the buttons and zip on his puffer jacket. As Jake had expected, hidden beneath the coat were six slabs of explosives strapped around his stomach. Almost identical to the one Abraham had been found wearing outside his bomb factory.

Except for one slight difference.

The front of this IED contained a timer in the centre. It said 04:46.

04:45.

This was against the plan. Nobody had prepared themselves for this eventuality.

It explained why the bomber hadn't been that worried about the phone dropping to the floor. He must have initiated the device when Jake hadn't been looking.

This was not good. Not good at all.

Jake, the terrorist and the armed officers around him, took in the gravity of the situation as Jake studied the device.

Somebody spoke. He didn't know who, just that he was going to listen and listen good.

'Nobody move a fucking muscle.'

CHAPTER 15

Even if he wanted to, Jake couldn't move. His feet were firmly rooted to the ground, melted into the concrete.

The voice behind him barked at him, but no matter how hard he tried, he was unable to tear his eyes away from the ticking countdown in front of him.

04:28.

04:27.

'What's your name?' Amir Khalid asked him.

At first, Jake wasn't sure if the young man had been speaking to him. In fact, he wasn't sure if he'd spoken at all; that it wasn't a figment of his imagination. A defence mechanism to force himself to loosen up.

He looked into Amir's eyes and saw a child staring back at him. A frightened twenty-year-old who had been brainwashed vehemently into believing that what he was doing was right. Was that fear on his face? Regret?

'Jake,' he answered. 'My name's Jake. What's yours?'

'You already know it. Otherwise you wouldn't be

here.'

'We're here to help you, Amir.'

Amir looked down at his chest. 'It's too late. The damage is already done.'

'What do you mean?'

When Amir didn't respond, Jake decided to change tactic. 'What happened to Abraham? Why was he murdered?'

04:02.

Just over four minutes remaining. Jake needed to find out everything he could in that time. Or else he – and all the other officers – would become scorch marks on the tarmac.

'Why was he murdered, Amir?'

Amir's silence concerned Jake.

'You didn't know, did you?' he asked.

Amir's expression remained blank.

'He was force-fed the same chemicals that are strapped to your body now. He told us about this attack before he died. Why would he do that? Why didn't he want it to happen?'

Nothing.

03:23.

Where the fuck was the bomb squad?

Jake pointed to Amir's chest. 'How do we diffuse this?'

'You can't.'

'Why not?'

'Because the moment you try, it'll be detonated remotely.'

Jake paused, his chest rising more heavily with every passing second. 'Is someone watching us?'

Amir nodded.

'Where?'

No response.

'Who? What's their name?'

'I'm not allowed to tell you.'

'What happens if you do?'

'They'll kill me. Like I said, it's already too late.'

'Then tell me what happened to Abraham,' Jake said. 'Who killed him? Why did he die?'

'He betrayed us.'

'How?'

'Disobeyed orders. Went behind our backs, created plans that weren't authorised.'

'Authorised by who?'

Amir opened his mouth to respond but caught himself.

'There was a mutiny?' Jake asked.

Amir nodded.

02:48.

'By who?'

Still no answer.

'You don't want to be doing this, Amir. You never wanted to be doing this. You got in with the wrong crowd. And one thing led to another. Now there's no way out. But there is an escape for others like you. Help me to help them.'

02:36.

Amir's lips quivered. He was consumed by fear, and as he tried to speak, his voice became hoarse and weak.

Then Jake felt a pair of hands on his shoulders, and the armed officers began dragging him away. Jake put up a fight, but it was no use against the strength of the men behind him. They retreated to a safe distance fifty feet away. There, Jake was able to take in his surroundings. In the short space of time he'd been talking, the rest of the armed officers had gradually retreated to the car park's entrance, over a hundred feet away. They had no idea of the blast radius, but they weren't taking any chances.

'Who's your leader, Amir?' Jake called, his voice echoing off the ceiling. 'Who is in control of this organisation? Give me the name!'

02:23.

'Give. Me. The. Name.'

02:21.

'Mole,' Amir said. 'There's a mole inside the police.'

02:19.

Jake froze. The officer behind him backed off.

'Who?'

'I… He has no name.'

'He must do.'

Amir shook his head.

Then, without warning, the device detonated, and a giant ball of flame erupted from his chest. The first thing Jake felt was the blast force knocking him off his feet. Then the thunderclap bursting his eardrums, followed by searing heat. By the time he came to, he was on the ground, debris raining down on him, smoke billowing along the ceiling. He rolled onto his back, chest heaving, and looked towards the pile of rubble where Amir had stood.

Casualties, none.

Dead terrorists, one.

Moles inside the Metropolitan Police Service, one.

CHAPTER 16

Several hours later, his mind still whirring, ears still ringing, Jake returned from the hospital and stepped into Room 1430.

'Jake!' Mamadou called from somewhere.

Jake turned, and the oversized man came bundling over.

'Jesus fucking Christ, son. Are you OK?' Mamadou asked.

'Never better. Doctor said I'm fine. My ears still hurt, but other than that I'm going to live.'

Shame the same couldn't be said for Amir.

'I think you need to go home,' Mamadou said.

'I was planning on it, sir. But first I wondered if we could have a word?'

Jake didn't enjoy being out in the open, where his inquisitive colleagues could overhear his conversation. What he wanted to discuss required the utmost discretion.

'Of course,' Mamadou replied. 'My office?'

Jake led the way and seated himself opposite his

boss's desk.

'I bet you could do with a drink,' Mamadou said as he found his seat.

'Better not. Doctors gave me some medicine for the smoke inhalation. Apparently the car park wasn't that well ventilated.'

'Well, you can have one on me later, Jake. You've earned it.'

Jake laughed. 'Just doing my job, sir.'

'Stop being modest. I mean, you and I *are* going to have words about you disregarding my direct orders, but I think I can keep some people off your back. For now. Given the way you risked your life, I wouldn't be surprised if they let me brush it under a massive carpet somewhere.'

'Thank you, sir. I appreciate that.'

'Now what is it you wanted to discuss with me?'

Jake swallowed and breathed in deeply, preparing himself.

'There's a mole, Mam. There's a mole somewhere in The Yard.'

'How do you know?'

'Amir. He told me.'

'And you believed him?'

Jake nodded.

'You can't be serious. You believed a terrorist who was about to blow himself up?'

'He didn't blow himself up, sir. His vest detonated with two minutes left on the countdown.'

Mamadou dismissed the claim with a shrug. 'It could have malfunctioned.'

'Possibly, but I don't think so.'

'Well, it's not about what you think. It's about what you know, and those are some very serious allegations to be throwing around, Tanner. I won't take them lightly. Not without concrete evidence.'

'I know who it is.'

Mamadou's face dropped, his expression relaxed and at once Jake could tell he'd piqued his boss's intrigue.

'You think or you know?'

'I think.'

Mamadou rolled his eyes. 'Go on then – who?'

Jake hesitated before responding. He looked over his shoulder back at the office.

'Chris, sir. Chris is the mole.'

Mamadou burst into laughter. 'You think Chris is a fucking terrorist? A genius mastermind capable of organising terror attacks on London?'

'Yes,' Jake said assertively.

'You're insane, Jake. Maybe you're a bit dizzy after that explosion. Did the doctors check you over for a possible concussion?'

'Mamadou, stop pissing about. This is serious. He's been working with them for at least a year, if not more. Give me some time and I can prove it to you. I can give you that concrete evidence you're asking for.'

CHAPTER 17

Jake stormed out of Mamadou's office and headed straight towards Green Team's corner of the room. The team of six were huddled around their desks, backs straight, eyes glued to the pixels on their three computer screens. It looked like they hadn't moved in hours, as they were in very much the same position as he'd left them.

He found DC Kate Osborne first and tapped her on the shoulder.

'Hi,' he said, smiling politely but avoiding the niceties. 'I was wondering if you could show me the CCTV outside the off-licence where Abraham was murdered. I remember seeing a small camera stationed in the corner. Have we managed to retrieve the data yet?'

'You're the first person to ask,' she said, moving the computer mouse rapidly. 'We sourced the footage and shared it with DI Bates, but nobody's had a chance to review it yet. It wasn't the priority at the time.'

'May I see it?'

Without much hesitation, she showed him. It was one of the pieces of evidence that, caught in the furore of the investigation, he himself had also overlooked.

Kate clicked through a series of folders until she found what she was looking for and enlarged the video on the screen. When Jake was ready, she prodded the spacebar, and the playback began.

Jake's eyes were glued to the screen as he watched a figure appear – heavily pixelated, dressed in a blue-and-white tracksuit. The figure hurried from right to left before disappearing out of shot. But in the short fraction he was on camera, Jake recognised his features immediately.

The man who had killed Abraham Al Bakir was Farsaid Dali. The registered informant who claimed to have defected from the group a little under a year ago. In the intervening hours, Jake had investigated Farsaid and committed the man's face to memory.

'Who else knows about this?' Jake asked.

'DI Bates,' Kate replied. 'We showed it to him before the incident. I think he's dealing with it now.'

Curious.

Jake tapped his feet and chewed on his bottom lip as he considered his next course of action. The evidence he'd been hoping to find in the off-licence footage hadn't been there. But that didn't mean to say it didn't exist.

The car park.

Jake's mind made the jump almost instantly, and he knew what he needed to do next. Thanking Kate for her time and support, he hurried towards Red Team on the other side of the office, keeping his head down.

Red Team were a larger outfit of highly skilled and technical detectives, who possessed the know-how to track anyone anywhere on the planet.

For Jake's purposes, they were perfect.

He accosted James Manning, a forty-year-old who always wore clothes that looked like he'd slept in them.

'Glad to hear you're all right,' was the first thing James said to him.

'Much better than the other guy,' Jake replied then immediately wished he hadn't. It was insensitive and a completely out-of-character statement. 'Sorry,' he added.

'What do you need?' James asked.

'Am I right in thinking the mobile phone that was found at the car park crime scene is being analysed?'

'You are.'

'And how far along is it?'

Janes perused through a set of files on his desk and retrieved a piece of paper. 'Digital forensics finished an hour ago. It was marked as high priority.'

'By?'

'DCS Kuhoba.'

You're not as stupid as you sometimes come across, sir.

'Do we know the last number that was called on the device?' Jake asked. His mind was moving too fast for him to keep up.

James prodded the top of the sheet and handed it to Jake. As he stared at it, he allowed himself to pause, breathe, process. In his hands, he potentially held the identity of the mole.

So far, he'd been right about everything else. He just needed to be right about this too. Not for his ego, but for the good of the team.

All the explosive devices that had been found on Abraham's body and inside the shopping centre had required a phone call to detonate them. The same applied to Amir's vest.

Except it had detonated early – and killed him.

There had been no malfunction. It had been a callous and destructive murder, a malevolent abuse of power, just as Amir had been about to unveil the name of the mole.

Jake looked at the mobile number for the fifth time.

'Can we call it?' he asked.

A look of surprise slapped James across the face. 'You want to call it?'

'Please.'

'I don't know, Jake…'

Jake had heard enough. Sighing, he turned his back on James and hurried over to his desk with the sheet in his hand.

There, he checked his phone for the first time all day. A few messages and missed calls from Elizabeth. Another message from Tyler, apologising for not being able to come in. And another message from his mum.

They would all have to wait.

Unlocking his device, he set the sheet on the table and readied himself. Once he was into the phone, he scrolled to the call log and entered the number.

A digit at a time.

His fingers began to sweat as adrenaline and fear coursed through his body.

Images of Amir and the explosion burst into his mind before disappearing again.

He stared at the number.

Staring…

Staring…

Staring…

Trying to summon the courage to call it.

And then he did.

The tone sounded in his ears, quiet against the persistent ringing from the explosion.

But he didn't need to hear anything on the other end of the line – the noise coming from inside the office was loud enough.

Slowly, Jake climbed out of his chair and rose over the top of his computer.

There, standing on the other side of the office, discussing with Mamadou, was DI Chris Bates. The man reached into his pocket and pulled out a small burner phone. His eyes widened with fear, and his head craned round the room like the beam from a lighthouse.

Until his eyes met with Jake's, and he knew it was all over.

THE EYE

CHAPTER 1

The live video feed illuminated Jake Tanner's face, his eyes fixed on the moving objects. The computer monitor beside him hummed in the background, drowning out what little noise from Counter Terrorism Command's control room filtered through the closed doors. The smell of an extra-strong espresso next to his keyboard wafted up his nose, but his mind paid it little attention. He was solely focused on the sounds and orders barking through the headphones cupped firmly around his ears.

He lowered the microphone to his mouth and began. 'This is Jake – street view shows Raman headed west on Robert Street.'

'Thanks,' Detective Sergeant Darren Reed replied.

'Lilly – I need you to hang back,' Jake said. 'Change your appearance. Darren's moving to the other side of the road to trail behind.'

'Received,' Detective Constable Lilly Hallam responded.

The screen in front of him was split in two,

vertically down the middle – Lilly's body cam on the left, Darren's on the right. Jake watched the shaky and distorted footage as Lilly ducked behind a parked car, removed her backpack, and began fishing inside for the wig and pillow that would alter her appearance. In less than five seconds, she'd become a heavily pregnant woman roaming the streets of London alone at dusk. It was a simple yet effective measure of counter surveillance and the perfect way to disguise her identity.

Jake then turned his attention to Darren's body camera. The images were clear and crisp, and in the low light showed a dark-haired man dressed in a Barbour jacket and jogging bottoms, prowling along the opposite side of the street over a hundred yards away. His name was Raman Al Hadid, and he was suspected of operating and owning a terrorist cell in West London. Jake and SO15's latest target. Recent intelligence gathered by the team suggested that a terror attack was imminent somewhere in the city. In the past couple of weeks, Raman had begun moving pieces on the chessboard. His next move, however, was unknown.

'Permission to speak?' Darren asked.

'Go ahead,' replied Jake.

'X-ray One is crossing the road and moving into Regent's Park.'

'Received,' Jake said. 'Keep calm and keep your distance. There's a lot of open space over there, which means it's just as easy for him to see you as it is for you to see him.'

'Is he meeting someone?' Lilly asked. 'This is against intel.'

'I don't know,' Jake answered. 'My guess is counter

surveillance. The field is the perfect place to draw us out. Be careful.'

'I don't like this,' Darren admitted. 'Do we know if he's carrying?'

'Not underneath that coat.'

Inside the control room, Jake was the eyes and ears of the operation – the king of the castle constantly feeding Darren and Lilly the intelligence they needed to pursue Raman as safely and inconspicuously as possible, while Detective Chief Superintendent Mamadou Kuhoba, and other members of Gold Group, put a plan in place for the suspected attack.

In the last few days, Raman had been displaying TAPIs – terror attack pre-indicators. Sudden, unusual movements in and out of his house. Complete radio silence on any of his mobile numbers and email accounts. The exact opposite of what SO15 had watched him do for the past three months. A routine of habits and exercises, sustained over a period of mounted surveillance, discarded at the drop of a hat.

The last move on the chessboard was imminent. Everyone could feel it. But their existing intelligence wasn't enough. They didn't know where the attack would take place, nor when.

Which was why Lilly and Darren had been deployed: they'd been sent to arrest and interrogate the snake's head, cutting the attack off at the source. But their investigation into Raman and his terrorist cell remained balanced on a knife edge. If they acted too soon, they risked blowing the operation wide open; if they acted too late, there would be untold and unthinkable consequences.

It was the job of SO15, the Met's counter terrorism department, to ensure that never happened. Every day, the team kept the public safe, through hard work, clear thinking, determination and remaining one step ahead of the people they sought to catch.

In the fourteen months Jake had been a part of the team, he'd uncovered the other end of the spectrum of human depravity. The lowest of the low. The diabolically evil. He'd risked his life during a hostage negotiation inside a cinema. He'd come face to face with a suicide bomber in the depths of an underground car park. But, on the flip side, he'd seen his colleagues go undercover and end up in the hospital after their cover had been blown. And, worst of all, an incel had slipped through their fingers and stabbed two people in broad daylight during a spring weekend.

He'd experienced the bad with the good. And yet he hadn't been disturbed or put off by any of it. It was the reason he woke up every morning and stayed late every night. It was his passion, his love.

His *raison d'être*.

'Keep your distance and stay eyes on,' he said. 'SCO19 are on standby. If he's headed to a potential bomb factory, they're ready to intervene.'

'Let's hope they don't blow up the fucking explosives along with him.'

Jake leant forward in his seat and watched Darren's monitor. Raman had come to a stop in the middle of the park and was standing perfectly still, staring into the sky. As if possessed by a demonic spirit. Or as if someone had just pointed a gun at his head and he was looking to the heavens for forgiveness.

What are you doing?

What are you up to?

What are you planning?

'This is Darren – suspect has stopped. I repeat,

Raman is no longer mobile.'

'OK. Hold back. Let Lilly handle it. She's wearing her disguise.'

Darren's mic went quiet. Then he reached inside his pocket, removed his phone and started speaking randomly into it, making it sound as though he was having a conversation with a relative. Jake was the only one who could hear the nonsense coming from Darren's mouth; he had complete control of their audio channels, so he was their only avenue of communication. The fewer distractions they had, the better.

After ambling around the outskirts of the park, still gossiping away to his imaginary interlocutor, Darren slipped through a gated exit, and Jake turned his attention to Lilly's feed. She was hanging well back, maintaining a thirty-foot distance to Raman on his four o'clock. Her view of him was broken up by trees and other passers-by: late-night dog walkers, joggers who'd been bitten by the fitness bug and couldn't help exercising at any hour of the day, and strangers coming and going as they continued on their path through life.

In the space of a few minutes, as the sun had dropped lower in the sky, the 13MP cameras placed on both operatives' chests had started to falter and were beginning to affect Jake's visibility. Instead of seeing high definition and colour, he was staring at a black-and-grey painting. Soon, total darkness would defeat his feed entirely.

'Update,' Lilly's voice echoed in his ear.

'Go for it,' responded Jake.

'Raman's on the move again. No sign of waiting for anyone. No sign of suspicious movement.'

'Understood,' Jake said. 'I'm losing visibility, so I

need constant reports. Keep it verbal. And make it loud enough for me to hear. The last thing I want is for audio *and* visual to go.'

'But, Jake, that's not how we—'

'I know, but right now we're doing it this way.'

His way.

My way.

Even if it broke a few rules in the process. The outcome of the surveillance operation weighed heavily on his shoulders. It was the first time he'd been entrusted with such a responsibility, and the pressure was getting to him. There was no room for failure, no room for mistakes.

'X-ray One is heading towards the end of the park,' Lilly stated.

She continued offering him the verbal updates he'd requested.

'Heading west towards the Sherlock Holmes Museum.'

'Suspect has now continued past Madame Tussauds.'

'And now… Wait…'

Jake held his breath.

'X-ray One has turned off Marylebone Road onto Chiltern Street… Now Porter Street… Now… you won't believe it. He's gone into a KFC.'

Jake let out a slow, steady breath. Never in his experience of monitoring and following Raman had Jake ever witnessed the man step into a supermarket, let alone a fast-food chain.

Curious.

Two minutes later, Raman emerged with a brown bag in his hands.

Jake prodded the control panel in front of him and

asked them both the same question. 'Anyone confirm visuals of what's in the bag?'

'Negative,' replied Darren.

'Negative also,' added Lilly, who'd just finished changing her appearance back to normal.

'OK. Proceed as planned.'

In the meantime, Jake turned his attention to another computer monitor on his left. He made a quick search of the restaurant and its location. Within seconds, the results threw up a list of names and home addresses for the restaurant's employees. Jake scrolled through them, feeding the names into another system that cross-referenced them against Raman. Any link between them, no matter how tangential and historic, would appear.

The search came back with a hit.

'One of the staff inside KFC knows Raman. The system flagged a Saeed Anwar as a person of interest, so approach with caution. It's possible Saeed handed something to Raman. He could be armed, carrying something.'

Unless this was it.

Unless this was the terrorist attack they'd been expecting: detonating an explosive device in a quiet street in West London?

Jake didn't think so, but he wasn't ready to play with his friends' lives so easily. He had a decision to make. Pull them out or let them continue. Knowing their lives would be endangered – not to mention the countless others caught in the crossfire – it wasn't a decision he was going to take lightly. He had to make absolutely sure there was no chance Raman was going to detonate the cell in a built-up public area.

Jake glanced at his watch – 9:30 p.m. An attack now

seemed ludicrous. There was no one around, no potential casualties. But something wasn't right. Jake sensed that much.

'I want you out, out, out,' he said.

'What?' Darren said. 'We've nearly got him. He's pulling into a cul-de-sac. There's no way out for him.'

'Don't be so sure.'

'It's fine. I'm following him down.'

'No, Darren. Abort. Abort! Darren. I'm giving you an order!'

Jake watched the screen with apoplexy.

Darren muted his mic.

'Lilly – do you have visual?'

'Yes.'

'What's he doing?'

'Who? Darren or Raman?'

'Darren.'

'I…' Lilly stopped, looked around, her body cam swinging left and right. 'I don't know.'

'What do you mean you don't know?'

'He's gone. He was just there.'

'Fuck.' Jake changed feeds.

Darren had moved down a small alleyway, branching off the side of the cul-de-sac. Trees and shrubbery hung low overhead, and the ground was littered with tin cans and wrappers and food and trolleys. Jake watched on in silence. Even the sound of the computer monitor humming in the background had disappeared. Half-consciously, he gave Lilly the order to return to a safe distance and ordered the armed teams to be on standby at the soon-to-be disclosed location.

Come on, Jake thought. *Listen to me. Turn around. Come back.*

But Darren couldn't hear his internal thoughts. And even when he tried voicing them, there was still no response.

Darren came to a stop metres away from an open door that led to the back of a decrepit building. On the computer screen, Jake saw Darren's thumb and forefinger touch together into the internationally recognised symbol for 'OK'.

Then Darren stepped closer, tentatively, cautiously. Yet there was no sense he was afraid. Instead, it was Jake who was worried. If something happened – if something went even remotely wrong – he wouldn't be able to forgive himself.

'What's he doing, Jake?' Lilly asked, bringing him out of his deeply focused state.

'I don't know. He's removed his earpiece. I can hear him, but he can't hear me.'

'Christ,' was Lilly's only response.

Jake continued to watch the screen. By now, Darren had moved forward, reached the door, peered through and stepped into the building. The screen turned pitch-black for a moment then gradually returned to normality as the lens allowed the low light to filter in. Darren was inside what appeared to be an old, abandoned building. A block of offices perhaps. Jake didn't know, but it was the perfect hideout.

The camera looked to the ground. Old cans, bottles and glasses of beer and spirits had been discarded on the floor. Alongside them were needles and shrivelled condoms; Jake was just able to discern them amidst the darkness against the other rubble that lay on the floor.

As Darren delved deeper into the complex, Jake's concerns increased. The narrow network of corridors made way for wider rooms and larger openings.

Darren's breathing became louder in his ears. Carefully, he tiptoed up a set of stairs, his footsteps nothing more than a whisper on the floorboards. At the top, he made a right turn and then stopped. Standing right in front of him was Raman, his back to Darren. He still held the KFC bag in one hand. And in the other, he held something much worse.

'Oh shit,' Darren whispered, yet when it came through in Jake's ears, it sounded like it had been yelled through a megaphone.

Jake tried to open his mouth – to order Darren to stop, to turn around and run back out, to jump out of the nearest window and get out of there as soon as possible – but nothing came out. Only a weak exhalation.

Raman turned. Faced Darren. His features were unusually pronounced in the low light. As was the gun in his hand. Behind him, on the floor, were bottles of bleach, nails, and other chemicals and active ingredients needed to create homemade IEDs.

Raman had led Darren straight to his bomb factory.

And they'd fallen for it.

'How long have you been following me?' Raman asked, his South London accent shining through.

'Long enough.' Darren coughed. The chemicals in the air had made their way into his throat, Jake was sure of it.

After he'd finished, he continued, 'What are you planning?'

'Something bigger than you'll ever know.'

'When?'

'Soon.'

'When?'

'Tomorrow.'

'What is it?'

'You'll have to catch me before I tell you that.'

Jake's pulse quickened, and his body went cold as Raman's words struck him to the core. He could only imagine how Darren was feeling.

'Tell me now, what have you got planned? What are you using these explosives for?'

Raman said nothing. Instead, he lifted his arm, pointed the gun above Darren's chest and pulled the trigger.

The explosion from the gun illuminated Jake's screen, and the supersonic sound of the bullet propelling from the chamber deafened him. He winced in pain and shock, yet he was unable to tear his eyes from the image of Raman's face.

Darren collapsed to the floor, his body cam sending the room into a whirlpool of black and grey.

For what felt like a long time, nothing happened. Then Raman came into view, standing over Darren's lifeless body. His dark features were made even darker by the camera angle.

Raman aimed the gun directly at the lens.

'Tomorrow, one of your city's greatest attractions will be attacked. Loss of life will be inevitable, and the blame will be your burden to carry.'

Raman pulled the trigger. The screen went blank.

The final move on the board was in play.

CHAPTER 2

Jake didn't know what to feel. A close friend of his, someone he'd got to know dearly in the fourteen months he'd been at SO15, was gone. At the pull of a trigger.

Dead.

'Son of a bitch.'

Jake threw his headphones onto the desk, and then put his head in his hands.

He was angry – angry at Darren. For ignoring his orders. For wandering inside that building. For getting himself killed. Why hadn't he listened? Because Jake wasn't authoritative enough? Because he was out of his depth? Had Jake made the wrong judgement call? Should he have called off the pursuit earlier?

His invasive thoughts plagued and crippled his ability to think comprehensively. He needed fresh air. But he couldn't leave. There was still a lot to do.

Lilly.

As he reached for the headphones, Jake was already speaking into the microphone.

'Lilly? Can you hear me? Report.'

A pause.

'Confirmed. What's going on, Jake? I heard gunshots.'

'Where are you?'

'Prince's Street. Why? What's going on, Jake? Tell me!'

Jake exhaled heavily and closed his eyes, almost unable to bring himself to speak the words. 'Darren's dead. Raman shot him. I need you to get out of there. I'm sending in SCO19.'

SCO19 was the name given to the Metropolitan Police's Specialist Firearms Command, home to several teams of counter terrorist specialist firearms officers, or CTSFOs. They were the elitist of the elite, and they were kept on constant standby for any terrorist or major crime incidents in London. Armed with Heckler & Koch MP5s and Glock 17s, they were capable of raiding buildings, boats, planes and trains, efficiently and effectively – and with as few friendly casualties as possible.

'Wait!' Lilly called.

'What is it?'

'Raman's still in there.'

'He won't be for long, which is why we need to get you out of there ASAP.'

'No, listen to me, Jake. He's still in there. I heard three gunshots.'

Three? Darren's video feed might have been destroyed, but his earpiece couldn't have been, could it? Unless Jake had mistaken the third bullet for another sound.

'You think Raman shot himself?'

'I don't know. But I need to find out.'

'No. Lilly, no. Abort. Get out of there. Leave it up to SCO19.'

Jake prodded a green button on the control panel and spoke into the mic. 'Kyle, can you hear me?'

'Loud and clear.' Sergeant Kyle Harding was the man in charge of the SCO19 unit positioned on standby down the road from Darren and Raman's location. They'd been tracking them from afar the entire evening. Watching, waiting, like an assassin in the night.

'We need all officers. Repeat all officers. One operative down. Three shots fired. Target suspected of being incapacitated. Approach with extreme caution.'

'Understood. Turning live feed on.'

The line went dead, then another image appeared in the bottom-right corner of Jake's screen. He enlarged the video and watched.

Please be dead, Jake wished. He had a terrible feeling that something disastrous was about to happen.

Kyle and the other men dressed in ballistic helmets and bulletproof vests approached the building, the sound of their steadied breathing and body armour shuffling up and down the only thing audible against the serene, still backdrop of the abandoned property. They wandered through the alleyway and then stopped at the same doorway Darren had used to enter. The unit of fifteen constables split up on either side of the door. Once everyone was in position, Kyle lifted his fist and, using his fingers, counted down from three…

Two…

One…

'Armed police!' Kyle roared as he burst past the threshold. The torchlights at the end of their weapons illuminated the hallways and rooms as the men funnelled into them, like water dispersing through cracks in the ground.

The shouts of the other men behind him almost burst Jake's eardrums. Someone out of shot gave the all-clear, and as soon as he heard it, Kyle led the charge upstairs.

As they arrived at the top of the staircase, Darren's dead body came into view. The hole in his head was almost perfect, and the blood at the back of his skull had spilt down the stairs in a waterfall of red. Jake had seen blood a hundred times, maybe more. He'd been trained, through years of exposure and experience, to deal with it, but nothing prepared you for the sight of it when it was one of your own.

'Jesus,' one of the armed officers whispered. Darren had been a prevalent member of the team, a friendly face to everyone – well respected and well-liked – and now he was just another statistic, another slab at the mortuary.

'Armed police!' Kyle shouted again at the top of his voice, making sure anyone who remained in the building knew they were there and that they weren't afraid to pull the trigger if necessary.

Kyle hopped over Darren's body and moved into the bomb factory.

Where are you? Jake thought. At first glance, Raman was nowhere to be seen. Then Kyle's head turned left and right, gaze sweeping the entire room. And then he looked down.

And found him.

Raman was lying on the floor, holding his stomach, weeping, begging for his life.

'Oh no,' Jake said aloud.

Raman's shirt was stained red. He craned his neck and peered up at Kyle.

'Ambulance,' Raman said, his voice nothing but a whisper. 'Please. Ambulance. Bleeding.'

Kyle bent down to his knees, looked at one of his constables and said, 'We need emergency evac. Casualty harmed. Suspected gunshot wound to the sternum. Go!'

Without needing to be told twice, the officer spun on the spot and sprinted out of the room. By the time he was out of the door, he was already speaking into his radio.

Kyle turned his attention back to Raman, who lay moments away from death. In the time it had taken him to look at his colleague, give the order and return his focus to Raman, the terrorist had deftly moved his left hand and now pointed the gun at Kyle.

'Die, bastard.'

A bullet fired before Jake had the time to register what had been said. Kyle's body collapsed to the ground. Still in the shot, Raman lifted himself off the concrete, amidst the shouts and screams and cries and roars, and pulled the trigger again. This time at the countless explosives that lay at the perimeter of the room.

The building erupted in a massive balloon of red and orange and white-hot heat. The live feed disappeared. Jake switched to an aerial view of the building from a drone that had been operated all evening by someone in another room. Flames licked and danced high in the sky, sending streams of smoke even higher.

Jake was speechless. Raman had single-handedly killed himself, seventeen officers and any evidence that might have led them to the location of the imminent attack.

CHAPTER 3

A few hours passed. In that time, the emergency services had swarmed the streets and shut off the surrounding area – police, the ambulance service and the fire brigade. It wasn't until well after midnight, some three hours after it started, that the fire brigade were finally able to extinguish the blaze. It was suspected that accelerant had been poured all over the walls, although it wouldn't be confirmed until the post-incident analysis had taken place. What had been more pressing, however, had been finding the casualties. And, fortunately for Jake – and everyone else in SO15 – they'd found them. Seventeen in total – sixteen armed officers, one plainclothes.

Which meant that there had been no survivors.

Which meant that Raman had single-handedly decimated an entire team of CTSFOs, and one of their own.

Jake was sitting in the briefing room with Lilly, DCS Mamadou Kuhoba, Commander Jasper Conrad and several others he cared not to recognise; his mind was too fraught to take in any more unnecessary information. Lilly had been brought back to Room 1430 for her initial debrief with Mamadou, and since then, the incident reports had been fed up the chain towards the Prime Minister and other COBRA members. As a result, the commander had been sent in to oversee the operation. Jasper Conrad was the man in charge of SO15. A man Jake had met a handful of times, who reported to the deputy assistant commissioner and commissioner of the Met. His inclusion in the meeting needed no explanation.

'While we wait for everyone else to filter in…' Jasper began. He was a man well into his fifties who possessed the knowledge and wisdom of someone twenty years his senior. He was tall, slender and cut his hair short in an effort to keep the appearance of age at bay; as a man very much near the retirement age, he was doing everything he could to avoid the dreaded day. 'I want to say how sorry I am to hear about Darren. I've worked with him a few times, and our paths have crossed many times before that, and not only was he a stand-up guy, he was also one of the most resilient and bravest men I've ever met.'

Darren.

Not Darren Reed, the father of one.

Not DS Reed, the sergeant with seven years' experience.

Just Darren. His entire life stripped back to one word. His name. His identity.

A gentle murmur rumbled around the room as everyone agreed with Jasper, each team member largely silent as they tried to process the shocking news. Sadly, though, there was little time to do so.

Tomorrow, one of your city's greatest attractions will be

attacked.

Tomorrow, which had now become today.

'As soon as everyone arrives, Mamadou and I will discuss the next plan of action.'

The moment he finished speaking, the door opened. Three people entered: DC Tyler Stuart, Jake's closest confidant in the team; DC Matilda Edwards; and DS Imran Malik.

'Welcome, team. Thanks for coming on such short notice. I fear it's going to be an all-nighter, so if you need to let any friends, families, boyfriends, girlfriends, and mistresses know that you're going to be home late, now's the time.'

At once, everyone in the room reached for their pockets, produced their mobile phones and dialled. Instead, Jake took his out and typed a message to Elizabeth, his wife of eight years. By now she would be fast asleep after a busy day of promoting her photography business online and managing the daily struggles of looking after their two young children, Maisie and Ellie. His message was simple.

Long night ahead. Will keep you updated. Speak to you when I see you xx

His grief was too strong for him to go into any further detail. After all, he didn't want to worry her.

As he hit send, he looked up and found Jasper staring straight back at him intently.

'Now that I think about it, Jake, Lilly – we're going to need some provisions. Can you both run down to the canteen and get us some coffee? As black and strong as possible.'

Jake thought about protesting but quickly decided against it. He could use the distraction. And the coffee.

Saying nothing, he rose from his seat and left the

room, letting the door close on Lilly behind him.

'Hey, watch it.' She chased after him and grabbed his arm, pulling him back. 'What was that for?'

Jake shook her off. 'What was *what* for?'

'Shutting the door on me?'

'Did I? Sorry.'

'How are you feeling?'

Depressed. Guilty. Fucking heartbroken.

'I'm fine.'

'You're not,' she said, her eyes burning holes in his lies. 'You're hurting over Darren, I can see it. We all are. But you mustn't blame yourself – it wasn't your fault.'

'It was. I led him down there. I should have told him to stop. I wasn't forceful enough.'

'Don't be ridiculous. You did everything you could. He was stupid for doing what he did.'

Jake stopped mid-walk. 'Excuse me? How dare you? He was a fucking good guy, and he was just doing his job. And now he's gone. He's never coming back.'

Lilly fell silent; Jake hoped the impact of his words struck a chord within her.

As she contemplated what he'd said, Jake left her behind and strode towards the lift on the other side of the room. By the time she caught up, the doors closed on her face. As the lift descended down to the canteen on the ground floor, he leant back against the metal railing and exhaled deeply. He only made it a few feet into the warehouse of his thoughts before the doors opened onto the canteen again.

The canteen inside New Scotland Yard was open 24/7 and catered to staff of all roles. During the day, it was manned by a team of fifteen, but here in the middle of the night, a skeleton crew of four were responsible for making sure SO15 – and all the other teams within the building – were kept fuelled with an unhealthy side of caffeine, sugar and pastries.

As Jake stepped out of the lift, Lilly emerged from the stairwell beside him, out of breath but trying her best to hide it. She'd been a solid member of the team for over three years, and had had several opportunities for a promotion but had always refused and chosen to remain as a constable because she loved the roles and responsibilities of the job. While many continued to chase the next rung in the ladder, she was happy staying where she was. Much the same as Jake. She had a wealth of experience over him, and the two of them typically saw eye to eye. But after her comments, she'd knocked herself down a step or two in Jake's estimations of her.

He ignored her as he paced towards the coffee machine – his second home. During his first few weeks, as part of his initiation process, he'd been dubbed the office's Coffee Bitch Boy, and as a result, had learnt everyone's order. It was both a blessing and a curse.

In total he made ten drinks. In his hands he carried four and left the remaining six for Lilly.

'Here,' he said, throwing a brown cardboard tray onto the surface. 'Use that.'

When they returned to the briefing room, they were welcomed by the sounds of happy and appreciative colleagues.

'About time,' Mamadou said jokingly as Jake stepped into the room. 'We've been dying of dehydration in here.'

Jake and the rest of the team chuckled. Awkwardly at first, out of respect for Darren. But then, as they all began to loosen up around one another, the room burst into proper laughter.

'Strange,' Jake said, 'I thought you were on one of those no-liquids diets, sir?'

Mamadou's smile dropped.

'No, you're getting it confused,' Tyler Stuart said. 'It's one of those all-you-can-eat diets. Where you eat everything and hope that by some miracle your body starts burning more fat than you're putting in. Mamadou's a sucker for a cheeky sausage roll. I saw him munching on one earlier.'

'Still fewer calories in this drink than a sausage roll,' Mamadou retorted quickly. 'So who's laughing now?'

'Definitely not your cholesterol,' Tyler replied to a chorus of laughter.

Mamadou extended a hand, and the laughter stopped. 'Shut the fuck up and give me my drink.'

Jake did as his senior ordered and found a seat next to Tyler. He felt better. Happier. Even if he knew it was only going to last a brief moment. Mamadou and Tyler were his rocks in SO15. They kept him grounded and provided him with the humour and inspiration he needed to carry on when things got tough. Together they were the Holy Trinity of counter-terrorism policing.

Lilly returned moments after, and as she handed the drinks out to the rest of the team, Jake caught her eye. There was no hint of remorse or reproach in her gaze.

After she'd found her seat, the commander cleared his throat. 'Let's begin then, shall we?'

Everyone turned their unwavering attention to the front of the room. On the wall was a large, flat-screen TV. The picture was split down the middle – an image of Raman Al Hadid on one side, and Darren's live feed on repeat on the other. Mamadou was standing beside Raman, and Jasper next to Darren.

'Moments before his death,' Jasper began, 'Darren managed to engage Raman in conversation about an attack that's due to take place at some point in the next twenty-four hours. We don't know where, and we don't know when. Which leaves us in a shit state, to put it lightly. Now, all of you in this room will be working together. So make a quick count of who's who, and make sure you remember them. I know there aren't many in S-Squad at the moment; the summer holidays have been an absolute ball-buster this month, but we're just going to have to make do with what little we've got. If you don't like it, tough. You can cry to your loved ones or into your cushions when you get home, but until that point, I want your absolute focus. Understood?'

Everyone in the room nodded, keeping their eyes fixed on either Jasper or the TV screen. Jake was part of the latter group. Raman's face stared back at him, mocking him.

Ambulance. Please. Ambulance. Bleeding.

'Excellent. Now, Mamadou and I have discussed this, and we assume we have an approximate eight-hour window at least to find out where the attack's going to take place and who's going to be carrying it out. Attractions and landmarks won't be open to the public until the morning—'

'Unless it's an inside job,' Jake interrupted, thinking aloud.

'Excuse me?' Jasper asked.

'I'm just saying, someone at the attraction may have already planted the explosives, and at a certain time it's going to go off, regardless of whether or not the suspect is there.'

Jake leant back in his seat, shying away from the prying eyes staring at him. He could sense they held him partly responsible for Darren's death. And he was inclined to agree with them. But that didn't stop their burning gazes hurting any less. 'We saw the same thing happen with Westfield last year.'

In the early hours of Christmas Eve, the head of a terrorist cell organiser had been found dead on the street, wearing a suicide vest. In his sock had been a clue notifying them of an imminent attack, similar to the one Raman had given them. After some decoding, they'd learnt that the attack would take place at Westfield Shopping Centre in Stratford, and that, overnight, one of the employees had filled the bins with explosives.

'What makes you think there's going to be an explosion?' Jasper asked.

'The bomb factory didn't exactly contain cuddly toys and dildos, did it?' put in Tyler.

'I don't want to know what goes on at your house,' Eloise, an intelligence analyst, remarked.

Tyler rolled his eyes. 'You knew what I meant.'

Clearing his throat, Jasper added, 'And what *I* meant was that we don't know what sort of threat it is. It could be CBRN or just a standard homemade IED.'

CBRN stood for chemical, biological, radiological and nuclear – the different types of attack that could befall the country. Largely considered the deadliest, they were also the hardest to defend against.

'None of the intelligence reports we have on Raman from MI5 suggest he's involved with any of those,' Eloise said, taking a sip of coffee. She grimaced as she swallowed and pushed the cup away from her on the desk.

'We can't rule it out,' Mamadou added.

He paused to take a sip from his drink. To Jake's surprise, he grimaced as well. Maybe he didn't know everyone's orders as well as he thought. It was shaping up to be a depressing night: first Darren, and now this.

'Jasper and I have decided to split you all up into three teams. Jake, Jason, Tyler and Lilly – you four will be investigating any known associates of Raman. I want their families checked, their friends, and even *their* friends and families. You've got to cram days' worth of information and tasks into a few hours. As soon as you get something, let us know.'

Mamadou pivoted on his heels to address the next group. 'Linda, Imran and Jerome – the three of you can look into any locations Raman or his associates might have visited in the past six weeks. Anything suspicious that screams out at you, report it. Even if it's something we might have overlooked or missed during the early phases of the investigation, count it. There are details in everything he does. Yours and Jake's team's discoveries will overlap, so keep one another in the loop.

'As for the rest of you – Tristan, Douglas, Alexandria – dive deeper into Raman. His social media accounts, email, film subscriptions, what he's been watching and listening to, internet history – anything that'll give us an inclination of where this attack might take place as well. Also – look at his purchase history. Credit- and debit-card transactions. Online orders. Both illegal and legal. Anything that suggests he might have planted a dirty bomb somewhere in London. I know we'll already have some of this information at hand, but I want it checked and triple-checked. Raman is the mastermind behind this, but that doesn't mean he hasn't left masterminds to take his place now that he's gone. Be vigilant, and be aware. If you think you've found something – no matter how big or small you might think it is – tell me. Darren's death was unfortunate and terrible, but we will mourn him later. Put your feelings of grief and hurt aside for the time being. We've got a terror attack to stop.'

CHAPTER 4

Seated at his desk, thirty yards away from the operation room, Jake's eyes ached. He'd been sitting in front of a computer monitor for over twelve hours, and he could already feel the incipient headache flexing its muscles inside his skull. The worst part was that he knew it was coming, and that if he didn't take a tablet soon, he would be in for an excruciating and unbearable morning. Especially when he needed to be hyper-focused and hyper-vigilant.

Beside him was Tyler, humming away, tapping his fingers on his mouse as he perused through a document on Raman Al Hadid.

He turned to Jake. 'You good?'

Jake looked up. Blinked. Rubbed the blue light out of his eyes. 'Not really. Been better.'

The brutal images of Darren getting shot and Kyle and the rest of the team dying continued to leech his mind. Sucking the energy from him, the optimism, the drive and the determination to succeed. If it could happen so easily to Darren, then it could happen just as easily to himself. Of course, that was true for every aspect of their job. But it was what set them apart from everyone in the police force. They were the ones willing to put their lives on the line in the battle against terrorism in order to save countless more.

It was their responsibility to protect as many people as they could.

The thought made him recall a quote he'd heard from his dad once: 'Good people plant trees knowing they won't be the ones to enjoy the shade.'

Good people were the ones willing to do the work for others.

The world needed more of that.

'You're gonna need some counselling after this,' Tyler said in his usual half-hearted manner.

'You're probably right,' Jake said softly. 'But right now I can't think about that.'

'Darren was a good bloke. Even though he waxed lyrical about his ball and chain, he was always more than happy to wingman me in the pub. And there was the odd occasion where I was happy to wingman him.' Tyler chuckled to himself. 'There was this one time—'

'Tyler,' Jake snapped. 'Please, mate. I know you're trying to make me feel better, but I can't think about that right now.'

Despite being a self-proclaimed man whore, and having lost over half his brain cells to overly casual drinks every Friday night, Tyler was incredibly intelligent. His work ethic was to work smarter, not harder. He was a gifted counter-terrorism detective who always managed to get results. But he was also a notorious source of distraction. It was one of the reasons Jake liked him. Their line of work was depressing, extreme and horrifying, and it made Jake and the rest of the team uptight, constantly on edge, and left them with a prevailing sense of never being able to trust anyone – a sensation that would never abate. But Tyler changed all that. He ameliorated it somehow. And he helped Jake switch off in the evenings or whenever he was back home with his family, rather than being insufferable and hyper-alert all the time.

Slowly, Jake returned his attention to his computer. Something about the surveillance operation had been bugging him. The man from KFC. The man who'd given Raman the bag that had led to Darren's death. The man who Jake held responsible for the explosion killing Kyle and everyone else inside.

Saeed Anwar.

Jake drew up the man's profile on the Police National Computer and consulted the first document for a few minutes.

'Gotcha,' he whispered.

'What's that?' Tyler asked, leaning closer to get a better view.

'Saeed Anwar.'

'Who?'

'British. Born in '92. Did time for eighteen months recently – been out for six months now.'

'What for?'

'GBH.'

'Wasn't Al Hadid locked up at the same time?'

Jake nodded.

'In the same prison?'

'Same cell.'

'Bloody hell.'

'And to make things more interesting, it looks like Raman is Saeed's newest landlord. It seems Raman's got him under his little wing…'

'Or in his debt,' Tyler added. 'Both are just as problematic as each other.'

Jake nodded. A moment of pause.

'You got an address?'

Jake pointed to the screen. 'I've already checked it out. It's not too far from the bomb factory.'

Tyler beamed. 'What are we waiting for?'

Jake and Tyler rose from their seats, set their computer monitors to sleep and started away from their desks.

'Where are you two going?' Lilly asked, sliding back in her chair.

'Speak with the commander.'

'You found something?'

'Yeah,' Jake said.

'Were you not going to tell us?' Lilly rose and wandered over to Jake. 'What about us working together?'

Jake looked into Lilly's steely eyes. 'You demoted yourself from the *team* the moment you blamed Darren for his own death.'

'I never blamed Darren for his own death.' Lilly stepped forward, their faces inches away from one another. She brought her voice down to a near whisper. 'I said he was stupid. *Stupid* for listening to you and thinking he was safe when he wasn't. It was obvious it wasn't safe. Raman was deliberately leading Darren to the bomb factory, and he fell for it. You should have pulled us out earlier. You should have got the drone in. You were never fit to run that operation – I don't know why Mamadou gave it to you, but he did, and now Darren's dead.'

The words slapped him. He felt enraged. Shocked.

Ashamed. He wanted to do something. Wanted to hit Lilly in the face. Make her bleed, cry, take back her words. But he knew deep down they were right. He'd been the one to push Darren closer for a better view, all the while risking the man's life without realising it.

Jake clenched his fist.

'Fuck off, Lilly,' Tyler said, pushing between them both.

Just as an altercation was about to begin, a deafening roar buffeted around the office.

'Tanner! Stuart! Get over here, now.'

Both men turned on the spot. Mamadou was standing in the doorway to the briefing room, his arms folded and his face a tapestry of disdain.

Jake and Tyler silently wandered over to the briefing room where they sidestepped past the chief superintendent, who made a point of taking up most of the doorway. It felt like they'd just been summoned to the headteacher's office for misbehaving during the lunch break. Except this was no time for games and playing; this was time for hard work and resourcefulness – the final revision stretch before the chaotic exam period.

'What the fuck's going on?' Mamadou demanded, slamming the door. His voice could be heard from outside the room.

'Nothing, guv,' Jake said, failing to meet his senior in the eye. He was usually the first to challenge and confront anything he disagreed or had an issue with. But some arguments with Mamadou just weren't worth fighting.

'It doesn't look like nothing to me. I'll ask again – what is happening between you and Lilly? What would have happened if I hadn't stepped in just then? I saw you clench your fist, Jake.'

Jake hung his head in shame. He'd been the victim of a moment of madness, pure stupidity, consumed by an immature and pointless rage.

'Nothing, guv. Nothing would have happened. And nothing *is* happening. Just a minor disagreement.'

'Jake and I forgot to mention we had a lead which we were about to check out,' Tyler started, coming to the rescue. 'She got arsey and didn't like it. Maybe she was jealous of the fact we got something and she didn't.'

'Shut up, Tyler. You sound like an arrogant cock.'

'I am, sir. It's how I get by in life.'

Mamadou rolled his eyes. 'What's this lead?'

Jake explained.

'Great. We'll add this info to the board and HOLMES. Hopefully, it'll help us build a bigger picture of the case.'

Mamadou moved to the other side of the room, grabbed a whiteboard pen and wrote Saeed's name in vibrant red ink.

'I want you to take some armed support with you. The last thing we need is another detonation. The moment you find anything, I want you to report back.'

'You got it,' Jake said, diving out of the room.

CHAPTER 5

The rental property registered in Saeed Anwar's name was a small, one-bedroom flat less than a hundred yards from the place where Jake had last seen Raman, Darren and the CTSFOs alive. The orange and yellow of the dying flames, combined with the pitch-black smoke against the starry backdrop, filled Jake with a burning sense of determination. Seeing the constant reminder of Darren's death induced a rage within him.

It was nearing 2 a.m., and time was wearing thin. It was, however, the perfect time to conduct an armed raid. Usually, most residents were asleep at this time in the morning, and an unsuspecting barrage of firearms officers was more than enough to bewilder and disarm even the deepest of sleepers.

A group of ten had formed outside Saeed's house. Just as Jake and the team at SO15 had done, the authorised firearms officers forced their colleagues' deaths to the back of their minds and focused on the job at hand. Even though they were all eager to exact revenge – delicious, sweet revenge.

With a clean swing, one of the heavily protected men swung The Enforcer onto the door. The heavy metal battering ram splintered the wood and forced the door to buckle under immense pressure. The AFOs then spilled into the building, like water down a plug, and covered every square inch of the property, fanning out in a fluid and efficient motion, canvassing every room.

The shout over the radio came a second later. 'Downstairs clear. Upstairs clear. Clear to proceed.'

Jake and Tyler looked at one another.

'You lead the way,' Tyler said, stepping aside as they approached the building's entrance.

'You scared?'

'Ladies first, that's all.'

'Ever the gentleman.'

Jake eased open the door and crossed the threshold.

The building was dirty, and the overwhelming stench of damp assaulted his senses. Either that or a weed farm had been growing somewhere in the building. The plaster on the walls was decrepit and falling off in different places.

Just as Jake was about to approach the stairs, he heard a noise from outside the flat – the sound of glass smashing and the unmistakable sound of a human grunting loudly as they clattered onto the ground.

Then Jake saw the figure burst past the small front garden, fully clothed, backpack draped over his shoulders and brushing himself off after falling from the height he had.

'He's bolting!' Jake cried, acting instinctively. He swivelled on the balls of his feet, sprinted out of the house and gave chase.

There, he saw where Saeed had come from.

Adjoining the side of the house was a row of garages, eight feet high. Alert to their sudden arrival, Saeed had been one step ahead, and had clambered out of the window and leapt onto the ground. With any luck, he would have twisted an ankle or buckled a knee.

Jake hoped.

As he sprinted along the darkened street, with the light from the area suffocated by the thick smoke in the air, Jake became vaguely aware of the army of individuals chasing behind him. Fortunately for him, he wasn't forced to lumber a firearm and protective clothing with him, so he could keep the distance between himself and Saeed Anwar short.

He pumped his legs furiously, keeping his feet light on the ground, and followed Saeed through a small alleyway. As he travelled through the undergrowth, Jake fought off the thorns and leaves and twigs and branches slashing at his body.

Saeed's silhouette was in sight, nearing the end of the alley. Jake pressed on, pushing his legs hard. As he reached the halfway point, he stopped caring about his face and powered through. By the time he approached the alley's threshold into civilisation, Saeed was on the other side of the road.

Jake hopped down from the kerb but, in his haste, misjudged its depth and stumbled.

The street was empty, save for the hundreds of gnats hovering underneath the street lamps – and the SEAT Ibiza that came out of nowhere and ploughed into Jake's right side. His body rolled onto the bonnet, over the windscreen and roof, and he swore as he landed hard, his head ricocheting off the concrete, like a rag doll. The sudden shock tore open a rip in the canvas of his vision, and very quickly, black began to seep through. Hours of training had taught him how to deal with such a situation: tuck into a ball and protect his vitals, the head and chest. Yet he'd been completely blindsided.

Before he could do anything, he heard the car speeding away, leaving him to struggle on the concrete alone.

Composing himself and lifting himself to his feet, he risked a glance at the licence plate. In his delirious and disorientated state, it was almost impossible to take in.

He punched the air furiously. 'Fuck!'

Tyler appeared, breaching into the light. 'Jake. Oh shit. Are you OK?'

He rushed to Jake's side and helped him to his feet. Jake winced as a blinding pain shot up and down his right leg, and the darkness in his vision spread.

'Don't worry about me, dickhead. Chase after him.'

Realising this wasn't the time to argue, Tyler shot past Jake and disappeared down the road. After he was gone, Jake turned his attention to his wound. He cried out in pain as he hobbled over to the kerb, his hip and upper thigh throbbing with every movement, and slid once more to the ground.

A short while later, the armed officers plodded past, carrying their weapons as though they were characters in a *Call of Duty* video game. They quickly surrounded him and helped him to his feet again. Cautiously, Jake placed more and more weight onto his right leg, gauging the extent of the damage. The initial diagnosis was not good.

When Tyler returned a few minutes later, all thought of the pain in his leg and head disappeared.

'What happened?'

'He's gone. The fucker's a quick little bastard.'

Jake swore internally and lambasted himself for being stupid enough to get himself knocked to the ground by a car – and losing the only lead they had.

'What happened to you?' asked Tyler.

'What does it look like?' Jake pointed to the small fragments of glass from where his body had struck the windshield. There were tyre marks a few feet away from where he was standing. Had the driver braked before seeing him? Or had they braked afterwards, while contemplating the decision to get out of the vehicle to help? Or were the skid marks from sudden acceleration as panic struck?

'Can you walk?' Tyler asked.

Jake tried. He couldn't.

'Come on – we need to get you to a hospital. And don't be stubborn about it – I know what you're like.' Tyler held his phone to his ear.

'What are you doing?'

'Getting you an ambulance. You can't carry on like this.'

Just as Jake was about to protest, Tyler began speaking into the device. Less than four minutes later, an ambulance arrived and carried Jake to the nearest hospital.

As he was stretchered inside, only one thought crossed his mind: where was Saeed Anwar, and what was his role in all of this?

CHAPTER 6

'What did the doctor say?' Jasper Conrad asked Jake as he, Tyler and Mamadou entered the briefing room.

'Heavy bruising,' Jake responded. 'Not much else.'

It was 5 a.m. and, after a solid three hours of tests, painkillers and scans, Jake had discharged himself from the hospital – much to the annoyance of the doctors and hospital staff who'd opposed the idea. The scans on his legs and hip had come back fine, but it was the head injury that worried the medical professionals. The initial investigations indicated a concussion – a violent and brutal one. Which Jake was already feeling the effects of. But he'd ignored their advice and returned to work. They couldn't afford to be another man down.

'That's it? Just a bruise?' Mamadou asked. Since Jake had last seen him, he'd changed into a Ralph Lauren polo shirt which now had a coffee stain running down the logo. 'They didn't keep you long.'

'No,' Jake said. 'I suppose if it had happened to you, they would've needed you to stay all day, what with your advanced age and everything.'

Jake let the insult hang there, a smug smile growing on his face. Now that he'd been a member for just over a year, it had become a tradition between Jake, Mamadou and Tyler to insult one another. Mamadou was the brunt of the old-age jokes; Tyler, the sleazy male whore who probably had countless sexually transmitted diseases but hadn't bothered to get them checked out; and Jake, the boring one who acted as if he was a middle-aged man punching well above his weight.

Tyler laughed. 'Maybe they would have been worried about your senility. Might have thought you were going to go wandering off until someone found you.'

Mamadou sat there quietly. Jake could sense he was trying to come up with a respectable retort, but inspiration failed him.

Jake turned the conversation back to his injury. 'They said I've chipped a bit off my hip bone but nothing life-threatening.'

'No gymnastics for you then. Or karate, come to think of it,' Tyler added.

'You're a lucky bastard, I'll tell you that,' Mamadou added. 'From the CCTV footage we managed to pull, it looked like they were going like the clappers. I'm surprised they didn't paralyse you.'

Shrugging, Jake asked, 'Did you run the plates?'

'Not yet. You think they're connected?'

'I don't know. But it seemed odd that it came out of nowhere, and then when we tried to look for Saeed, we couldn't find him again.'

Jasper opened his mouth to speak, but the door beat him to it. Standing in the way was Matilda Edwards.

'Guv – we ran the plates through the database, and the car is registered to a Miss Samira Khan.'

Jake and Tyler looked at one another. Tyler gave him a bemused look that said, 'You got run over by a *girl*?'

'Any affiliation with Anwar?' Mamadou asked.

'Yes, guv. They're stepsiblings.'

'Stepsiblings?' Mamadou repeated.

'That's what happens when sometimes two different mummies and daddies who love each—' Tyler began.

'I know how it fucking works, Tyler.' Mamadou rose to his feet. 'Have we got a tracker on Anwar or Khan's phones?'

'Doing it now.'

'Good work. Keep me updated.'

Matilda closed the door behind her. As soon as it was shut, Jasper addressed them all.

'Jake – I need you indoors for the rest of the operation.'

'Why?'

'Because you're not fit to work.'

'Yes, I am.'

'No, you're not – you've just been run over. If anything, you shouldn't even be here. If HR knew about this, they'd have an absolute field day.'

'It's a good thing they don't start work until nine then, isn't it?'

'That's not the point. The point is, I can't let you go out on the field when we finally find out what's going on.'

'Still nothing?' Jake asked, fighting away the waves of pain that kept washing over him. He could feel the painkillers the doctors and nurses had pumped through his body beginning to wear off.

'Nothing yet. So far, Green Team has backdated

Raman's credit and debit transactions as far as six months ago, ever since he was released from prison. Not that long ago, in fact, he bought large quantities of bleach – and other substances you already know the capabilities of.'

'No surprises there. Any mention in text messages, emails? Codes of some sort?'

'None have been found in the team's investigations so far.

Jake was about to speak but was interrupted by the door opening again.

This time it was Lilly hovering in the door frame.

'What is it?' Jasper asked tartly.

'Sorry to interrupt, sir, but we looked into both Raman's and Saeed Anwar's recent whereabouts, and there was one place they both visited within hours of one another. Twice in the last two weeks.'

Finally, Jake thought, *something concrete.*

'Where?' Jasper asked.

Lilly pointed to the window behind Jake. 'The London Eye.'

CHAPTER 7

'The London Eye?' the room repeated simultaneously. The meaning of the words came crashing down on them like the car that had collided into Jake in a moment of stunned silence.

'That's what I said, yes,' Lilly replied.

'What's our plan of action now?' someone in the background asked. Jake's mind was too focused on what Lilly had said to pay attention to anything, or anyone, else. He tried to move in response but couldn't; despite the painkillers, his leg and hip still pained him, and he was forced to keep movement to a minimum.

Doctor's orders.

Jasper checked his watch. 'It's nearly 6 a.m., and the Eye opens at 11 a.m., which gives us a little over five hours to pool our resources together and work out a solution. We know the where, we just don't know the when. Or the who.'

'What time did Raman and Saeed visit the Eye respectively?' Tyler asked to Jake's right.

'What's that got to do with anything?' Jake snapped. His head was beginning to pound, aggravated by the surrounding lights. And he was rapidly becoming irritable and abrasive – a character trait that only appeared when he felt under immense levels of stress. It was also the character trait he hated most about himself.

'Believe it or not,' Tyler continued, this time speaking sardonically, 'it might give us a time frame for when they're going to attack.'

'You know what they say about people who assume…'

Tyler shook his head. 'You can be such a condescending prick sometimes, you know that?'

Jake did. But sometimes it was better to turn a blind eye to his faults and fallacies than it was to spend all his time apologising for them. 'Let's say – hypothetically – you discover they're going to attack between one and three, the busiest period of the day, but then they don't. They attack early in the morning instead and cause absolute fucking chaos. Dozens of lives lost. And we did fuck all about it because of some stupid guesswork. No. I don't think so.'

The room fell silent.

'Tanner's right,' Mamadou responded. 'But he needs to watch his attitude.' He glared at Jake, who remained steadfast in his stare. 'We're a team, remember. And we can't afford to fall out with one another, not this close to something happening. Whatever your problem is with someone, put it aside and out of mind. Otherwise I'll find some coffee mugs that need cleaning in the canteen. We need to assume they could attack at any point throughout the day, whenever we least expect it.'

Mamadou paced from left to right in front of the TV screen. 'Here's what I'm thinking. We have a window of five hours to stop the attack from taking place, with a little spare at the end. Which means we have four hours to plan for every eventuality. I want all of us at the London Eye, on the lookout for Saeed Anwar. He's our prime suspect – and if we find anyone of interest in the meantime, we add them to the list. I want us to work in shifts. I can see around the table you're all looking knackered, and the coffees aren't helping, which is why I want you to split in half. Some of you go take a nap while the rest of you continue the investigation.'

'How's that going to help?' Tyler asked.

'Because you'll be more refreshed, you'll have recharged your batteries, and you'll be less likely to make any fucking mistakes.'

Then Jasper took over and began calling out a handful of Jake's colleagues' names. Slowly, those addressed rose to their feet, left the room and disappeared off into a small, secluded room somewhere in the building which they would return from in a couple of hours.

At the end of it, Jake and Tyler remained, along with DC Matilda Edwards, DS Natalie Jones, DS Imran Malik and DC Jerome Bennett.

'You guys, on the other hand,' continued Jasper, 'will be working non-stop while they're resting. I want you to set up an OP somewhere at the foot of the Eye, or somewhere in one of the buildings. Inform uniform, and have them arrange a series of patrols around the area. And then we're going to need SCO19 on standby. In case things get hairy. I know you don't have long, but it's all we've got.'

'Our biggest priority should be finding who's going to carry out the attack, no?' Jake asked. 'Saeed Anwar might be higher up the food chain than we think; there could be a group of underlings beneath him.'

'Which is why I want you in charge of that,' Jasper said.

Jake didn't know how to feel about that. Again, he was the one being lumbered with a huge amount of responsibility. The same man who, only hours before, had carried the same weight on his shoulders and watched one of his colleagues die. If he identified the suspected attacker or attackers and caught them before 11 a.m., then he would be labelled a hero and would receive a well-deserved congratulations and a pat on the back. But, on the other hand, if he didn't, then he would not only be responsible for seventeen deaths – Darren, Kyle and the rest of the CTSFOs – he would also be responsible for the deaths of countless others inside the London Eye.

He saw it as his personal mission to make sure that didn't happen. A chance to redeem himself.

It ain't about how many times you get hit…

'Fine,' Jake said, biting his tongue. 'I'll get started now.'

Saying nothing more, Jake hobbled out of the room and wandered to his desk, unnerved by the silence in the empty office. The battle against terrorism was a twenty-four-seven job, and he was used to seeing it filled with at least a handful of officers. But now it had the atmosphere of a hotel in the middle of the night.

At his desk, Jake logged in and quickly began his search of the other prison inmates that had served a sentence at the same time as Saeed Anwar and Raman Al Hadid. Both men had been arrested for different offences – Saeed for GBH, and Raman for preparing acts of terrorism – but after spending several months in a cell with one another, Raman Al Hadid had radicalised and brainwashed Saeed Anwar into joining his endeavour. Jake's concern was that Saeed wasn't the only one. That there were more out there. Unknown, invisible. Silently working their way towards the London Eye.

'Here you are, champ,' Tyler said, walking over to him. In his hand, he held a plastic cup of instant coffee. A peace offering for their earlier argument. 'Thought you could do with this.'

It wasn't often they fought and argued, but whenever they did, they always made up and forgave each other within a few minutes. Like the perfect marriage – or bromance, as others in the team referred to it.

'Another one? If I have any more, my blood pressure's going to go through the roof.'

'It might numb the pain of life.'

Jake chuckled. 'If the painkillers I got at the hospital aren't taking care of that, I doubt coffee's going to make much difference. What did Mamadou and Jasper say after I left?'

'As soon as the Eye opens, we're going to be stationed in the pods two apiece. All day.'

'How? There are thirty-odd capsules on that thing and only twenty of us. That doesn't add up.'

Tyler shrugged and passed the coffee to Jake. 'He's finding a few more people from different teams. Mainly SCO19 and uniform.'

Shaking his head, Jake said, 'I'm always here to help.'

Tyler turned coy. 'You'll have to speak to him about

it. I'm staying out of it. Sorry, mate, got to go. We're setting up an OP in one of the river boats and another in the hotel nearby. I've got me a one-way ticket to a special, never-before-seen river cruise on the Thames!'

Tyler turned and disappeared out of the room, and Jake continued his investigation. As he sat there, staring idly into the screen, his eyes hovering over the words on the page but not actually reading them, an idea came into his head.

'*One-way ticket,*' he whispered, rising out of his seat.

He hobbled back to the briefing room and entered without knocking.

'I have a concern, sir,' he said to Jasper.

The commander swivelled on the spot, seemingly unfazed by Jake's abrupt entrance. 'What's that?'

'I want to source a list of names of people who have purchased tickets for the Eye today – cross-reference it with our files, and fingers crossed it should come up with a match.'

'Great thinking. Now, what do you need me for?'

'The warrant sign-off, sir.'

Jake hesitated, and both men knew he had more that he wanted to say. 'Because…' Jake continued, 'I want to be out there, sir. We're low on bodies. I can help.'

'You are, Jake. You're helping by being in *here*. Please don't fight me on this. Like Mamadou said – you need to watch the attitude, otherwise we can find something else for you to do.'

Dejected, Jake nodded and started out of the room.

'Wait, Tanner!'

Jake stopped. Turned on the spot. Ignored the pain in his leg.

'I don't want you taking a nap.'

What.

'Why not?'

The.

'Because,' Jasper began.

Fuck?

'Because what?'

'Because you said so yourself – we're running low on people. I need you in charge of the control room while everyone else is out there.'

Jasper nodded to the outside world, on the other side of the brick wall facing south. 'You're one of our best and brightest. You've already thought of looking at the ticket holders for today, well before anyone else did. I can't afford for you to miss out on anything, even if it is for thirty minutes.'

CHAPTER 8

After three relentless hours of searching and waiting, Jake still had no answer, no leads. Finding a person to speak to about the ticket holders had quickly become impossible: the warrant had been signed, but it was still early, and everybody in the management company was either not awake yet or just beginning their long slog in the office. The only silver lining, however, was that, while he waited, Jake had continued his efforts into finding associates connected to Saeed Anwar – though as far as he could make out, there were none. Which meant Saeed was likely a single cell, acting alone. The problem that remained, however, was finding him. If they could catch him before he ventured anywhere near the London Eye, the investigation would be a success. But if Jake couldn't – as he'd assigned it his own mission to find the suspect himself – then the prevalent risk of attack remained.

Jake eased back into his chair in frustration, and as he glanced at the rows of desks around him, he saw reasonably refreshed faces, their bodies understandably grateful for the short pitstop. He, on the other hand, was struggling. His body felt fatigued, and his mind dipped in and out of consciousness every time he lost focus. The headache was unrelenting, and his nausea had worsened. But he'd kept it to himself. The team needed him to be on his A game, without fault. He couldn't let them down. Again.

'All right, everyone!' Mamadou shouted, bolting Jake awake. 'It's time.'

At that, his colleagues erupted from their seats, grabbed their ID cards and headed down to the stockroom where their bomb bags were kept.

Bomb bags contained various items, including a chequered blue police baseball cap, uniform rain coat and epaulets with SO15 on them, as well as a white armband, a bomb whistle, reinforced boots, knee pads, gloves and a respirator. They were used during terror attacks or hostage negotiations to alert civilians to their presence.

After everyone had disappeared, Mamadou approached him.

'Channel three on the radio, OK?' Mamadou said. 'Keep in constant contact with everyone. Lilly's supplied you with the CCTV footage from inside each capsule and at the foot of the wheel, so you've got eyes on everything. Any questions?'

Jake shook his head. 'If I think of anything, I'll let you know.'

Just as Mamadou turned away, he stopped, reflected and turned back. 'I'm assuming still no luck finding Anwar or any other potential suspects?'

Jake looked down at his desk and then the floor, and shook his head again. 'Nothing.'

Embarrassing.

'OK. Well keep searching, and if something comes up, give me a bell.'

Mamadou left the room, leaving Jake completely alone.

With his thoughts.

With the nausea.

He didn't appreciate being left behind like this. Right now, more than anything, he wanted to be on the front line, making a difference – since his endeavours in the office had already failed miserably. Perhaps it was his ego, wanting to prove itself. Not to himself directly but to others. Or perhaps it was the deeply rooted desire to protect. To ensure others' safety. If he couldn't do it behind a desk, he could do it in person. Even with a cracked bone in his hip and a concussion. A part of him wanted to rip his keyboard from his desk and smash it into the monitor, but he knew that would leave him worse off than before.

His pulse raced, and in the aridity of the office, he could feel the onset of a malicious anxiety attack. His first in months. They'd started after he'd been swept up in an avalanche and almost suffocated. As a result, he suffered from debilitating attacks, typically when he was under severe amounts of stress, in a high-pressure situation, or in danger. He was surprised he hadn't had one after the car incident.

Before he allowed it to overcome him, he began his calming exercises to distract himself. Breathing in through the nose, out through the mouth.

In for four.

Out for four.

In. Out.

Just as he finally calmed, his phone rang.

'Tanner,' he answered, without checking the caller

ID.

'Hey, honey.' It was Elizabeth. It was so good to hear her voice; even though he'd only been away from home for twenty-four hours, it felt as though it had been a week.

'Hey. How you doing? Sorry I didn't call to say I wouldn't be home. I didn't want to wake you and the girls.'

'The text was enough, thank you. Is everything OK?'

'It will be.'

'Good. I just wanted to let you know that I'm bringing the girls into London with Monica and Vicky.'

'What?'

'The play date. Remember?'

This was the worst possible time for her to be calling.

'Right. Yeah, I remember.'

He didn't.

'Anyway, if you're around, we'll pop by on your break or something.'

'Yeah, yeah, sure. OK.' He needed to get rid of her and focus back on his work. He'd already spent too long talking to her.

'We're planning to take a wander along the South Bank.'

Something on the screen caught his eye, distracting him. 'Oh yeah? That sounds like a good idea.'

'Yeah.' There was a pause. 'Are you all right? You seem distant.'

It took him a while to comprehend what Elizabeth was saying. 'Yeah.' Another pause, this time longer. 'Yeah, I'm fine. It's just…'

'I know you can't tell me what's going on, but if

something's troubling you, I want you to tell me.'

Jake exhaled deeply. Their marriage hadn't always been sunshine and rainbows, but after several hours of counselling, they'd learnt the first step was being open and honest with each other.

'Jasper's being a prick,' he blurted out then checked around to see if anyone had overheard.

Then he remembered he was alone and had the place to himself so he could say whatever he wanted.

'Why?'

'Because he's doing his job.'

Elizabeth scoffed. 'Not usually the reason people are called that, Jake. What's he done?'

'Essentially kicked me off the team. Forced me to stay back while everyone else is out doing something.'

'I'm sure he has his reasons.'

'If that car hadn't—'

'What car? What did you just say?'

'Nothing.'

'Jake Isaac Tanner, tell me this instant.'

Jake breathed in. It was funny – he could have been the hardest, most aggressive man on the planet, yet the most important woman in his life had the power to bring him back down to size and make him seem like a child about to be berated for doing something he shouldn't.

'Car. I got hit by a car,' he said, hoping the silence that followed would end with Elizabeth hanging up.

'You did *what*?'

Maybe not.

'A car hit me.'

'And you didn't think to tell me?'

'You were asleep. I didn't want to wake you. I didn't want to worry you.'

'*So* thoughtful of you, Jake,' she replied sarcastically. 'What are you going to do next time something happens – send me a letter and wait until it arrives in the post before you think about coming home?'

'Elizabeth…'

'No, Jake. You foolish, foolish man. No wonder Jasper kept you back. What happened? Are you injured?'

'Just my hip. It's just a bruise. Nothing too serious.'

'I'll give you "nothing too serious" when you get home.'

The line went dead – Elizabeth had hung up. Her words rang through his ears as he placed the phone on the desk.

The first step to a happy marriage was being honest. And he'd just lied.

The time rolled around to 11 a.m. – opening time for the Eye and the ticket management company. Grabbing the phone from his desk, Jake dialled the number and waited. And waited. The final piece of the puzzle hinged on this vital piece of information. If he could access the names of those with bookings, he could then cross-reference it against the names of Raman and Saeed Anwar's family, friends and historical associates. And he could then find out what time Saeed Anwar had booked for his slot.

If they answered the bloody phone!

Eventually, after a ten minute hold, he managed to get through to someone and quickly explained the situation. The person he spoke to seemed accommodating and friendly, and less than five minutes later, he had the details delivered directly to his inbox. Passing a studious eye over the information, his mind searched for any red flags. But he found nothing untoward. No names of either Raman's or Saeed's associates. And, more worryingly, no mention of Saeed Anwar's name at all under the booking slots.

What?

Jake checked for Saeed's known alias names or anything similar.

Still nothing.

This was bad. Very bad. If he couldn't find Saeed, or a name associated with him, then everyone on the ground would be working blind, in the dark. They would be susceptible to a surprise attack from an unknown figure at an unknown time of day.

Jake ran his fingers through his hair when he heard a voice in his ear.

'This is Mamadou. Jake – can you hear me?'

'Loud and clear.'

'Good. We're in position. The gates have been opened for a while now. We've circulated images of Saeed Anwar's face to one another so we know who we think we're looking for. Have you got anything else for us?'

Jake took a moment to think. It was better to be honest than lie and risk their lives. 'Negative. None of the ticket reports came back with anything.'

He made a point of making his frustrations known.

'OK. Let me know if anything changes.'

Jake clicked the button on his mouse, and the screen changed. Live CCTV footage of each of the Eye's capsules appeared in separate squares on the monitor, with a final one displaying the queue to get on the wheel.

'Where is everyone?' he asked.

'In their pods.'

Jake enlarged the first thumbnail. An image of the inside of one of the capsules opened, and Jake instantly saw Lilly staring out of the window, pretending to take photos of the city below.

He spent the next couple of hours waiting, clicking, searching.

But still nothing. In the meantime, he continued his investigations into Saeed Anwar, their prime suspect, by speaking with his stepsister, Samira Khan. After bringing her in for a chat in one of the interview rooms, Jake had questioned her about her stepbrother's life. His birth, his childhood, his adolescence, his education, his arrest, his time in prison and his subsequent release. In the space of his twenty-three years on the planet, the furthest Saeed Anwar had travelled had been from Lambeth to Wandsworth, where he currently lived, and the most he'd experienced had been an eighteen-month stay in one of Her Majesty's finest.

The conversation had then turned to the missing SEAT Ibiza. According to Samira, she'd been asleep during the time of the incident but had informed Jake that there were several other names on the insurance: herself, Saeed and a woman called Rasha, who was Saeed's blood-related sister.

Rasha, full name Rasha Al Abdi, had a four-year-old son and worked with her brother at KFC. The two had lived together for a few years after their parents' death, but following Saeed's incarceration, she'd been forced to work several jobs to pay for rent and put food on the table for her son. It hadn't been easy, but she'd done what she could to get by.

Samira didn't know whether Rasha had been driving the car, but Jake thought it was more than likely. The only question that remained was why?

But before he could think about it anymore, back in his chair in the office, something caught the corner of his eye. A figure in one of the CCTV thumbnails.

Saeed Anwar.

Dressed in a long, dark coat, wearing a hat and sunglasses, standing at the back of the queue. Alone. His face was clean shaven, fresh, prepared.

Shit.

'Attention, attention, suspect Saeed Anwar is currently in the queue. Repeat – confirmed visual of Saeed Anwar in the queue.'

But his message was unnecessary.

His colleagues, who'd blended themselves amongst the other patrons in the queue, had immediately spotted Saeed Anwar's oversized winter coat – incongruous under the summer sun – and pounced on him. Three detectives, each communicating through their earpieces, surrounded him from all angles and grabbed him. Their movements had to be precise and decisive. Any less so and they risked enabling Saeed Anwar, with the briefest of opportunities, to detonate whatever he was wearing beneath his coat.

Jake watched the computer screen intently. Within seconds, the crowd dispersed as the Met's finest manoeuvred Saeed onto the ground.

And then the call came over the radio.

'Saeed Anwar arrested and detained. We have him in custody.'

Somehow, through hard work, determination and a helping hand of luck, they'd managed to knock Raman's queen off the chessboard.

Check. Mate.

CHAPTER 9

The atmosphere inside Room 1430 was one of immense relief. They had Saeed Anwar in custody, and all fears of a detonation at one of London's most iconic landmarks had disappeared with him. Shortly after his arrest, Jake had learnt that Saeed had been carrying a suicide vest beneath his winter coat, and that Imran Malik, the usually quiet and unassuming detective sergeant, had been the one to tame his inner lion and pry the detonator from Saeed's grasp. Jake was, more than anything, incredibly proud of everyone on the team. They'd put their lives on the line to save the civilians who were oblivious to the realities of what had happened – and would continue to remain so. They'd put their lives on the line without a thank you from the general public, without a pat on the back, without a 'well done'; he just wished he could have been there to help.

'You did,' Tyler said to Jake as they made a coffee in the canteen. Jake's hip was still aching, but he'd started to get used to the pain of walking and had stopped using furniture for support. His head, however, was far from OK.

'How do you work that one out?'

'We all heard you over the radio. You saw Saeed first. Without your call, we would've missed him. And who knows what could have happened.'

Jake knew that was a lie. But he also knew that his friend was trying to cheer him up. Ever since the injury, Jake's emotions had been all over the place. One second he was alert, the other vacant. One moment he was angry, the next he was depressed, the next elated.

The motherboard inside his head was frazzled. And it needed rest.

Sadly, there was no time.

As he and Tyler returned to Room 1430, coffees in hand, DS Imran Malik and DC Billy Vance were in the middle of the room talking with Mamadou. The two officers were in charge of interviewing Saeed Anwar at Paddington Green, the station designated for terror suspects and convicted terrorist offenders. Jake caught the end of a sentence as he passed, and listened in at his desk.

'... I wouldn't be surprised,' Vance said.

'And he didn't want a solicitor?' Mamadou asked.

'No, sir,' Vance replied. 'He just sat there in silence. Didn't say a single word.'

'And he had this weird smile on his face,' Imran added. 'Like he knew something we didn't.'

'That's typically what happens in an interview, Detective.'

'I know, but this time it was *different*.'

'Another attack?'

Imran shrugged.

'Do we have any intelligence to suggest another

one's been planned?'

Jake, in his delirium, had been lost in the conversation. It wasn't until the profound silence in the room caught up with him that he realised they were all waiting for a response from him.

The master with the key to the information.

'Jake,' Mamadou started. 'Do we have any intelligence to suggest that he's got another attack planned? Another associate in control perhaps?'

Jake held his breath. Searched his mind. He wasn't sure of the answer himself.

But everyone else on the team had done their part. He couldn't let them down now.

'No, sir. From... from my investigations, I was unable to find anything of the sort.'

'Well, that may be, but we need to make absolutely certain. I'm not discrediting any work you've done, Jake, but an extra pair of eyes never hurt anyone.'

CHAPTER 10

Those extra pairs of eyes had quickly turned into ten, then fifteen, then twenty as Mamadou's paranoia and concerns had multiplied. While Imran and Vance continued to interview Saeed Anwar and question him about the possibility of another attack by a wider cell, Jake and the team ramped up their investigations, cramming months' worth of work into hours.

Again.

If ever there was a time where Jake had felt foolish and insignificant, it was nothing compared to the way he felt watching others in the office conduct his own work. A different team, with a fresh set of eyes, had been tasked with accessing Saeed Anwar's financial records, email history, message history and social media history, while another had been sent to raid his house and search it for evidence, and another team of two had been sent to speak with Saeed's probation officer, who'd last spoken to Saeed several months ago.

Jake, on the other hand, was part of the team looking into the CCTV footage of Saeed Anwar's movements in the previous twelve hours. Now that they had him in custody and knew his movements before the attack, they could follow him in reverse order. Where he'd come from. Who he'd seen along the way. Trying to ascertain his thoughts, his behaviours and what relation they bore to the investigation, if any.

'I'm Hank Marvin,' Tyler declared.

Jake hadn't realised it, but he'd been staring into the pixels of the screen, lost in their brightness.

'You what?' he asked.

'Starving. Hungry. I need some food in my belly or I'm going to pass out.'

Jake grunted, his mind unable to process what Tyler had said. He was vaguely aware, from the rumbling in his own stomach, that it was long past lunchtime and he was hungry too. Not only his stomach but also his head – hungry for rest, medication and water.

'Yeah,' he replied eventually. 'Nice.'

'Are you feeling all right?' Tyler asked.

'I've been better.'

'How's your hip?'

'Fine,' he lied.

'You sure you're feeling all right?'

'Why wouldn't I be?'

'Because you don't *look* right.'

'I often think the same about you, but at least I keep those thoughts to myself.'

A smirk grew on Tyler's face, and he slapped Jake jovially on the arm. 'There he is, good old Tanner. The one who thinks his banter's on point but has still got a lot to learn.'

Jake chuckled. Then he laughed. The sensation felt strange. But then it all came crashing back down on him as images of Darren appeared in his mind. It had been such a long night that he'd almost completely forgotten it had happened. But now that he found himself laughing, it reminded him of his former colleague. And a wave of guilt rolled over him.

Follow by a tsunami of nausea.

'I need a moment,' Jake said, jumping out of his chair. 'Excuse me.'

Without saying another word, he hurried out of the room as fast as his hip would allow, and raced towards the bathroom, where he found the first available cubicle and dived inside, unable to suppress the heaving in his throat for much longer. Before he had the chance to shut the door, the vomit erupted from his mouth and splattered into the toilet basin, splashing back onto the seat and his hands and face. He retched and convulsed as the meagre contents of his stomach exploded from his body.

Twice.

Three times.

A fourth.

When it finally finished, he flushed the toilet and wiped his mouth clean. Then he sat on the seat and rested against the cistern, spent, left with the acidic taste of bile in his mouth and throat.

A pounding started in his head, squeezing from every angle. And then the blackness returned. Blotchy at first, but then as he struggled to catch his breath, it worsened.

Water. He needed water.

Air. He needed to breathe.

Get out of there. He needed out.

Slowly, cautiously, as if his life depended on it, he rose from the seat. As he did so, another wave of nausea pummelled him from all sides, and the darkness worsened the pounding in his head. He felt like he wanted to throw up again and pass out, preferably in that order. But he couldn't. Not in a cubicle on his own. What if no one found him? Or what if it was too late by the time they did?

Summoning what little energy hadn't been spent vomiting, Jake unlocked the cubicle door and shuffled towards the sinks. His fingers fumbled over the tap until he switched it on.

As soon as he heard the sound of running water, he cupped his hands beneath the stream and pressed it against his face. Then swallowed a mouthful. The cool, refreshing liquid instantly rejuvenated him, replenishing his lost fluids. Never before had he felt so grateful for a fully functioning tap.

As he took another gulp, his phone vibrated against his leg. Delirious still, he fumbled the device out of his pocket and answered.

'Hello?'

'Jake? Are you all right?'

'Hey, hon.' He switched off the tap. Composed himself. 'What's the matter?'

'Nothing,' Elizabeth replied. 'We've just got to the South Bank. Are you free? I thought you might be able to spare a few minutes for a coffee by the Eye.'

Air.

All Jake could think about was air.

'Sure,' he said. 'I'll come down now. Give me ten.'

He paused a moment, and as he stared at himself in the mirror, realisation entered the bathroom and slapped him across the face. 'Wait, what are you doing at the Eye?'

'We decided to get tickets seeing as we were going to be in the area. We're booked for four o'clock – the girls will love it.'

'What…' He didn't understand – couldn't process the how and why of his family being right outside in the midst of all this through the relentless pounding in his head.

While he struggled to come up with a coherent response, she added, 'I'm with Monica and Vicky. We took the girls out for the day. I told you this earlier, remember?'

CHAPTER 11

She had told him, but he'd completely forgotten. Or not listened in the first place.

The reasons for his forgetfulness were unimportant. What mattered was that his family needed to evacuate the area as soon as possible. Something which, stubborn as ever, Elizabeth didn't want to do given that he hadn't offered her any explanation as to why – something he didn't want to do over the phone. Plus, the tickets had already been bought – over a hundred quid for the three of them to visit.

According to Elizabeth, that was money they would never see again.

Well, Jake would much rather never see the money than the alternative – never seeing *them* again.

But Elizabeth wouldn't have any of it. She was persistent and stubborn, and in part, it was one of the reasons he loved her. But, on the other hand, it was also one of the reasons he hated her sometimes too.

Shortly after hanging up on her, he hurried out of the bathroom and raced out of the building. Suddenly, his mind and body felt better, as if the fear of his family dying had rejuvenated and elevated his senses, and cleared the fog in his head.

As he exited New Scotland Yard and paced over Westminster Bridge, two thoughts occupied his mind.

One: how could he have possibly missed his own wife's name on the booking list for the day?

Two: this was the first time he'd set foot on the bridge since his final showdown with The Cabal, the head of an elaborate underworld crime syndicate responsible for making his life, his marriage and his career a misery.

That altercation had ended badly. And he hoped history wouldn't repeat itself a hundred yards downriver.

Ten minutes later, he arrived at the base of the London Eye, exasperated and gasping for what little air his lungs could inhale. Now he had a new type of headache. And a stitch. For the first time in ten years.

God, you're getting old, Jake.

Stitches were for unfit teenagers who didn't have any experience running. Not relatively fit men in their mid-twenties.

'Did you just sprint over here?' Elizabeth asked as he arrived. She was dressed in a thin jumper, and Maisie and Ellie were wearing the matching raincoats they'd begged for in Primark.

'How did you expect me to get here? Helicopter?'

'Yeah!' screamed Maisie, having only heard the last word of his sentence. 'Helicopter! Awesome!'

Jake bent down and gave his daughters a kiss and a hug before returning his attention to Elizabeth.

She pointed to the brunette woman beside her. 'This is Monica. Remember?'

He didn't, but Jake leant in and embraced her anyway. 'Hey, how you doing?' he said politely, then turned his attention to Monica's daughter, who clung to her like a baby chimpanzee. 'And who do we have here?'

At first the girl seemed coy, pensive, her hand lodged firmly in her mouth.

'You can tell the man,' Monica said, coercing her daughter into speaking.

'My name's Victoria,' she said sweetly. 'But you can call me Vicky.'

'That's a pretty name,' he said, smiling ebulliently. 'And very clever – shortening your name like that. It doesn't work so well on my name. I'm Jake, and if you shortened it, you'd get Ja.'

'Like jam without the M!'

'Very good! Like jam without the M. Maybe everyone should start calling me jam!'

It was better than his initials: JIT.

He was eternally grateful that his parents hadn't called him Tom, or some other such name…

His response elicited a vibrant and beautiful laugh from Vicky, the kind only a child possessed. The laughter of pure, untarnished happiness. He loved it and didn't want his daughters to ever grow out of that same phase, though they were already showing the signs.

'What are you guys doing here?' Jake asked Elizabeth once the laughter had died down.

'I told you – we're here for a play date. A spontaneous, fun thing to do. Is that all right?' Elizabeth was unable to hide the accusation in her voice.

'I'd prefer if you weren't here,' Jake replied.

'And why not?'

'Because of work.'

The hidden meaning behind his words slowly registered on Elizabeth's face. 'You mean…?'

'Yep.'

'And…'

'This morning, in fact. And there's still more to come, we think.'

'Right…' Elizabeth's face paled.

'So I need you guys to be anywhere but here. Does that make sense? Forget the money. I'm sure we'll find it somewhere.'

'I haven't paid for them yet,' Elizabeth said, her body and mind suddenly coming to.

'Who has?'

'Me.'

Monica.

'The reservation was under my name.'

That explained why he'd missed the name on the list at least.

'Liz was going to pay me back when she gets the money.'

Jake was just about to respond when something out of the corner of his eye distracted him. A woman pushing a pram. Typically an innocuous sighting, not only in London but anywhere in the world. Except there was something about this woman that concerned him, that alerted the tired and broken senses at the back of his brain.

'Jake, what's the matter?' Elizabeth asked, although her voice sounded distant. He was drowning her and everyone else out, the cogs in his dehydrated and concussed brain only able to focus on one thing at a time.

'Get out,' he said, keeping his eyes fixed on the woman. 'Leave. Go, as fast and far as you can. I'll speak to you later.'

Before leaving, he kissed and embraced his family, not knowing if it would be the last time he would see them again. He forced his mind not to think about that.

For now, he sensed a threat. A terrifying and deadly threat.

He recognised the woman's face from somewhere. Somewhere recent, somewhere nearby.

And then he had it.

It was the same woman he'd seen on the CCTV inside the KFC Raman had entered.

The same woman Samira had told him about.

The same woman who'd likely run him thirteen hours before.

Rasha Al Abdi.

Jake watched her slip through the crowd and join the front of the fast-track queue: Raman's final – and this time it was final – piece on the chessboard moving into position.

CHAPTER 12

The first thought that crossed his mind was to alert someone. Anyone who could do something about it. Mamadou. Tyler. Jasper.

But when he tried their mobile numbers, he was met with voicemail every time.

'When I need you, you don't fucking answer,' Jake mumbled under his breath vehemently.

Aware that, any moment now, Rasha was about to board the Eye, Jake started after her, hurrying down the aisle for the fast-track queue. If no one could help, he was going to have to take matters into his own hands. He couldn't let her board that capsule. Under any circumstances.

Ten metres separated them.

Nine.

As he drew closer, Rasha's head pivoted left and right as she surveyed the area for any signs of a threat. Jake had to pause and blend back into the crowd lest he give himself away. A few seconds passed, and then it was too late. She and the boy inside the pushchair had boarded the capsule. They were inside.

Jake stopped to think. He had a twenty-second window before he lost Rasha – and everyone else on the London Eye – for good.

He needed a contingency plan, something that meant, if he failed, he would be able to evacuate the area and risk as little life as possible.

It was no use. He was going to have to go for it.

Ahead, following Rasha and the boy, was a small petite woman pushing a pram with the aid of an employee onto the capsule. Jake took that as his cue.

Dipping underneath the barrier, Jake sprinted over to the woman and shouted, 'Honey!'

Just as he was about to board, an arm impeded him.

'Excuse me, I can't let you on without a ticket,' one of the employees said. He was a lanky thing who looked like he'd long since had enough of working with the general public, despite his young age.

'Please,' Jake said forcefully, reaching into his pocket for his warrant card. 'My wife and kids are on there. I don't want to miss it. Look, here's my ticket.'

Jake handed his warrant card to the spotty teenager, who inspected it. When he realised who Jake was, his eyes bulged, and his larynx moved up and down his slender neck.

'I'm sorry, sir,' the guy said. 'Come with me – I'll let you in.'

Jake followed him over to the pod. The doors were just about to close as the capsule reached the end of the platform. But the teenager pressed a button on his belt, and the doors froze. Jake stepped in, turned to face the man, nodded and allowed the doors to close behind him.

Before Jake could take in his surroundings – and he

sensed almost everyone in the pod was watching and judging him – he had to set his cover story up. To his left was the mum who'd entered seconds before him.

'Honey,' he said to her. 'I thought we almost got split up then.'

At first, the woman looked at him in confusion. But before she could say anything, Jake hugged her, placing his right arm over her back and his left in front of her face, making sure his ID was abundantly visible. He prayed she wouldn't react, that she wouldn't blow his cover before it had even begun.

To his surprise, she just patted him on the back and said, 'That's all right, hon. At least we're together now.'

Good. Very good. She was smart. And also a little worried. She had questions he was sure, but right now he couldn't afford to answer them; he needed to keep up appearances.

Smiling at the woman, he pulled her closer into his chest, and then looked down at the small child in the pushchair.

'You all right, little one?' Jake asked, playing with the baby's hand. She took his fingers in his, and at that point, it reminded him of his daughters, and how it had only seemed like yesterday when they were both that age, giggling uncontrollably. Now they cared less and less about him, and more and more about any screens they could get their hands on.

'Chloe's been fine, haven't you, my darling? Been missing her daddy.' The woman bent forward and picked the child up. She bounced her in her arms, looked around her and then turned to Jake. 'What's going on?'

She kept her voice low and pretended to play with the baby as she spoke.

Jake didn't know what to tell her. What could he? That there was a terrorist cell on board, ready and waiting to blow themselves up, and that he was their only chance of survival? He didn't know how she would react, and that was a risk he couldn't take.

'I can't tell you the details,' he said. 'But I might need your help. What's your name?'

The atmosphere in the capsule seemed relaxed. Conversations flittered around the enclosed space as groups and couples and families took photos and selfies and videos of themselves wandering around the cabin and the sights of London beyond. In the background, gentle music played through a set of speakers built into the ceiling.

'Jennifer,' she murmured, giving him a nervous look.

'Nice to meet you. I'm Jake. Do as I say, and everything will be fine.'

Jake wasn't sure if he believed himself.

He was alone, locked inside a small capsule, with a family of terrorists to call his co-passengers. And nowhere to go. He – and everyone else with him – was trapped.

The next thirty minutes were going to change his life forever.

CHAPTER 13

Thirty minutes. That was how long one revolution of the Eye took. And Jake estimated he had half that. A small window of approximately fifteen minutes until their capsule reached its peak height. The furthest away from the bottom of the wheel, the furthest from any form of rescue and safety. The perfect place to detonate.

Fifteen minutes to save the lives of the twenty people onboard with him.

It wasn't an exact science, but it was all he had.

Either way, it meant he needed to act. Fast.

But he couldn't. Something was stopping him, stepping in his way. Was it his leg? No, the fresh painkillers he'd downed before leaving the office had all but done their job on that. Was it his head?

No. It was something else. Something deeper. The sense of claustrophobia, the sense of impending doom, closing walls, no air, no escape – it was all getting too much for him. An anxiety attack. Suddenly, Jake was transported to that place high in the Alps and everything began to bleed white. Jennifer, Chloe and everyone else in the capsule had turned to white. His body went stiff, and his teeth chattered. The nightmare was still alive.

It had been years since the event had taken place, and in that time he'd undergone countless hours of therapy to combat it, but no matter how much he pretended it wasn't an issue, it lay there, dormant, buried just beneath the surface. Ready and waiting to burst into his life and attack him whenever it was least convenient.

Jake's head felt light, and the world began to sway from left to right. Please God, don't let him pass out now. He couldn't draw more attention to himself. There was too much at stake.

He held his breath. This time, the voice of his therapist sounded in his mind. Relaxed him. Controlled him. Then he felt a strong grip on his arm, breaking him out of his stupor. Before the white disappeared, an image of Rasha smiling at him, detonator in hand, finger poised over the trigger, appeared in his mind. When the image melted into the background, it was replaced with Jennifer, gripping his forearm.

'Are you OK?' she asked.

Nodding, he said, 'I'm fine. I just… I just needed time to think, that was all.'

'Do you know what you're doing?'

'No. I'm still working on it. Give me time.'

Jennifer turned away from him and cuddled her baby closer to her chest. She knew her moments on this planet were numbered if Jake didn't do anything – he could see that much from her wilted and morose expression.

Jake turned his attention away from her and cast his eye over his surroundings. The pod was ten feet wide and almost twenty feet long. Metal railings circled the perimeter, and in the centre was a large wooden bench for tired and bored legs to sit on. Two families were huddled together on the other side of the capsule, taking photos, discussing quietly. A couple moved about the space from left to right, front to back, gasping as every new angle revealed something exciting and unexpected. A group of children were chasing after one another, dodging everyone else inside, while the rest of the parents were sitting in the middle – Rasha included. And lastly there was a man with a backpack on, holding a professional DSLR camera – reminiscent of the ones Elizabeth had at home for work – pointing it out at the London skyline.

Each of them oblivious to who was in there with them. Each of them oblivious to what was about to happen.

Jake ignored them all and wandered over to the bench. There he found a space beside Rasha and reached for his phone. Six missed calls – four from Tyler, two from Mamadou. He could only begin to imagine what was happening back in Room 1430. Whether they knew what had happened to him. Whether they'd uncovered Rasha and Saeed's plans. Or whether they thought he'd gone for a stroll and got lost along the way.

Jake pressed Tyler's name and waited for the call to connect.

'About fucking time!' Tyler screamed in his ear. 'Where are you?'

'I'm on the London Eye,' he said convincingly then moved away from Rasha, hopefully out of earshot. 'I'm glad you've called. I've been trying to get through to you for ages, but the signal's been terrible.'

Jake needed to maintain a façade. He needed to keep up the appearance that he was a regular person, with a regular job, with a regular family, and not, in fact, a terrorist hunter.

He looked around the capsule, as if he was describing to the person on the other end of the line the scenic views from inside. As his head rotated ninety degrees, his eyes caught Rasha's. They were pitch-black, like an abyss. He froze, then feigned a smile. If she'd clocked on to what he was doing, he would have no chance. If she hadn't, then he'd been given a lifeline.

A very thin and pale lifeline.

'Are you alone?' Tyler asked in his ear.

'*Yeah*, that's what I thought, *yeah*.'

'How the fuck have you ended up there?' Tyler asked. He was flustered and getting panicked, and Jake sensed he was trying to flag someone down in the office.

Jake kept talking on the phone while he waited. 'I've been meaning to talk to them about it, but things have just been so busy with work.' He moved beside Jennifer and rested his back against the pod window.

He continued. 'We decided to take a little break for a couple of days. Show Chloe the London sights. We managed to get tickets on the cheap. They were under Jennifer's *sister's* name. *She* ended up giving them to us.'

'You have visual of an X-ray?' Tyler asked.

'Yeah, that's the one.'

'Who?'

'Can't remember, sorry. But how've the *family* been?'

'Understood, Jake,' Tyler said, calmer this time.

'Yeah, it's been the same here. Jen's mum's been in hospital with pneumonia for the past few days. We've tried to see her as much as we can.'

'Pneumonia? Confirm.'

'Yeah. The doctors said she should be OK though. They're monitoring her now.'

Pneumonia was their code word for an explosive device and had been decided several months before by Darren. His mum had died unexpectedly from it, and he'd wanted her memory to live on. It was like an explosion in her lungs, he'd said.

'Received, understood,' Tyler replied.

A moment of silence followed.

'Hold on – Jasper wants a word.'

'Thanks. I'll pass the message on.'

'Jake. Can you hear me?' came the voice of the commander.

'Yes.'

'OK. Good. Listen carefully. We need you to incapacitate the target. We're trying to find out what you know. If you can give us names, that would be great.'

Jake looked at Jennifer, deep into her eyes, half paying attention to them, half not. 'They've run some tests, and they've found other illnesses. Two more, to be exact. One small and one big.'

Then Jasper began calling out the names that Jake had put together during his investigations. He envisaged the list on his desk, and he waited until he heard Rasha's name.

'Yeah, that's it unfortunately. We'll have to see how she goes.'

'Is *she* alone?' Jasper asked.

'No.'

'With a man?'

'No.'

'Child?'

'Yes. I remember you saying now. *He* and Chloe could be good friends one day.'

To the outside world, his conversation probably made no sense, but he didn't care. So long as he conveyed the valuable information across to the people that mattered, he was happy.

A problem shared was a problem halved after all.

And a problem shared with some of the finest detectives and thinkers in the Metropolitan Police was a problem considerably reduced entirely.

'Right,' Jasper continued, 'give it five minutes. We're all acting blind on this one. We have no way of knowing whether she's carrying anything, or what it might be. You need to tread carefully. We're going to set up an observation point in the hotel opposite. Do everything you can to stop her, Jake. Good luck, and be safe.'

He swallowed.

'Anyway,' Jake continued, 'it's been lovely, but I need to get going. We're going to be at the top of the Eye in a few minutes, and I want to make sure I don't miss it. My phone's got the best camera. Need some good photos for my Facebook!'

Jake rang off. He hoped his final message had been conveyed: that the rest of the team had minutes to save him and everyone else inside the capsule. But there was no way of knowing.

Not until it was too late.

He pocketed the phone and smiled at Jennifer. A part of him was grateful that his real family wasn't with him. He couldn't bear the thought of them perishing in an explosion, their limbs and organs and blood and bones being flung into the River Thames, never to be found again. Though instead, they might get to watch *his* decimated body explode into the atmosphere.

'Everything OK?' Jennifer asked.

'As OK as it can be.'

Jake looked out of the window, deep in thought. Behind the calm exterior, far inside the recesses of his brain, his mind was putting together a plan.

And he had one opportunity to execute it.

CHAPTER 14

The pieces slowly fell into place. Now all he had to do was find a way to execute them. Twenty other people shared the same cabin as him. The problem he faced was getting them out of the way. They were going to be the catalyst in his decision-making; their actions determined his.

He couldn't let them mess this up for him.

But first he had to identify where the explosives were. Whether they were on Rasha or inside the pushchair. Or somehow on her little four-year-old son.

Jake nudged Jennifer. 'Come on – let's go to the other side.'

'Is that… safe?'

'Wise, you mean. Is that wise?' Jake paused to look around him; no one suspected him of anything. 'And no. In both instances, it is not a sensible thing to do. But I need you with me on this. I don't know how yet, but I'm working on it.'

Nodding slowly, Jennifer placed Chloe in the pushchair and moved with Jake over to the other side of the capsule. The north side of London came into full view. The gushing, murky waters of the River Thames cascading beneath their feet. The archaic, gothic Houses of Parliament. The familiar building Jake knew too well – New Scotland Yard. It was crazy to think less than half an hour ago he'd been inside, safe, not about to come face to face with a terrorist.

With death.

Jennifer and Jake stood for a moment, neither able to appreciate the glorious blue skies and the dazzling sun in front of them.

'I need you to shout at me,' he whispered to Jennifer, throwing his arm around her.

'What?'

'I need you to pick a fight with me.'

'How? Why?'

'Because it's important. Is there anything you've forgotten in the pushchair?'

Jennifer considered a moment. 'No, but I ran out of wipes on the way down.'

'Perfect, I need you to pretend like I forgot to pack them. Cause a scene, make sure everyone hears us. Then go and speak to the lady in the middle with the pushchair.'

'Why?'

'I need you to see if she's carrying any…'

Jake didn't finish his sentence. He didn't need to. Both he and Jennifer knew the answer. He just didn't want to be the one to confirm it.

'Bloody hell,' she said. A maternal instinct seemed to come over her; she stroked Chloe's cheek and gave her a kiss.

'Check her coat and the inside of the pushchair. Report back to me what you see.'

'Why can't you do it?'

'It'll look suspicious.'

If he could, then he would. But he'd already made eye contact with Rasha once. He didn't want to have to do it a second time in case it spooked her.

Jennifer inhaled deeply, then let out a long, heavy sigh. She was clearly psyching herself up for the performance of a lifetime.

'On the count of three…' he said, then rounded the front of the pushchair and bent down beside Chloe, who was smiling and giggling at her reflection in the window. Keeping his fingers hidden from view, he counted down.

Three.

Two.

One.

'Erm, Jake,' she started. The tone of accusation already in her voice sounded like she'd done this before. 'Where are the wipes?'

'What wipes?' he said, looking up at her, confused.

'The wipes I told you to pack.'

'You didn't ask me to pack any wipes.'

'I did. The ones in the kitchen, right by the kettle. I explicitly said to you, "Don't forget to pack the wipes."'

'Oh, sorry, love. I don't remember. Have you not got any already in there?'

'Do I look like a witch? You think I can just magic some wipes from thin air?'

Jake hadn't been expecting this performance, but he was mightily impressed. Jennifer played the part of aggrieved wife very well. And with a deep sigh, she slammed the roof of the pushchair and sauntered towards Rasha, shooting Jake a look of derision as she went.

While she was speaking with Rasha, Jake tried to listen in on the conversation, and, with one eye on Chloe and the other on Jennifer, he tried to watch it too.

But a small child stepped in front of him and stopped. The young boy was transfixed with a toy car, and it was then that Jake recognised him as the boy that had come aboard with Rasha. The fact that she was willing to kill herself and an innocent life – no less her own son – was absurd. How she could bring herself to do it he didn't know. And where she fitted into Raman's master plan, he really didn't know. Sadly, there was no time to ask her.

The boy turned away from Jake and, as he did so, he bumped into Jennifer.

'Sorry, sweetheart,' she said as she passed Jake a couple of baby wipes.

Still keeping up the act, Jake wiped Chloe's hands clean and then bopped her nose with his finger. She let out a little squeal of excitement. And for a split second, he forgot about the situation, about the immense pressure he was under.

But then a clock appeared in his mind and brought him somersaulting back to reality. By his estimations, they were already eleven minutes into the journey. Nearly at the top.

And nowhere near close enough to stopping it.

'Hey,' Jennifer said, calling to Jake from the window.

He pocketed the wipes and joined her. 'What's up?'

She pointed to the sky. Up in the air, above the Houses of Parliament, a police helicopter hovered parallel to them.

'What's that doing here?'

'There's a helicopter pad just down the river. I think it's where the police fly out of when there's an emergency. If we're lucky, we'll get to watch them land.'

Jake reached into his pocket and drafted a message to Tyler. It read: *Land heli ASAP. Spook inevitable.*

A few seconds later, the helicopter listed to the right and headed east, towards the Tower of London, before eventually disappearing out of sight behind The Shard.

Jake relaxed a little.

And then he was pulled back into the capsule.

'What did you see?' he asked Jennifer, gently tapping her on the shoulder.

Without asking permission, Jennifer wrapped herself in his arms and nestled into his shoulder. 'She got the wipes from the back of the pushchair. She moved slowly, but I couldn't see anything in her coat. She's zipped all the way up.'

'And you couldn't see anything in the pushchair itself?'

'No. Just baby stuff.'

Jake breathed deeply. Armed with the information Jennifer had given him, he was now certain that, if Rasha was going to detonate anything, it would be a suicide vest strapped to her body beneath her coat. The same way Saeed had planned on doing it.

'You do have people working on this, right?' Jennifer asked.

'Yes. Don't worry. They're working on it, trust me. They're doing everything they can.'

'They better hurry up before it's too late.'

'Everything's going to be OK,' he reassured her – even though he didn't believe it completely.

Any minute now, Rasha Al Abdi was going to

martyr herself and her son, and detonate a suicide vest inside the London Eye.

And it was up to him to stop her.

Typically, decisions such as this didn't require top-level approval from the most powerful person in government; the burden of advising lethal force during a terror attack usually fell to himself. But this time, it was different.

Jake Tanner had a matter of minutes to disarm and disable the terror attack from taking place. And if they weren't quick enough, another good man was about to die. Fortunately for Commander Jasper Conrad, he had a direct line to the Prime Minister's office.

'Jasper?'

'Yes, Prime Minister. I don't have much time to discuss. We have an emergency at the London Eye. A suspected terror cell is currently on board, potentially carrying explosives.'

'You don't know for certain?'

'Negative, Prime Minister. Our intelligence, however, does suggest that the cell is wearing a vest.'

A pause.

'What do you need?'

'We have an officer in the capsule with the cell. We're trying to leave it up to him but, failing that, do we have permission to use *lethal force*?'

The other kind.

Another pause.

'How many casualties?'

'Between twenty to twenty-five, Prime Minister.

Another pause. This time longer. Eating into the

time they didn't have.

Then came the message he'd been waiting for.

'Proceed as necessary.'

CHAPTER 15

'You understand what you need to do?'

Jennifer nodded. 'Jake… I'm – I'm scared.'

'I know. I am too. But everything's going to be fine, OK? So long as she doesn't realise what – and who – you are, you'll be fine. If you see her, or anyone else, reaching for a phone, do what you have to. Beat them up if you have to. Knock them unconscious. However, this is only a last resort, if all else fails – if *I* fail, all right?'

'Yes. Oh God. Please just let it be over.' Jennifer was quickly becoming hysterical, and she began scratching the back of her hand until the skin became red.

As Jake looked at his watch, his phone vibrated. It was a text from Tyler, letting him know that he, Jasper, Mamadou – and the rest of the team – were watching and waiting and praying. It wasn't the message he'd been hoping for. It wasn't the message telling him it was just a joke, that there was no way Rasha was carrying a vest of explosives, even though she was wearing a large jacket in the summer London heat. It wasn't the message telling him that he could relax because help was on the way. To him, it felt like Tyler's way of saying goodbye.

An alarm went off somewhere in the pod, bringing Jake out of his reverie. He spun on the spot and saw Rasha looking at her watch, transfixed. She had gone pale, afraid of what was about to come.

Jake made his move.

Without thinking, he lunged towards her, placed his hand on her shoulder, and said, 'Don't you fucking dare do what I think you're about to.'

Rasha looked up at him in abject horror, and as the reality of who he was suddenly dawned on her, she threw Jake's hand aside and pushed him backward.

Jake stumbled into someone behind, and together they collapsed to the floor. Screams of confusion and panic erupted from around the capsule, echoing, deafening him inside the confined space and inside his broken mind.

For a moment, the two of them tussled on the floor, until Jake felt an explosion in his crotch and an agonising pain flare in his stomach. He rolled to the side, allowing Rasha to leap to her feet.

By the time Jake joined her, she'd unzipped her coat and revealed his worst nightmare – a suicide vest, almost as large as her entire torso, with four separate packages wrapped in cellophane, strapped to her stomach. Dozens of wires protruded from the charge in the centre of her body, and Jake could see, beneath the thick layers of plastic, hundreds of pieces of metal buried deep within the material. If the explosion wasn't enough to kill everyone inside, then the shards of metal perforating skin and flesh would.

'Don't come any nearer!' she roared.

At the sight of the vest, a cacophony of screams erupted, disorientating Jake. He stood still, his chest heaving, his mind working overtime.

He looked at the crowd of people scrambling and banging on the windows on the other side of the capsule, begging for escape.

'Please,' he began, talking to Rasha while pointing at the people, 'don't do this. You don't want to. It's not going to achieve anything. Rasha, *please*.'

At the mention of her name, Rasha's expression dropped, and her face contorted as she began working everything out.

'You're the person from last night?' she began. 'The one who chased Saeed. The one we ran over.'

'We?'

'Yes, the rest of us. The faceless figures hiding in the depths of the city, planning more attacks than you'll ever know. More attacks than you'll ever put an end to. You won't stop us – *can't* stop us. Our network is too big, too strong. There's nothing you can do, so you may as well give in, let it happen. *Scum*.' Rasha spat the last word with venom.

'These people are innocent. And so are you. What did Raman tell you and Saeed to make you believe this was right?'

Rasha shook her head. 'You will get no answers from me so long as you fear me.'

'I don't fear you,' Jake said. 'I pity you.'

'Enough. Stop talking!'

Rasha reached inside her pocket, her hand and arm trembling. In that instant, before she had a chance to remove the detonator she was no doubt reaching for, Jake jumped atop her, his body acting as a human shield against the incoming explosion. They collapsed to the floor again. Panic ensued in the cabin, and Jake felt the volatile explosives crush underneath his weight.

Rasha howled as Jake's knee plummeted into her abdomen, incapacitating her. Jake then rolled her onto her side and pinned her hands behind her back. Adrenaline surged through his veins, giving him a new lease of energy that masked the pain in his body.

But it didn't last long.

'Jake!' Jennifer screamed, breaking his focus and momentum.

He turned to face her. And there she was, pointing to the man with the camera. The man who had, until this point, kept his back turned to Jake at all times.

And he'd now swapped the camera in his hand for a mobile phone.

CHAPTER 16

Twenty storeys later and his pulse had risen only by a fraction. The key to maintaining a low heart rate was a healthy lifestyle and diet. Many tried to overcomplicate it with supplements, artificial products and fad diets that did more damage than good – but it was all a con. A marketing scheme to rob from the poor and give to the rich. And everyone fell for it.

Up here, on the roof of the Stoughton office block, sitting just over several hundred yards from the London Eye, wind whipped and whistled around the building like a steam kettle finishing its boil. Hissing, screeching. Ominous. It brought with it a bitter chill. The kind that reminded you of winter and made you wish you'd worn a coat despite the season.

With him was his sniper rifle. An Accuracy International AW50 to be accurate. And within a matter of seconds, he'd turned it from a mass of individual pieces of metal into the killing machine it was known as. He loaded it onto the bipod and waited.

As far as he knew, the target was somewhere on the

London Eye. He was waiting for the clearer details to come through. And the final approval to pull the trigger.

While he waited, he took in the view. Big Ben. The Eye. The River Thames. The boats ferrying passengers to and fro. St Paul's in the distance. Good old London. Except this time he sensed a solemnity about it.

Before he could dwell on it much longer, the mobile phone he'd placed beside the AW50's bipod started vibrating. He answered the call.

'Are you in position?'

'As instructed,' he replied.

'Sending you the target now. Are you alone?'

'Yes.'

'Were you followed?'

'No.'

'Good. Make sure it stays that way. One bullet, one casualty. Don't miss. And don't forget to tidy up after yourself.'

The call ended, and as he lowered the device from his face, he looked at the text messages that had just come through.

He stared blankly at the screen. Looking directly back at him was the face of his next target. A woman he'd never met before. A woman he'd never have the care of noticing on the street. Yet she was a woman who wanted to kill people, and he was the government's secret response to that.

As he adjusted himself into position, he felt his pulse begin to quicken.

CHAPTER 17

Jake froze, suspended by fear. He didn't know who the man was but he had less than a few seconds to stop him from pressing the large green dial button on the phone.

As he propelled himself from Rasha's body, he tripped on her hand and stumbled, catching the man's heel as he collapsed to the floor. It distracted him for only a moment, but it was just enough time for Jennifer to act – his temporary wife jumped atop the bench in the middle, arms soaring high like a bird's wings, and leapt onto the man's back. The two of them then fell to the ground, landing atop Jake, crushing his already damaged hip. The capsule felt as if it had shaken from the sheer force of their weight. Jake bellowed in agony, reeling in pain on the floor. Amidst the noise and furore of the situation, he could hear Chloe wailing in the background.

In the fall, the phone in the cameraman's hand had skittered across the floor to the centre of the capsule, metres away from Rasha. Now free from Jake, she saw her opportunity and took it: scrambling to her feet, grappling at the slippery surface for grip.

But she wasn't the only one with an advantage.

Jake was a foot behind her, close enough to reach out and trip her up.

After she'd smashed face first onto the floor, Jake climbed over her and used his body weight to pin her to the ground. Together they wrestled for superiority. Rasha – consumed by an anger and desire she hadn't had thirty seconds ago – swung at Jake, her nails narrowly missing his eyes. Jake ducked in defence, grabbed her arms and pinned them against her back, before punching her repeatedly in the ribs, kidney and stomach, knocking the wind from her lungs. It wasn't in his nature to hit a woman, but right now he didn't care what sex, race or creed she was. What mattered was that she didn't get anywhere near that phone.

Once she was sufficiently subdued, Jake clambered off her and started towards it.

He reached out a hand for the device, which had landed just beneath the bench, but someone beat him to it.

The little boy.

Despite his age, the boy's hand dwarfed the phone.

Jake watched on in fear, overcome with paralysis and disbelief that a child so young had been told what to do. Had been told how to martyr himself and kill dozens of other people. There was no fear or compassion or humility in his expression, just hate.

In the face of a four-year-old boy.

'Do it!' Rasha screamed. 'Do it now!'

The boy pressed a button.

Then everything seemed to happen in slow motion.

First, Jake heard the sound of the explosion. The ear-shattering, sound-barrier-breaking noise that sounded all too familiar.

The next sense to be disrupted was his vision.

Fractured and splintered glass rained down from above as the bullet penetrated the window, entered the back of the boy's head and exploded the front. A mist of blood, brain matter and bone burst into the air, dousing Jake and Rasha as the boy's little body collapsed to a heap on the floor, followed closely by the mobile phone.

Covered in the boy's blood, Jake wiped his face clean with the back of his sleeve and shuffled over to the phone – ignoring the piercing cries from around him – then removed the SIM and battery and stamped on it. The device buckled underneath his foot, bits of plastic and metal sticking to the bottom of his shoe.

As the gravity of what had just happened dawned on him, Jake spun on the spot and looked through the small hole in the glass. On the other side, somewhere in the distance, was the sniper who'd fired the shot, lurking on the roof of a building nearby. Jake tried to find his saviour but couldn't – they were too far away.

Then he checked himself for bullet wounds, in case the bullet had continued through the boy and found a home in his body, and shock had covered up the pain. But it hadn't. And when he swivelled to pick up Rasha from the bottom of the capsule, he found out why.

A flower of blood bloomed on the bottom of her shirt, rapidly staining her clothes. She clung desperately to the wound, but it was no use. She was too weak, and the blood escaping her body moved too fast. Life was leaving her eyes as he hurried towards her.

Despite who she was and what she'd tried to do,

preservation of life came above everything else.

'Keep pressure on it!' he yelled at her, placing his own hand on the wound.

Rasha's eyes opened and closed as she dipped in and out of consciousness, her blood warm beneath his fingers.

Pressure. The only thing he could do was apply pressure. He didn't have a magic wand to retrieve the bullet from her stomach. Neither did he have the morphine that would numb her pain. She needed a hospital – urgently. And by his estimations, they still had another ten minutes to go until they reached the bottom.

Ten minutes that ran the risk of her bleeding out.

'Just keep pressure on it,' he told her again, even though he could see from her face that his words were falling on deaf ears. 'Everything's going to be OK.'

He said that just as much for his sake as everyone else's.

Keeping his eyes and attention focused on Rasha, he called to Jennifer behind him, 'Are you OK?'

When he didn't get an immediate response, he cast a look over his shoulder and found her still atop the man. Except this time she was surrounded by the other passengers who, over their initial shock, had assisted her and now pinned the man to the floor.

'Looks like you've got it under control!' he said.

By the time he turned his attention back to Rasha, the dying woman had now become the dead woman. Her small frame was slumped against the window, her hand fallen by her side, the life gone from her eyes.

One bullet. Two fatalities.

Two for the price of one.

Whoever had taken the shot had known exactly

what they were doing.

A part of him was happy: it was done. He'd avenged Darren's death, and he'd protected dozens of innocent human beings in the process.

But the other part of him was afraid, tired, worn out. Then the effects of the last eighteen hours caught up him with and assaulted him. With a vengeance. His brain was filled with too many emotions, too many thoughts, too much fatigue and he passed out, the image of the boy's brain matter the last thing he saw before the blanket of darkness cushioned him.

CHAPTER 18

Jake awoke minutes later thanks to a forceful prod in the chest. When he opened his eyes, he noticed the entire capsule had been evacuated, except for the dead bodies, and had been replaced with a figure in a white suit. Behind them, the capsule doors were open, and beyond that was emptiness. It felt as if he'd woken up mid-dream.

'Jake, can you hear me? Wake up.'

He recognised the voice as Tyler's. His friend. Coming to his rescue.

As he opened his eyes wider, Jake's head began to pound. 'What? Yeah. I can hear you.'

Tyler lifted him to a seated position, with his back pressed against the window a few feet from Rasha.

'Are you OK? Are you in pain?'

'Apart from the ringing in my ears, and the fact my leg feels like it's about to fall off, and my head's about to explode, I'm fine.'

As Jake surveyed his surroundings, it dawned on him that Jennifer and the cameraman had disappeared.

He bolted upright, clutching Tyler's sleeve tightly. 'Where – where's he gone? Did he get away?'

'Easy, Jake. Easy. Calm down. Everything's fine. Everything's been taken care of.' Tyler helped Jake to his feet. 'When we got here, there was nowhere for him to go. He's down at Paddington Green now, being booked in as we speak.'

'And Jennifer? Chloe?'

'They're safe. They're being looked after by a paramedic somewhere. They'll be fine. As will everyone else. *You* saved them.'

'I didn't. Someone else did.' Jake pointed to Rasha to highlight his point.

'But if it hadn't been for you, we wouldn't have this other guy.'

That reminded Jake. 'I need to get to Paddington Green.'

'No.'

'I need to speak with—'

'Jake, sit down.' Tyler placed his hands on Jake's shoulders and pressed downwards. 'You're in shock. You need to take it easy. We need to get you checked out.'

'Where have I heard that one before?'

'After that, Mamadou wants you to go home. You've been through a lot today, you're exhausted, and you need rest.'

'No. What I *need* is to speak with Saeed and that guy. There was something Rasha said earlier that I need to check out.'

'What? What did she say?'

Jake swallowed before speaking. 'Let me speak with Saeed, and I'll tell you.'

CHAPTER 19

The air inside Paddington Green seemed sterile. Jake supposed it was to match the interior. Dull. Unattractive. Plain.

He stepped into the interview room Saeed Anwar had been moved to. The suspected terrorist was sitting in the middle of the room, behind the desk, with a plastic cup of water and his thoughts to keep him company.

Both Jake and Tyler pulled out their chairs, allowed the sound of metal on concrete to finish its echo and sat down.

After they'd completed the legalities, Jake began.

'Saeed Anwar, under the Terrorism Act 2006, you are being charged with attempting to commit an act of terrorism. My colleague and I would like to ask you a few questions, if that's OK?'

Saeed remained silent.

'No problem. We'll ask them anyway,' Jake said. He always found these interrogations differed from those during his days in CID; when dealing with terrorists, he spoke with a lot more contempt.

'I'm going to start with my main question: Rasha, who is she to you?'

'My sister.'

'Not your partner?'

'No.'

Jake swallowed hard before continuing. He didn't know how Saeed was going to respond. 'And what about the boy?'

'He... he was my nephew,' Saeed said softly. Something caught in his throat and he choked.

'And the man you'd snuck in there as well?'

'A friend.'

'What friend?'

'*My* friend.'

'How did you get involved in this?' Tyler asked. 'What forced you to do it.'

Saeed looked around the room, as if searching for someone to tell him the answer. 'I don't know,' he replied.

'What do you mean you don't know? Sounds like bullshit to me. Who are you working for?' Tyler pressed.

'Rasha mentioned there are more of you,' Jake added. 'More of the faceless...'

Saeed paused a moment to collect his thoughts. 'That's because it's bigger than you know.'

'And what does that mean exactly?'

Saeed leant forward, a hint of a smile on his face, but Jake couldn't be sure if he noticed it for certain. 'There are more of us. Way more than you can imagine or even begin to comprehend. And we will never stop. We will never be beaten. There are more attacks planned. More lives are going to be lost.'

'When?'

Saeed suddenly turned tight-lipped, although Jake could see on the man's face he wanted to speak.

'Tell us. Give us a clue.'

The smile on Saeed's face grew. 'Another attack. Right here in the city. Tomorrow.'

AFO - Authorised Firearms Officer. A police officer who has been trained, accredited and authorised to carry a firearm.

ANPR - Automatic Number Plate Recognition. A highly accurate system capable of reading vehicle number plates.

ARV - Armed Response Vehicle. Specially adapted vehicles that accommodate specialist equipment and transport authorised firearms officers to incidents that require their presence, usually in high-risk situations.

BDU - Bomb Disposal Unit.

CID - Criminal Investigation Department.

CSI/SOCO - Crime Scene Investigator / Scenes of Crime Officer. Forensic analysts who attend crime scenes searching for fingerprints, DNA, etc.

DC - Detective Constable.

DCI - Detective Chief Inspector.

DCS - Detective Chief Superintendent.

DI - Detective Inspector.

DS - Detective Sergeant.

EO - Exhibits Officer. Officer in charge of cataloguing and controlling the exhibits gathered throughout the course of an investigation. Exhibits include, but are not limited to, forensics, interview tapes, CCTV seized and items created by police officers in the course of the investigation.

EOD - Explosive Ordnance Disposal. Team responsible for the safe removal of explosive devices.

FLO - Family Liaison Officers are specially trained officers who work with families as part of the investigation team. They are the family's first point of contact.

HOLMES - Home Office Large and Major Enquiry System. The national computer database for storing all the entries in a large and major enquiry. Capable of logging decisions, actions and statements, allowing analysis of the intelligence to be made.

H-to-H - House-to-House is a technique that enables investigators to identify suspects, and to canvass for witnesses in areas that are connected to an incident.

IMEI - International Mobile Equipment Identity. A fifteen-digit number unique to a specific mobile phone that can be traced and tracked.

IPCC - The Independent Police Complaints Commission is a public body responsible for overseeing the system for handling complaints made against police forces in England and Wales. As *The Community* is set in 2010, the story refers to The IPCC, but it was later changed into the IOPC in 2018.

MG11 - Name given to the witness statement form taken from witnesses by police officers.

MIR - Major Investigation Room. The hub of any major investigation. Usually a dedicated room where all the officers collate, organise their work and work through the evidence.

MIT - Major Investigation Team.

MLO - Media Liaison Officer. Responsible for dealing with the media and the press during a major investigation.

OFC - Operational Firearms Commander. Responsible for ensuring the strategy set by the Strategic Firearms Commanders is put in place.

PC - Police Constable.

PS - Police Sergeant.

RTC - Road Traffic Collision.

SFC - Strategic Firearms Commander. Responsible for ensuring a strategy in response to a high-risk situation is in place.

SIO - Senior Investigating Officer. Officer in overall

charge of a major investigation, usually the rank of a Detective Chief Inspector.

Printed in Great Britain
by Amazon

37075992R00182